THE PANORAMA EGG is the smallest of fantasies. What is it, after all? An egg. Not a real egg, as a general rule, but an egg made of glass, or paper, or porcelain, or styrofoam, or sugar. An egg with a peephole in one end. An egg with a world inside.

The poorest and cheapest of them are the styrofoam Easter eggs with paper rabbits and flowers inside them. There are larger eggs, and better eggs. Some are frozen dreams. There are eggs with mountains painted on the shell, and silver threads of rivers running into distance. There are china eggs holding figures frozen in a dance forever.

And there is the ideal egg, the egg that no collector has ever found, the egg that no craftsman has ever made: the egg that contains a world. I have searched for this egg for nearly seventy years. All collectors search for it. It is our El Dorado, our unattainable goal, the dream that kills those who would find it. For, we who collect these fantasies, we are the dreamers of dreams. We are the keepers of the soul.

                Sir Henry Patterson
                (from "Keepers of Dream,")
                Diorama Book 1974

THE PANORAMA EGG

by
A. E. Silas

DAW BOOKS, INC.
DONALD A. WOLLHEIM, PUBLISHER

1301 Avenue of the Americas
New York, N. Y.　　10019

Copyright ©, 1978, by A. E. Silas

All Rights Reserved.

Cover art by H. R. Van Dongen.

FIRST PRINTING, AUGUST 1978

1 2 3 4 5 6 7 8 9

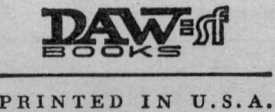

PRINTED IN U.S.A.

PART ONE

Chapter One

Tuesday, November 23

"Mera, m'dear, you're always welcome here," said Sir Henry Patterson into the telephone. "But if you come tonight, you'll have to behave."

"What do you mean?" said the voice of Mera Melaklos.

Patterson grimaced. "I mean that you are to avoid cryptic remarks and riddling speech and leaps into fantasy. As far as possible, that is. Wear an agreeable mask."

"You've a guest," she said. "Who?"

"You don't know him, m'dear. He's interesting. He thinks he's an ordinary man."

"Thinks he's an ordinary man?" she repeated thoughtfully.

"I'd like you to meet him," said Patterson. "But you're not to make him nervous. Understood?"

"Understood," she said. "Who is he?"

"His name's Archer."

"Archer," she said. "And he thinks he's an ordinary man."

Ragnell's Cove, Connecticut, was old enough for a core of New England Yankees, picturesque enough for a small artists colony, and close enough to New York for a growing commuter population. It had all three. They lived in perpetual hostility.

Sir Henry Patterson got along with all of them. For five years he had lived in a house in the no-man's-land that bordered all three areas, talking to everyone he met and collecting panorama eggs. It was a panorama egg that took Archer to dinner with him instead of to the theatre and supper in New York with his wife and four friends.

That was the night before it happened.

Patterson let him in and took his coat. At seventy, the retired actor was short and spare. His hair was white, his comic triangular face lined, but his features were as mobile and his voice as rich and flexible as they were when George VI knighted him for his contributions to the English theatre.

"It hath arrived," he said conspiratorially, as they went

down the short hall to the library. "Sit down; I'll fetch it forth."

There were, as always, three armchairs in front of the fire. Archer crossed to the one farthest from the door and sank into it with a sigh. For a few minutes he sprawled there, letting the peace in the room seep into him.

He liked Patterson's library. It was an island of quiet in the chaos that surrounded him more and more. It was restful after Diane's constantly changing decor (currently back-to-earth with Colonial overtones, dried grass and pewter and remnants of Neo-Plastic).

Patterson's walls were the mellow color of old ivory, with mouldings and bookshelves in dark oak. At one end of the long room a fire burned in a big brick fireplace with a tiled hearth and a wide oak mantle piece. Before it stood a satin-dark tea table and the three deep leather armchairs on an Oriental carpet of rich colors subdued by age.

Archer sat up straighter in his chair and idly tabulated the objects on the mantelpiece. They never varied: three ceramic eggs, two silver candelabra with white tapers, the unobtrusive ebony clock, the capering bronze jester.

Above them was the only disturbing thing in the room: Berini's portrait of Patterson as Lear's Fool. The background of angled grays and blacks, suggesting stone walls, the half-crouched figure of the Fool, ragged in dark-green motley with cockscomb and bauble, the mocking innocence of his face, hinted at things dark and horrible. Archer shivered and glanced over his shoulder, half expecting to see the mad king listening to the pointed jests of his fool. He had seen the portrait a hundred times at least, but he couldn't get used to it.

"Berini was mad. Like the best of us."

Startled, Archer turned his head. For the first time he saw that the chair nearest the door was not empty. A small dark-haired woman in gray was curled up in it, watching the fire.

He was almost sure she hadn't been there before, but he hadn't heard her come in. And had she spoken? She looked as though she had been watching the fire in silence for hours. He opened his mouth to ask if she had said anything.

She turned her head toward the door, just before the electric lights came on and Patterson entered.

He carried a wooden box about fifteen inches square, which he set on the tea table before sitting in the central chair.

The gray woman uncurled like a cat and sat forward. As her face came into the light, Archer saw that it was oddly alien, with exquisite fine bones and large dark eyes. He thought that she did not look quite human.

Patterson turned toward her, not at all surprised. "Ah, Mera, m'dear. I didn't know you'd come. This is Archer, a fellow collector, and a performer of some promise. Archer, Mera Melaklos."

She inclined her head slightly. "Good evening."

As Archer returned the greeting, he was uncomfortably aware that she was studying him. Why? There was nothing to study about him. He was just a rising professional man—there were thousands like him in New York City alone. The only unusual thing about him was that he collected panorama eggs.

That reminded him of Patterson and the box, and he turned to the old actor. "Is that it?" he asked, knowing that it was, but wanting to build a barrier of words between himself and her gaze.

"It is." Patterson had unlatched and unfolded the sides of the box, so that they lay flat around a cube of cotton-wool packing. He carefully began to pull the packing away.

"Where did you get it?" asked Archer, although he had heard the story before.

Patterson glanced at him curiously, but replied, "I first saw it nearly twenty years ago, in Australia. It was made by an old station-rider, a man with good hands and time to employ them."

"Scrimshaw," murmured the gray woman.

Patterson half raised a hand in her direction, a gesture that she acknowledged with a twitch at the corner of her mouth.

The actor continued, "He would not sell it for all the jewels of India, but when he died six months ago he left it to me in his will. There was some legal trouble; the old father antic released it to me only last week." He blew at it gently, dislodging the last wisps of packing.

It was an ostrich egg, not as large as Archer had expected it to be, but large. It rested in a velvet-lined cradle in the box, slightly angled so that the lensed peephole in the smaller end was raised. The outer shell was unadorned.

Archer rose to reach for it, eager to see what was inside.

"Don't pick it up," said Patterson quickly. "Had I lifted it when first I looked inside, I should have dropped it."

That must be quite an egg, Archer thought. He knelt awkwardly at the table and leaned forward to peer into the egg.

Green land opened before him, rolling grassland that was never in Australia. White sheep grazed on a distant hillside;

9

far beyond them marched blue-hazy mountains. A silver thread of stream ran toward the mountains, with willows and poplars leaning over it. Wool-white clouds echoed the sheep against a summer-blue sky.

Archer's throat tightened. It was beautiful. It was larger than the shell that contained it. He looked at it all—the green land, the summer sky, the cotton-wool clouds—and then he knew that he had looked too long. He had seen the inevitable flaw.

The gray woman must have seen disappointment in his face when he sat back, for she half smiled and quoted softly: " 'For sixty-five years I have looked into panorama eggs, always hoping for the miracle: for mountains that are not painted on the shell, for grass that stirs in the wind, for light from a tiny impossible sun. I know that it is useless. I know that the animals are paper, the lake a looking-glass, the mountains and sky mere paint. Yet I continue to peer through tiny windows, hoping to be transported.' "

"My blushes, m'dear," murmured Patterson.

Archer recognized her words: they were part of a piece that Patterson had written for the *Diorama Book* two years before. He recalled reading and re-reading them, liking this proof that someone else saw the eggs as he did. That was what had prompted him to tell Patterson he was a collector, two years ago.

Back in his chair, he looked at the ostrich egg and said, "It's remarkable. It seems larger than the shell." Then he saw the distorted reflections in the glass that covered the peephole, and knew why. "Magnifying lens?"

"Yes," said Patterson. "The man was a genius. There is no distortion in the image."

He was right, there hadn't been. Archer said slowly, "If I'd stopped looking three seconds earlier, I'd swear it was perfect. I looked just long enough to see what was wrong. It's dead. Nothing moves."

Patterson chuckled dryly. "Motion can be dead. I have had several clockwork eggs—most of them pornographic."

That startled Archer. It was a possibility he hadn't thought of. He visualized a pornographic egg, and laughed. Ridiculous. Like something they advertised in true detective magazines.

The gray woman was shaking her head. "Pornovisual," she said, as if trying to find the right word. "Pornopictic. Pornoptic."

Again Patterson made that silencing half-gesture, not turning toward her, and again she acknowledged it with a microscopic twist of her mouth.

Archer realized abruptly that these two were close, closer than he had been to anyone in his life. The murmur, the scarcely-lifted hand, the mouth twitch, were the communication of two people who were accustomed to each other. He didn't know who the gray woman was, but he envied her that rapport.

He looked away from her distant gaze, still on him, and said to Patterson, "I've never seen a clockwork egg."

The old actor said, "They always remind me of the first one that I had—an uncle gave it to me when I was seven. It contained three deer that leaped about a pine tree. At first I was enchanted. But always they went in the same circle, with the same motions, and as it ran down they moved more and more slowly until they stopped in mid-leap. There was a macabre quality to it. I finally hid it away where I wouldn't have to look at it."

Archer had a sudden vision of the law firm partners leaping solemnly about a tin Christmas tree: dry M'Laughlin, crisp Burns, fat cranky Whistlin. Then they all turned into solemn Archers, and he pushed them out of his head and concentrated on Patterson's voice.

"The ideal panorama egg, I suppose, would be a roc's egg." He chuckled. "I seem to recall that they were as large as the dome of St. Paul's, or at least large enough to contain a small menagerie. One could get into an egg of that size."

"But the mountains would still be painted on the shell," said the gray woman quietly. She spoke with an odd precision, as though English were not her native language.

"You, my dear, are an obstructionist," said Patterson mildly.

She smiled with one side of her mouth. "And you, my old, are that best of things, a romantic."

Archer heard them absently. Something was taking shape inside his head, an idea that must have been waiting for something like this to crystallize it. He voiced it hesitantly. "An ideal panorama egg would have to be large enough to get into, yes. But you should be able to hold it in your hand. It would have to be a—a paradox."

"A most ingenious paradox," murmured the other two simultaneously. They looked at him, Patterson attentive, the woman waiting from her distance for him to continue.

He went on, gathering speed and confidence as words came to him. "It would have to be so large that you could walk in it and never find the edges. So large that if you climbed the mountains, there would be more lands on the other side. So large that you could cross the sea and find strange countries. It would have to be a whole world that you could hold in your hand." He stopped abruptly and looked at the fire, feeling his face grow hot. He was talking nonsense. He just hoped they wouldn't laugh at him.

Patterson was laughing, a comfortable chuckle. "I could be bounded in a nutshell and count myself a king of infinite space," he said, and laughed again without elaborating.

It didn't sound like the laughter of derision. It was the laughter of someone who has seen something new and wonderful. Archer let out his breath, realizing for the first time that he had been holding it. Patterson was just the man to understand what he had said.

The woman said thoughtfully, as if speaking to herself, "Small enough to hold in the hand."

Something in her tone made Archer turn to look at her. She was still curled in her chair. Her alien face was unreadable, dust-brown in the light. But now she was not looking at him. He followed her gaze. She was looking at her hands, cupped together on her knees as though she held something small and fragile and infinitely precious.

It was three o'clock in the morning. Archer had left half an hour before, astonished at the time. Patterson and the gray woman sat before the fire in comfortable silence.

Finally, he said, "You're thoughtful tonight, m'dear."

"Am I?" She turned her head and smiled absently at him, a small sad smile, "I have a puzzle to solve."

"May I lend assistance?"

She shook her head. "I think that I have a key." She dismissed it with an abrupt gesture. "I talked to Andersen last week. He wants to consult you about the background for the Harlequinade."

"When will he be here?"

"After the New Year." She stood up in one flowing motion. "I'll tell you just what he said when I return."

He turned his head sharply, surprised. "I didn't know that you intended to go anywhere."

"It is a recent decision—quite recent." She moved toward the fire, stood looking into it. Without turning she said, "I shall be gone for a while—two weeks, I think. Perhaps more. I should be back for the darkest night of the year."

He frowned at the back of her dark head. "Where are you going?"

Her shoulders moved impatiently. "Nephelecoccygia."

He looked worried. He said, "Take care, m'dear."

"Never you mind about me." She turned and looked at him; her eyes shone out of the shadows of her face. "I know what worries you, my old. I'm quite sane."

He shook his head. "That doesn't worry me any more. It's the way you affect other people. You're going to try something tricky—I know the symptoms. People don't like to be tricked as you trick them."

"What do you mean?"

He spread his hands, a stage gesture. "I mean nonsense. I mean that you mesmerize people. They talk too much to you. It makes them vulnerable, and they resent it."

She made a motion as if in denial, then said quietly, "You do not resent me."

"I think I understand you. You've never mesmerized me."

She was thoughtful. "I do not know that I could. I am thy fool, my old. Even the fool, they say, must have his fool, so universal is the spirit of folly."

He said sternly, "You're avoiding me."

She did not look at him, but turned toward the door. "I must go, Patterson. I must do dark deeds ere dawn."

He stood up and walked with her. Quietly, casually, he said, "You seem intrigued by young Archer."

She was silent for a moment. "Intrigued? No. Interested."

He draped her long gray cape over her shoulders. "I've never heard him talk so much, or so freely."

She did not reply, but fastened her hood.

Patterson reached for the doorknob. "He's a good man, Mera. Don't play tricks on him."

She slipped out into the chill November wind. "I never trick people, my old," she said in a low voice. "They trick themselves."

He shook his head. "You mesmerized him, m'dear. I've never heard him say so much."

13

Chapter Two

Wednesday, November 24

What had he said?

Hiding behind his paper on the morning commuter train, Archer tried to sort out his thoughts. One question kept returning, however he tried to avoid it: What had he said to the gray woman? She kept intruding with her distant considering gaze, even when he tried to remember the fight with Diane.

Diane had been furious when he got home at nearly three in the morning. She had shouted at him while he tried to go to sleep, nothing in particular, the little things that quarrels are made of, and he had finally lost his temper and shouted back. Somewhere along the line she said that she was leaving in the morning, and he had gathered up bedding and the alarm clock and gone to sleep in the den. He hadn't seen her before driving to the station; she was probably still asleep.

What had he said to the gray woman?

He pushed the question angrily away, staring at his opened newspaper without seeing it.

He and Diane had never fought like that before, not even when she "confessed" about Paul Baird. She wasn't serious about Paul. He was all right, smart, ambitious, sharp dresser, the whole image. But he was dull. Diane had always liked people who could talk. Now she didn't believe that he could talk until two-thirty in the morning.

What had he said?

He yawned behind the paper. It wasn't a good idea, staying up that late. Not something to make a habit of. He needed sleep. Patterson might make a habit of it; he never seemed to run out of energy. Archer sometimes felt ancient compared to him, although the actor was nearly forty years older than he.

What had he said?

He gave up and faced the question.

He had talked a lot. The gray woman seemed to compel him to talk, sitting curled in her chair with her grave dark eyes on him. It was as though she could look into his head and choose what she wanted to hear, and compel him to say it.

He had the uncomfortable feeling that he had betrayed something. But exactly what had he said? He couldn't remember.

He closed his eyes, recalling the conversation after dinner. Sitting before the library fire with the lights off, he and Patterson talking, the gray woman saying hardly anything, but watching him.

Who was she? Patterson called her "m'dear." Maybe she was his mistress. Actors were supposed to have mistresses.

No. There was something untouchable about her. Something unnatural in the idea. Besides, it didn't account for her interest in him. She had studied him as though she were somehow testing him. He didn't like the memory. He didn't like her.

He remembered what they had talked of. Not panorama eggs anymore. They had started with little theatre. Then Patterson, reminiscent, talking about growing up in an English traveling troupe just after the turn of the century. And somehow he had started talking about his own five summers in repertory.

The gray woman had led him on with murmured words, inquiring turns of her head.

Five summers in repertory, with everything that went wrong and everything that was so good, the best time of his life. Badly lighted auditoriums, makeshift sets that collapsed. The redhead who giggled through love scenes. The trapdoor that swallowed Sherlock Holmes just as he was revealing the murderer's name. And things that went right, of course, but they weren't as memorable. There was never a night when everything went right.

Patterson, laughing. "In seventy years I have learned that it doesn't happen. Something always goes wrong."

Five summers. Then the family made him give it up. After all, he was in law school.

"No future in it?" murmured the gray woman.

Getting through law school as fast as possible. Diane, marriage. A successful career, a house in Ragnell's Cove, a partnership soon. And himself somehow left behind, lost somewhere with flats and lights and panorama eggs.

Ice formed in Archer's stomach. He had poured out his soul to that alien-eyed woman. He had betrayed himself and ten years of his life to a stranger.

Why had she wanted that?

Who was she?

The gray woman and the fight with Diane made it impossible to concentrate on his work all morning. His secretary had to recall him to his letters half a dozen times in an hour. Her fingernails were purple today, and for some reason that fascinated him. Every time he looked at them he saw, like a triple exposure, the gray woman's hands cupping something small and precious, and Diane's hands clenched in white-knuckled fury.

Diane called just after the secretary left. Her voice was small and distant.

"I'm leaving now, Hal."

That shocked him. He hadn't thought she meant it. He said, "Where are you going?"

"To the Bahamas. With Paul."

He went cold all over. His brain refused to work for a moment. He looked at the surface of the desk, forcing his head to clear. One thought came immediately: she couldn't have arranged it this quickly. It must have been planned before.

He said, "How long has this been on?"

"He—" She stopped, started again in a stronger voice. "He's had it arranged for a month, but I didn't say I'd go until today."

She hadn't planned it, then. She had decided after the fight. Or had she? She had started it, without much reason. He'd stayed almost that late at Patterson's house before, and she hadn't made a federal case of it. Maybe she'd wanted an excuse to go with Paul. She wouldn't go without being able to justify it. But if she did want to go—maybe she was serious about Paul after all.

That hurt. He had to move, to do something. He wanted to shout questions at her.

He straightened things on his desk, making himself concentrate on them as if they were the most important things in the world. The photograph of Diane. The octahedron paperweight. The calendar. His head was clearing. The calendar leaf said:

wed

NOV

24

Diane said, "Hal?"

"Hm?" He made it casual, careless. The next move was up

to her. He gripped the receiver to keep from shouting, concentrated on the calendar. There were two notes in his secretary's round schoolgirl hand.

"Hal, aren't you going to say anything?"

(Dr. Boyd 11:30. Mr. Whistlin 3:00)

There was an edge to her voice. He wasn't following the script that she undoubtedly had in her head. He grinned mirthlessly at the photograph of her and said steadily, "Will you be home for Christmas?"

"What difference does it make?"

(The secretary dotted her i's with circles. That meant something—faddist? Something like that.)

The words came out before he could stop them. "Diane. Don't go."

"Why not?" She said it too quickly.

So that was the game. He looked at the photograph again, Diane blonde and arrogant in a peacock-blue satin. He knew her. She wanted to justify leaving him this way. He was supposed to ask her to stay, perhaps beg, finally demand, so that she could hang up and leave in righteous anger. Well, this time he wasn't going to play.

"You haven't answered me," she said.

"Say hello to Paul for me."

She gasped. "Hal. I never—don't you care?"

"Sure, I care." He swivelled in his chair and looked out the window. He watched puppet-people move in the offices across the street, keeping his voice even while he said, "So what? Is anything I say going to change your mind?"

She said nothing. He could picture her at the telephone in her fur-collared coat, eyes bright with rage. Anger heightened her color under her makeup.

When the silence had grown uncomfortable he said, "Won't you miss your plane?"

She said in a desperate voice, "If you don't care enough to ask me to stay—"

Anger made his hand shake as he gripped the receiver, made his voice shake. "I've asked you to stay. I don't want you to go. But if you want to take a trip with a—" He stopped, trying to calm himself. He straightened the things on his desk again, but his hands shook. Diane's portrait fell face down. He reached for the ceramic egg that he kept in the office. It slipped from his hand, rolled onto the floor, bounced on the carpet.

Diane said coldly, "Are you finished?"

He drew a deep breath, looked at the calendar. Whistlin

3:00. He said, "Whistlin wants to talk about the partnership this afternoon. With M'Laughlin and Burns retiring they want someone else."

There was a short silence. She had been after him about a partnership for years. Maybe that would keep her here. He should have mentioned it before, instead of losing his head.

She spoke at last, icily. "Congratulations. You've been talking partnership for months."

She was building up to the angry walkout after all. Archer felt cold rage at this final rejection. At least she wouldn't have the last word. He said gently, "Good-bye, Diane," and hung up.

It was that simple. Only it wasn't. If she really was off with Baird nothing would ever be the same again. It was all right when she went to the theatre with him and used him as her escort and played golf with him. Archer didn't care about that anyway. But if she went away with him, even for a short time, Archer had lost her forever.

He couldn't imagine that. They had been married for ten years. He loved her—or he had loved her once. Now, it didn't make any difference. Ten years is a long time. Her absence was too great a change to picture.

Maybe she really wouldn't go. She'd think better of it. Maybe she was just trying to make him mad. He could call, apologize perhaps, try to make a little more sense. Anything to keep her home.

He reached for the telephone, picked up the receiver, dialed.

His secretary put her head through the door. "You'd better hurry, Mr. Archer, or you'll miss your doctor's appointment."

He nodded at her impatiently, and she withdrew. The telephone was ringing. He let it ring twelve times. Then he pressed the cradle button and dialed again. This time he counted twenty rings, then hung up.

She was gone.

He stood up, unable to sit still. His foot came down on something that rolled. He clutched at the desk, regained his balance, glared down at the carpet. The ceramic egg knocked against the desk.

He picked it up and hurled it against the wall. It shivered into a thousand shining splinters.

"You're killing yourself," said Dr. Boyd. "Not that it does any good to tell you."

"There's a lot of that going around." Archer followed Boyd

from the examination room into the doctor's cramped office, buttoning his shirt. He sat down and said, "Cigarette?"

"Not in *my* office. You need to quit, Hal. Your lungs look like coal sacks."

Archer shrugged and put the cigarettes back into his pocket. Now came the lecture Boyd gave every time he came in. He tried not to listen to it.

"You want it all this time?" Boyd leaned back in his chair and straightened his glasses. "Okay. Maybe you don't like it, but you are damn well going to sit through it."

"I'm listening," said Archer impatiently. He got up to tie his tie in the mirror on the wall. Boyd's voice pounded into his head. He couldn't shut it out this time.

"You're thirty-three years old," said Boyd. He snorted. "In a dim light you could pass for forty-five. You eat too much, you're getting fat. You smoke too much, your lungs are rotting. You drink too much, your liver is going and your brain is dying. You work too much, you're developing an ulcer and you're heading for a good old-fashioned nervous breakdown. The only thing going for you is a strong heart, and the guarantee on that just ran out."

Archer, fumbling with his tie, met the eyes of the man in the mirror. He hadn't looked at his face for years, not even when he shaved in the mornings. A stranger looked back at him, pasty-faced, features thick and blurred. The stranger's eyes were red-rimmed and muddy and quietly desperate. He was a sorry specimen to be loaded down with everything Boyd had just listed. Archer yanked the tie into some semblance of order and turned away. He didn't want to look at that face any more. It showed him the truth of Boyd's assertions, and he had been trying to ignore Boyd for years. It wasn't Boyd's business if nothing was important enough to keep himself in shape for.

Boyd went on. "Parkin downstairs says that you're still on the sleeping pills. He's got your last refill for you today. That right?"

Archer was irritated. This was an invasion of privacy. He nodded.

"They'll just help you along. As you said, there's a lot of this going around. I make my money trying to get guys like you off the one-way street to the cemetery."

Archer reached for a cigarette to give his hands something to do, remembered the ban. A funeral procession was passing through his head, with thousands of hearses and no mourners. He tried to dismiss it. He said, "Mass suicide."

"Damn right. About the only thing you're not overdoing is sex, and chances are you've slowed up or stopped that."

Archer grinned to cover any betrayal. How did Boyd know that? Keep it light. He said, "What's your prescription? A call girl's number?"

Boyd shot a finger at him across the cluttered desk. "Ideally, you should give everything up for at least a year, and try to live like a human being."

"And realistically?"

Boyd sat up and looked at him angrily. "Take a couple of months off. Get away from here, forget about everything for a while. You can afford it. There are too many men working themselves to death in this country as it is. Take a long vacation."

He couldn't leave until Diane came back. If she came back and found him gone, everything would really be over. He couldn't tell Boyd that, couldn't tell him that she had left him. He said lamely, "There's no place to go."

Boyd slammed an open hand onto his desk. "No place to—of all the—go to the Bahamas and get sunburned. Go to Colorado and break your ankles. Go to Canada and hunt moose, or California and hunt girls. Go to the moon and collect rocks, for Pete's sake, but go somewhere and do something besides helping idiots cut each other's throats so you can have a bigger funeral than your neighbor's."

Archer winced. One of his neighbors had been buried just last month. But it wouldn't happen to him. But then, Simpson had probably thought the same thing six weeks ago, before he collapsed at his desk.

Archer shivered. He felt cold, colder than he had ever been. This must be the "wild chill of mortality." It was as if a grave had opened before him, and he knew that it was his.

Boyd was talking. He concentrated on the voice, letting it override his macabre thoughts.

"Why the hell didn't you stick to acting, Hal? You were good in college—I thought you liked it."

Archer said shortly, "I'd never have gotten anywhere."

Boyd snorted. "Where have you gotten in business law?"

Archer considered. A wife who had apparently left him. A partnership soon in a good law firm. Plus everything that Boyd had listed. It wasn't impressive any more. He answered literally, "Ragnell's Cove."

"You make me sick," Boyd stated. "Take a long vacation. You're killing yourself. Now get the hell out so I can get some work done."

There was a line at the prescription counter in the third-floor pharmacy: people on their lunch hour, collecting tranquilizers and diet pills and sleeping tablets to help them survive themselves. Archer joined the line and looked around the cellophane-wrapped shop. On a crowded display near him styrofoam angels simpered in artificial snow, alternated with bottles of an after-shave apparently named after a British mythological hero. Archer turned around and saw a reflected ghost in a glass-fronted cabinet. A young man, beginning to go prematurely middle-aged. Just like millions of others.

He turned away from the ghost, feeling uncomfortable. He hadn't thought like this before, but now all day he had been questioning himself and what he was doing. Why?

The answer came immediately: Patterson's little friend in gray. The Melaklos woman with her distant gaze. She had awakened doubts in his mind last night. By making him talk about himself, she had made him see himself. Who did she think she was, Til Eulenspiegel?

He recaptured that thought. Why Til Eulenspiegel?

Something Patterson had told him once. "And on his gravestone he had carved an owl, because he brought men wisdom, and a looking-glass, because he showed them themselves." Til Eulenspiegel, Howleglas, Owl-Glass, Owl-Mirror.

She had looked rather like an owl, curled up into a gray egg shape, with her great eyes shining in the firelight. And she was responsible for the way he was thinking now. He had been happy enough, or at least not unhappy, until she had shown up last night. Well, with luck he would never see her again, and he could—

Someone jostled him. "Wake up, mister."

He blinked. He was at the head of the line, and the girl behind the counter was watching him with a martyred air.

He got the sleeping pills in their bottle in the ridiculous pink paper bag. He finally pushed into a crowded elevator, made it to the lobby, burst into the street—and discovered that he had left his overcoat in Boyd's waiting room.

Somehow he managed to have a tasteless lunch and get back to the office by two-thirty. His secretary was painting her mouth purple to match her fingernails. She stopped long enough to say something about no callers and Mister Whistlin in hafnour.

Archer muttered something and dodged into his office. He didn't want to see Whistlin in half an hour. He didn't want to do anything. He ran a hand back over his bare head, automatically, and encountered his bald spot. One more reminder of lost time.

No more of that. He crossed to his desk, sat down. Whistlin in half an hour. Wearily he closed his eyes.

"Good afternoon," said the gray woman.

Chapter Three

Wednesday, November 24 (cont'd.)

His first reaction was fear. It passed quickly. Then came anger that she should be here, and curiosity. What did she want with him?

How had she gotten in? His secretary had said there were no callers. She would have to explain herself. He turned his head to look at her.

She sat in the pseudo-leather chair beside his desk, composed, making no restless motions, apparently unaware that her feet dangled two inches above the floor. She was covered from throat to feet in a pale gray cloak, as if she had just materialized out of mist.

She said, "I must apologize for calling without warning."

Archer thought briefly, irrelevantly, that she had a beautiful voice, a true contralto, low and rich and musical even with her precision of speech.

He cleared his throat, said tightly, "My secretary didn't say you were here."

"No."

He waited, but she made no attempt to explain. She just watched him gravely, like a cat or a child, as though she were weighing him in some balance in her head. Her eyes were as dark and distant as they had been at Patterson's house last night.

He started to ask how she got in, hesitated. She had probably slipped in while his secretary's back was turned. He could ask at the main desk. But they would have mentioned her when he passed on his way in.

He said, "How did you get in?"

She moved one shoulder, a hint of a shrug. "No one notices me unless I choose that they should."

It was possible, just possible, that she had slipped past everyone. He hadn't known she was in the office until she spoke. All right. That wasn't important. Now he had to find out what she wanted and get rid of her before he had to go listen to Whistlin.

He said, "Can I do anything for you?"

She had one eyebrow slightly raised, as if she knew what had passed through his mind. A corner of her mouth twisted. "I have something that may interest you."

"What is it?"

"A panorama egg. A unique panorama egg."

A warning went off in his head. If she had a rare egg, surely she would take it to Patterson. She was the old actor's friend, after all. Archer said, "Why bring it here? Why not—"

"To Patterson?" The mouth-corner twisted, turned up into what was literally a half-smile. "The egg responds to only one person."

That was a strange thing to say. As if it were alive. A one-man egg, like a one-man dog. She sounded like a madwoman, possibly dangerous.

He glanced toward the row of buttons on his desk. He could tell his secretary to get someone—who? Police? A doctor? Police. They'd know what to do. His hand twitched, ready to move. He looked at the woman.

She was regarding him steadily, and again he felt that she knew his thoughts. She looked from him to the buttons and back, still with one eyebrow raised inquiringly.

He knew what she meant, although she said nothing. He couldn't say how he knew, but he knew what she was saying with that slow thoughtful glance. She was saying that, small and slender as she was, although she was across the desk from the panel, with no purchase on the floor, she was strong enough and swift enough to stop him if he tried to call for help.

He believed her. He settled back, assuming casualness. When she relaxed her guard, he would move. Now it was a matter of waiting, of humoring her.

She was watching him with her look of last night again, the judging look. She seemed to watch from a great distance, as though she were far away, manipulating her body like a distant puppet. He had thought so last night, too. It was uncanny.

The silence stretched, became tense. Archer cleared his throat. He should keep her talking, keep her occupied. He said. "What about this panorama egg?"

She seemed to reach some decision. Her eyes were suddenly shuttered, opaque. She nodded slightly. Her hands appeared through her gray cape, empty. They flickered, and something was in them. She held it toward Archer.

24

He took it in his hands. It was an egg. An ordinary sort of egg, the size that supermarkets call small: he could easily close his hand around it. In color it was dust brown, mottled with darker brown. It was so light that it had to be empty, and it had the dry papery feel of real eggshell.

He turned it, looking for the peephole. It was tiny, and in the wrong end, the larger end. A Blefuscudian egg. He glanced at the gray woman. She was watching him with an amused twist to her mouth.

He looked at the egg again. Might as well see what was inside. He raised it to his eye.

Forest stretched away to the edge of sight, dark forest specked with tiny flashes of color—birds? In front of the forest, a small irregular patch of grassland. Beyond it, far beyond, the smoky line of mountains, beyond them a blue infinity of sky, with torn clouds scudding across it.

Scudding. They moved. The forest rose and fell in an unseen wind. The birds flashed in and out of the darkness. He could almost hear them piping against the sea-like sough and sigh of branches.

Something stirred at the edge of the clearing. Two tiny reddish-brown animals, like deer, sped across the grass and vanished below his line of vision. He tried to look after them. The forest came nearer—he could hear the wind, the birds— he was slipping into the egg, slipping—

In panic, he closed his eyes and lowered the egg. He sat still, hardly breathing. He was surrounded by silence. Beyond it, familiar noises came: the distant surf roar of traffic from the street below, the faint clatter of his secretary's typewriter, the almost inaudible hum and stir of a human hive. His heart stopped pounding; his breathing became easier.

He opened his eyes. The gray woman—he remembered her name abruptly—the Melaklos woman was watching him without expression. She did not speak.

He looked down at the egg in his hand. He didn't believe what he had just seen and felt. It was impossible. This was an egg, no more. He could crush it with one hand. He tried to curl his fingers around it, but they wouldn't respond.

He put the egg on the desk as if it burned his hand. He didn't want to touch it. It frightened him. He looked at the grave face of the Melaklos woman, and found his voice.

"Where did you get this?" It was a whisper.

"I made it. You gave me the suggestion last night."

"Last night," he repeated mechanically. What had he said about panorama eggs? A world that you can hold in your hand—something like that. So she had taken him at his word and made—

No. It was impossible. You couldn't put a whole world inside an egg.

Then how was it done? He thought wildly of film, of projectors. But no man—or woman—alive could make a projector, or film for it, that could be hidden inside a small egg. That was even madder than the idea that it was real. How, then? Hypnosis? Illusion?

He closed his eyes and pinched the bridge of his nose. He didn't want to think about this. Boyd was right, he needed a vacation. He was having hallucinations. He told himself that, made himself believe it. When he opened his eyes, she would be gone, and the egg with her.

He opened his eyes.

The Melaklos woman said, "You are showing less stability than I had hoped for, but more than I expected."

Not hallucination, then. And he didn't think it was hypnosis. She had said something—what? Something about his being unstable. He'd show her how unstable he was. As long as this egg seemed to be real, he would act as though he believed in it.

He drew a deep breath and tried to speak casually. "How did you do it? Make the egg, I mean?"

"I built it around a world." She moved a hand. "I cannot explain it in words that you would know."

Meaning that she wasn't going to try. Which was probably just as well. He didn't need new confusions. He said, "What place is inside it?"

She seemed slightly embarrassed. The hand moved again, an abortive gesture. "It contains all worlds."

"Including this one?" He was surprised that he could speak madness so calmly. She was really insane, but he didn't mind any more. They were isolated now on a tiny island of insanity.

She said, "Yes, this world is within it. I—expanded your idea. It was easier so. Still, this is what you meant, is it not?"

"Ah—I guess so." He looked at the egg again. An ordinary-looking egg, although he could not recall ever seeing one with just that coloring. A small egg, less than two inches long. Hadn't he said something else about the ideal egg? Yes. He said, "I also specified that you should be able to get inside."

"You can."

He looked at it again. So, he could get inside it. All right. "How?" he asked. "Does it grow, or do I shrink, or what?"

"It is not necessary. The egg is large enough to contain you. Indeed, you are within it now."

Given her premise that it contained all worlds, that made sense. That was what was so beautiful about it. There was something exhilarating in an insanity that made more sense than sanity.

He said curiously, "If I want to get in, what do I do?"

"Look into it."

He remembered his sensation of slipping into it. As simple as that? He liked it. Boyd had told him to get away from it all. Well, another world was about as far away as you could get.

He lifted the egg toward his face. Then he realized what he was doing.

He was catering to insanity. For all he knew, he was letting himself slide into it.

He stared at the Melaklos, angry, afraid. She was drawing him into her own madness. He couldn't allow that. He was Hal Archer, with a wife and a position of responsibility in the firm. He couldn't afford insanity.

She was watching him. She was testing him. He was on the brink of success or failure—in what? He stared at her. Around them, time froze.

The night and the day unrolled before him in one pattern of people. Patterson, Diane, Boyd, the secretary, Whistlin. That was the pattern of his life, until this creature with her distant eyes wove her alien thread into it, distorted it, made him see it.

He could be rid of her easily. If he crushed the egg, she would never appear to him again. The pattern would be restored.

Or he could break the pattern. He could accept the egg. He believed in it now. He could go into it, smash the pattern.

That was the choice she was offering him. That was the test she was making.

The desk intercom buzzed, buzzed again. Jarred back to reality, Archer jerked his head up, looked at the wall clock. Three o'clock. Time to see Whistlin.

Around him, the world was coming to life again, the pattern resuming. Only the Melaklos sat still, watching, waiting.

The intercom buzzed.

Then he could move. He raised the egg to his face. Even if it was only a gesture—

The trees were still moving, the birds flying. Clouds sailed over the forest, their shadows slipping over the trees after them. The sound of wind in trees grew louder, like the sound of the sea in a shell, louder and louder, until everything was lost in gray sound.

Chapter Four

Spring: first quarter, day 3

The gray faded. Archer stood on green grass, facing the dark trees. Wind murmured in the spiky branches, and the bright birds called and sang. The air was transparent as crystal.

He turned around slowly, hardly daring to breathe. It was real. He didn't believe it. But he could see it, hear it. The breeze was cool on his face. He was standing in a small clearing, surrounded by tall rough-barked trees. He could smell them, the rich damp smell of earth, the pungency of the broad leaves.

Fear took him, made him shake. Either he was insane or it was real and he was alone in a strange world. He could not think clearly, and that made him mad. Anger didn't clear his head, but it drove the fear away. He was angry at the Melaklos woman for dumping him here without warning, and angrier at himself for listening to her, much less humoring her. He should have gotten rid of her as soon as he saw her in his office.

No. He looked around again. He was still angry, but his mind had started working again. Something impossible had happened. The only thing to do was to act as though he believed in it. He had managed to climb inside a panorama egg and into another world. It looked like a pleasant world. "All he had to do now was find some way to stay alive in it. It would have been easier if—

A sudden noise startled him, a sound like an explosion turned inside out.

The Melaklos appeared out of nowhere, looking shaken. She put her hands out to steady herself.

She looked around, not seeming to notice Archer. "So," she said, half to herself. "The place is right. As to the time—" She closed her eyes. After a moment her face tightened, and she seemed to pull away from something that clung. Her eyes opened, she said uncertainly, "It is of small matter."

Archer couldn't stand being ignored any more. He said, "What are you doing here?"

"Good afternoon, Archer." She didn't look at him as she spoke: she was watching the sun, as if calculating something. "We must go," she said abruptly. "It is late, and we must reach the *kos* before nightfall."

"Wait a minute." Archer clung to his shreds of purpose. He wasn't going anywhere with this odd creature until she answered some questions. "Where are we?"

"You are inside the egg."

"I gathered that," said Archer, trying to sound patient. "But what is this place?"

"In the south of the Long Forest, near the western coast of the Lesser Continent. It is—or should be—early spring." She turned and started toward the trees.

Exasperated, Archer shouted, "A lot that helps!"

Before he could say more, she turned and looked at him for the first time since her appearance. She said, "What is in your hand?"

He looked down automatically. His right hand held the panorama egg.

She'd said he was inside it. He was in the place he had seen inside it. But he was holding it, so something else must be in it now. That made sense. What was in it now? Probably his office, that seemed logical.

He raised it and looked inside.

Forest, clouds, grass—it was the same scene. Almost the same scene. There were two figures in it now, a dark-haired person wrapped in gray, and a man in a gray business suit with his hands at his face.

Archer jerked his head back and stared wildly at the sky, half expecting to see an enormous eye looking down.

The Melaklos said calmly, "You are trembling."

Archer bit his lip and closed his eyes, fighting the chaos in his brain. He had accepted the egg as real, but how could he be in it and outside of it at the same time?

As if answering his unspoken question, the Melaklos said, "The egg contains all worlds, and so contains itself."

That didn't really explain it, but it sounded good. Archer opened his eyes and asked unsteadily, "What would happen if I went into it?"

"You would be here again."

Archer looked at the egg. He took a deep breath. He looked straight at the Melaklos and said, "Is this magic?"

She said, "No." Before he could react she continued, "It is sorcery. Material portals are borderline cases, I admit, but I maintain that a portal made by sorcery is sorcerous."

"That seems logical," said Archer, not sure why he said it. What she had said made no sense to him, except to tell him that there was some difference between magic and sorcery, and that both of them worked here. That wasn't really upsetting: he'd always liked the idea of magic, although he didn't tell anyone. He asked, "Are you a witch?"

She shook her head. "I am a sorceress." She looked at him thoughtfully and said, "You must learn the differences and the terminology. There is a magician who may cause trouble."

"Who?"

She shook her head again. "I do not know. He attempted to block my passage into this place, and may have misdirected us in time."

So that was why she'd been shaken and uncertain, Archer thought. He was vaguely surprised that he was accepting this so easily. Once he'd swallowed the egg (or it had swallowed him), the rest was not hard. He looked at the egg affectionately. Whatever happened inside it was evidently going to be interesting. He started to put it in his pocket, hesitated. It was fragile to the touch. He said to the Melaklos, "Will it break?"

She turned from studying the trees. "Give it to me." She held it between her hands for a moment, eyes closed. Then she handed it back.

It was heavy in his hand, covered and filled with glass, or crystal. This was so transparent that he could see the tiny scene inside as clearly as before.

"It will not be crushed," she said, "but it will break if you throw it with force against stone or drop it from a great height."

"What happens if it breaks?" said Archer, curious.

"You will return home, I believe. I am not certain. It may kill you."

Archer shivered and looked closely at her; she was quite serious. He put the egg carefully into his pocket, resolving that he would be sure to keep it safe.

The Melaklos turned away again and started for the trees. "We have wasted time enough in talk," she said. "The forest is not safe after dark. We must reach the *kos* by nightfall."

Archer caught up with her as she passed into the shadow of the trees. "What's a *kos*?" he asked.

"A trade village on the forest river," she said with finality, as if to discourage further talk.

Archer soon found that he wouldn't have been able to talk,

anyway. He needed all his breath to keep up with her. She was smaller than he, short-legged, taking three and four strides to his two, but he was out of condition and she wasn't. She traveled at a steady tireless pace that took her up slopes and through brush tangles and over streams without pause. He tripped over roots and got tangled in creepers, and once nearly slipped down a treacherous mud bank into a brook.

After what seemed hours, she glanced sidelong at him and called a halt. He dropped gratefully to the leaf-covered ground under a green-skinned tree. He was more exhausted than he had been for years, streaming sweat, scratched by brambles, and his feet hurt. He wasn't sure he had the strength to get up and hit the Melaklos if she grinned at him.

She didn't grin. She took off her long cloak, which had somehow avoided getting tangled in briers, and folded it and put it away in a large leather shoulder bag she had carried under it. Then she sat down against another tree and took a wooden pipe, like a recorder, out of some concealed pocket. She played on it fitfully, as if she were thinking aloud with it.

Archer took off his tie and jacket and watched her enviously. She was dressed for a forced march through forest, although most hikers wouldn't have approved anything so much like a dress. She wore pale gray, a loose knee-length tunic with a shorter, closer one over it, a belt of black flat-braided leather with a hand-sized double pouch and a sheathed knife attached to it, and soft gray boots, just above ankle-high, thick about the ankles. Reinforced, he thought—hiking boots.

He looked ruefully at his own shoes. They were expensive shoes, but not made for running around in forests. Neither was his suit: it was ripped and stained, and clung to him uncomfortably. Something on the order of jeans and flannel shirts would be more appropriate. He wondered if he could get them somewhere. From the way the Melaklos was dressed, he doubted it. Surely she would wear something more practical if it were available. She was probably dressed in the fashion of the people.

He realized abruptly that he had no idea what kind of people lived here. She had mentioned villages, so presumably there were people, but for all he knew they could be cave men or super-civilized beings. He turned to ask her about them. Then he saw the creature perched on her wood-flute, and gaped at it.

"What's that?" he whispered, afraid to startle it.

"An unearthly creature," she said, and pushed it gently off

the pipe until it gripped her fingers. She leaned toward Archer, holding it out.

Clutching her two outstretched fingers with long thin claws, balanced on three slender bird-legs, it was like nothing he had ever seen or heard of. Its body was the size and shape of a ping-pong ball, covered with what looked like off-white peach fuzz or plush. Spines like cat whiskers stood at intervals all over it, moving in tiny restless patterns.

"What is it?" Archer asked again, still whispering. Several of the spines tilted toward him.

"In the *sezhkai*, the trade tongue—which you must learn—it is called *imnye*, but the people of the *kos* call it *torp*."

"*Torp?*" It sounded so odd that Archer laughed. He put out a hand to take it, extending two fingers as she had. She pressed the creature's legs against them. It wavered, groped, gripped with one foot. Quickly it brought the other two up and stood with spines swaying on its long bird-leg tripod.

It's grip was like a bird's. It dug tiny claws into his fingers. How could it stay alive? How did it eat, or breathe? It had no visible features except for the spines. It was just a plush-covered ping-pong ball on three legs.

That was when he really knew that he was in an alien world. In the back of his mind the suspicion had lurked that he was in some part of the world that he did not know—Australia, perhaps, or South America. Now he knew that this was another world. The knowledge chilled him.

He looked at the Melaklos in the light of that knowledge. She apparently knew this world—it might be her home world. In any case, he was going to be more or less dependent on her for a while. Until he learned enough of the language to get by one, at least. She'd said something about a language for him to learn—*sezhkai*, the trade tongue. That was the first order of business—learning the language.

She was getting up, picking up her shoulder pouch. The pipe had vanished. She said, "We must go."

He groaned and got to his feet; he was stiff already. He said, "How far away is this *kos* of yours?"

"Three hours. We may be there by twilight."

Chapter Five

Spring: first quarter, day four

They had tracked him to the glade, Diane in her mini-skirted Robin Hood outfit, and Whistlin in his Santa Claus costume. Archer crouched in the green-skinned tree, scarcely breathing, watching. Three-legged ping-pong balls played leap-frog along his arms.

"There," said Whistlin in his unctuous Peter Lorre voice. "In that tree. He can't run out on a partnership. Give me the bow and arrows: I'll shoot him."

"Nonsense," said Diane, her voice high, Hollywood-British. "I'll shoot him myself. That'll teach him to go running off to imaginary worlds—and not even his own imagination. Panorama eggs indeed!" She snorted and fitted an arrow to the bowstring.

"But I insist," said Whistlin. "I'm a better shot."

Diane said haughtily, "You forget that I am an Archer, by marriage at least." She raised the bow.

Archer threw a ping-pong ball creature at her. It flew into her face—it had blue wings, it was a parakeet, squawking. She tried to wave it away with the bow, but it perched on the nocked arrow.

She looked so foolish that Archer had to laugh. He clung to a branch and laughed as she waved the bow about, trying to shake the creature off.

Another of them perched on Archer's nose, making him cross-eyed, and began to whistle in three shrill tones. Things started to dissolve. He was crouched in a tree—or lying on something hard—with something tickling his nose, possibly a ping-pong ball with three legs. His nose twitched. If I sneeze, he thought hazily, I'll know where I am.

He sneezed, opened his eyes. Where was he?

He was lying on his back on something hard. He brushed at the thing that was tickling his nose; it felt like a coarse blanket. That was all right. But the ceiling was big and slanted, made of evenly spaced strips of wood woven with leaf-covered branches. He had never seen a ceiling like that. What was this place?

The shrill whistling was still rising and falling, three half-tones, like an oboe gone mad. It was remote—outside, he thought. There would be someone outside who could explain this to him.

He sat up and groaned. He was stiff, and his back hurt. He swung his legs over the edge of whatever he was on top of, and looked around.

He was sitting on a table in the big dim room, lit by pale sunlight coming through an open door. He was alone. There were other tables, boards set across trestles. There were benches at them and ranged along the wooden walls. The floor was strewn with dead weeds, and there were dead torches in brackets on the walls. One end of the room was blocked off by a waist-high counter; there was a door in the wall behind it. The arrangement was familiar, although he was sure that he had never seen this place before.

The familiarity was easy to define. It was set up like a short-order restaurant, or a tavern of some sort. But why would he be sleeping on a table in a primitive tavern?

He slid off the table. Someone had undressed him to his underclothes. His clothes lay on a bench, neatly folded. They were in bad shape, as if he had been hiking in them.

He pulled on trousers and shirt, picked up his jacket. Something bulged in one of the pockets. Something heavy. He reached for it, pulled it out.

It was the panorama egg. He remembered all of it now. He was in a wine shop in the village, the *kos*. They had come in after sunset. He had been sleepy and stumbling—he remembered passing between long low buildings, slipping down a steep path. There had been the gleam of moonlight on water, and then the red light of torches, the sound of voices. He must have gone to sleep as soon as the Melaklos guided him to a bench.

The Melaklos. She must be outside with that maddening whistle. He padded barefoot to the door to find her.

The wine shop stood back from the river bank, which was an expanse of black mud. Behind the shop rose an abrupt earth bank; the opposite shore was gentler. Alluvial, thought Archer.

The mud flat was crowded with people watching children splash about in the water—an odd activity for a chilly morning, if it was morning. He could not see the Melaklos. He grimaced and started toward the shore.

Coming closer, he saw that a net on stakes enclosed a large area of the shallows, and the children were inside this, apparently chasing something. As he watched, one dived and came up with a fish in his hands. Grinning, he splashed to the bank and put it into the net basket that someone held out to him.

Archer caught a glimpse of gray. That must be the Melaklos. All the men and women he could see—the villagers, he decided—wore belted loose tunics of green or brown or dull red.

He passed the whistler, a thin young man blowing a short reed pipe. He looked hypnotized. No wonder, he played the same notes over and over.

Pushing through the crowd, he saw the Melaklos calf-deep in water and mud, talking to three naked children. As Archer came up, they laughed and splashed back into the water.

Archer stooped to roll up his trouser legs, waded out until he was just over ankle-deep. "Good morning," he called over the babble around them.

The Melaklos turned her head. "Good day, Archer."

He gestured at the net. "Fish harvest?"

"Yes. A very old custom."

A dripping red-headed boy bounded up to her, clutching a fish half as big as himself. He slammed its head against a stone and put it into her long netting bag, saying boastfully, "*La kor.*"

"*Si kro,*" she replied gravely, and gave him a small silver coin. He put it in his mouth and turned back into the river.

The Melaklos weighed the bag. "Enough," she said. "Are you hungry?"

He was. He was more than hungry, he was famished. "But—we don't eat them raw, do we?" he asked apprehensively.

A corner of her mouth twitched. "No. Come." She started toward the wine shop, carrying the net bag.

She haggled with the bald tavern keeper. Half an hour later, they had breakfast, sitting at a table in a corner. There were fish, baked and wrapped in leaves, and hard-boiled blue eggs, and strong-smelling white cheese, and coarse hard bread, and pale green wine. Archer was hungry enough to find it all excellent, but not too hungry to ask the Melaklos about some of the things that were bothering him, and to listen to her answers.

"There will be no disturbance about your disappearance," she said, in reply to his first question. "You have not disappeared. Your secretary has—or will—go into your office to see why you have not acknowledged your summons. She has—or will have—found you unconscious on the floor."

Brushing aside the riddle of her uncertain tenses, Archer said, "And she'll find you unconscious with me—that should be interesting."

"No doubt," said the Melaklos dryly. "However, she will not find me. I made the transfer in this body."

Archer picked up a blue boiled egg and frowned at it. "That body? What about me? If I'm unconscious on my office floor, what about this body I'm in? It's solid enough."

"It is a duplicate."

Incredulous, Archer said, "How did you do that?"

"I didn't. You did." She glanced at him, looked back to the sour black bread that she was cutting. "My formal colleagues call it psychic regeneration. Your intelligence, soul, spirit, psyche, or whatever you care to term it, has regenerated a body. The twins are usually accurate to the contents of the pockets, with the possible exclusion of lint."

Archer decided to let the explanation go, at least for a while. It sounded like the sort of thing that led to metaphysical arguments, and he didn't feel up to that. He decided to test another part of what she had said. Accurate to the contents of the pockets, eh? He couldn't check on most of what she had said, but he could try that. He emptied his pockets onto the table.

Keys, wallet, change, lighter, knife, handkerchief, pen and pencil, sleeping pills, a small hard-bound book, rubber bands, various junk. No lint. And he couldn't remember carrying anything else. In fact, he didn't remember one of the things on the table: the book.

Puzzled, he picked it up. It was pocket-sized, bound in faded gray-green cloth, with the title too worn to be read. He opened it, saw the black and white bookplate: a stylized fool's cap, *Ex Libris* printed above it, and below, in a slanting flourished hand, the name Henry Patterson. Of course. He remembered now: last night, or the night before, rather, Patterson and the Melaklos had argued—

He looked up and saw her gazing at the book with one eyebrow raised.

"He thinks well of you, to lend you that," she said, and added inconsequentially, "I designed the plate for him."

Defensively, Archer said, "He lent it to me so that I could read the notes—you were arguing about some point in it."

"Lear, of course."

Archer nodded and closed it. "Don't know why I had it with me," he said.

She met his eyes, and her lifted eyebrow angled farther up and then subsided.

He looked away, unable to stare her down. He was embarrassed and a little angry. She looked as though she knew why he had it. He had planned to start reading it at lunch, but he hadn't. It wasn't the sort of thing you read in restaurants, not if you were a lawyer. Newspapers, a few of the soberer magazines, perhaps. But not books, and certainly not something like Shakespeare. So he hadn't read it, and now he wondered if she knew, if she considered him a coward for it. He thought there had been amusement in that glance: a grave amusement and a searching glance that he knew he was going to dislike if they were together so much as a week.

She said something.

Glad of the chance to change the subject, Archer said, "What?"

"Most of this must go." She indicated the pile on the table. "Choose what you wish to keep. Not the cigarette lighter. The rest must be destroyed, buried, or sunk in the river. I have bought clothing for you—it can be replaced in kos-Alar."

"Wait a minute," said Archer stubbornly. "It it's going to be replaced, why buy it at all?"

She picked up a blue egg, cracked it on the table, rolled it between her hands. Concentrating on peeling it, she answered, "*Imprimis*, your clothes might not survive the journey, and are in any case unsuitable for travel. *Secundo*, if you appear within ten miles of the coast in trousers, you will be shot on sight."

Archer shuddered. That was a convincing argument.

It was convincing enough to get him into the clothes, once he figured out how to wear them. They consisted of: a loincloth (a long cotton rectangle with a cloth-strip belt); knee-long woolen tunic that was two rectangles sewn together on three sides, with openings left for the head and arms (the loincloth was new, the tunic second-hand: it had been boiled to get rid of the insects); a greasy leather jerkin; and calf-high boots, thick around the ankles. When Archer returned to the tavern's main room, feeling like an extra in a costume epic, the Melaklos produced a belt, a hooded woolen cloak, and a leather traveling pouch. Into this he put his four remaining possessions: his pocketknife (it might be useful), the sleeping pills (he wasn't sure why), the little gray-green *King Lear* (to read, and to remind him of home), and of course the panorama egg.

The Melaklos promptly added more to his load, mostly food: eggs, sausage, cheese, dried fish. Her own gray bag was already laced shut and slung across her shoulder. A wine skin balanced it at the other side.

Archer slung his own pouch and skin in imitation. He picked up the small gray bundle that was his clothes and his rejected possessions. "What do I do with this?" he asked.

"There will be a bonfire on the mud flat," said the Melaklos. "We shall pass it on our way."

It was a good large bonfire, zealously tended by a troop of smoke-grimy children. Archer held his bundle, not wanting to throw it in. He was holding his past between his hands. Thirty three years of life. The fire seemed to reach for it greedily.

Self-consciously he glanced at the Melaklos, but she was not looking at him. She stood gazing beyond the river, beyond the forests, as though she looked far down the roads that they would travel. If she felt Archer's eyes on her, she made no sign.

Archer looked back at the fire. A log near the center cracked and fell, sending up red-golden sparks. He threw the bundle hard into the heart of the flames. There was a sudden flare as the cloth caught fire.

Archer laughed. He felt that he had just cast away a great burden. This was a new world, and he was starting afresh.

Light-headed, he turned to the Melaklos and made a slight mocking bow. "Lead on, MacDuff," he said. "Forward to Byzantium."

"Kos-Alar," she corrected, with an amused twist to her mouth.

Archer waved the correction away. "Kos-Alar, then. But forward nonetheless."

Chapter Six

Summer: 4th quarter, day 30
(last day)

The *tsol* forest meets the sea two hundred miles above Dragonspaw Gulf, along part of the line of bluffs that forms the western coast from the stone lands just above Dragonspaw to the Great Salt Marsh in the north. The cliffs rise and fall irregularly from a height of a few yards to the five-hundred-yard point north of Ker. In the *tsol*-forest range, they are between ten and fifty yards high.

The sea undermines these bluffs. The trees nearest it tilt crazily over the edge, roots half-exposed, ready to topple to the coarse sand below. When enough of the sandy soil falls, the land begins to encroach on the sea in its turn.

"Increasing store with loss and loss with store," murmured the Melaklos when they came upon a landfall south of kos-Alar. "The coastline above Dragonspaw is constantly changing." She spoke several times of this, until Archer half expected the city to be drastically changed from the first time he had seen it.

Traces of the coastal change could be seen in kos-Alar itself. Broken wall foundations crumbled on the shelving shore, half buried in the sand, showing how far the city had once reached. The stone piles of the Long Pier, destroyed in some forgotten holocaust, ran up the broad main street to the now-useless sea wall, marking some ancient limit of the waters.

Kos-Alar sprawls in the lower inward curve of a small natural harbor, shallow in the south where the docks are. The water is deeper in the north, where the Yrtsol (the forest river) pours into it. The basin of the river had been widened behind its mouth, to allow piers to be set up to handle the extensive river trade. No one knew how long ago this had been done. The docks were silting up; nothing seemed to work against that. The Melaklos said that kos-Alar was in her long decline.

She didn't look like a dying city that year, Archer thought as he and the Melaklos walked down the broad main street.

Kos-Alar, river-seacoast city, was frantically a.
been so filled with life and noise in the early spr..
first saw it.

"Festival begins tonight," said the Melaklos, as if ..
plain.

They were behind the old seawall, then, in the section of the city that was built mostly of stone. The buildings were long, low, flat-roofed and windowless—possibly for protection from the occasional violent storms. Here lived the moderately wealthy merchants, and such minor aristocracy as the city boasted. Wealthier merchants and the two ruling families had more elaborate houses of wood and stone in the fringes of the forest behind the city.

The old sea wall was now the boundary between rich and poor. As they passed through the great bronze gates, Archer was as always struck by the sudden change. At one moment he was passing painted stone buildings and elaborate fountains; twenty steps later, he was passing the small wooden dwellings of the tavern keepers and prostitutes. They lived nearest the broad street, crowded against the Long Pier piles as against cage bars.

In the narrow crooked streets beyond, cheap wine shops were cramped among the tenements, the flimsy wooden island houses of the poor. As they shouldered toward the sea, they grew flimsier and more crowded, until they smashed like waves against the blank back wall of the city guards' barracks.

Here, under the walls of the watchmen, was the worst part of the city. Few families lived in this last narrow strip of tenements. Only those who had business here slept in the rotting houses. Taverns outnumbered all other buildings and businesses: lizard nests, where the wine and the girls were cheap and coarse and quick, and life often the same. This was the killing quarter. The city guard did not patrol here.

The blank-backed barracks against which the tenements flung themselves were narrow and long, housing the city guard, dock workers from the major warehouses, an occasional important traveler, and (unofficially) at least half of the dockside whores.

Between the barracks and the docks rose the warehouses which reached almost to the boardwalk that ran along the shore. The little custom houses were spaced along the boardwalk, one to every pair of piers.

There was a usable sea wall, but it was under water most of the time. Only a triple-moon tide would uncover the almost slimy stones. It made a ten-foot drop five feet from the boardwalk, ample for the shallow-draught ships of the time. In early summer ships would have been crowded as close to it as the harbor officials dared, the docks full. Now it was late summer, the day before Autumn Festival, and a third of the piers were closed, the rest only half filled.

They would be closing more docks after the festival, Archer thought as he scanned them. Most of the ships would probably leave after the five-day stay.

The Melakos, at his shoulder, made a small sharp movement.

"What is it?" Archer, attuned now to her almost imperceptible reactions, was instantly alert. "The people we're meeting?"

"One of them." She was peering toward the northward docks. "His ship is in. For the other—" She turned her head and looked southwest, shading her eyes against the late sun. "They left Gurn six days ago," she said, half to herself. "The way is not so long."

Archer was used to her thinking aloud by now. He leaned against a post and looked out over the bright water of the harbor. He had stood here before, looked at the same scene, but he could scarcely recall that first glimpse. That had been on his fourth night in this strange world, and that was—how long ago? He wasn't sure. He turned to the Melaklos.

"How long have I been here?" he asked.

Startled, she turned her head quickly. "Two seasons," she said. "Half a year Dolesar, about eight months Earth time. In that half year you have lost weight, trained into good condition, learned how to use a sword and more about archery, and grown a beard. The beard suits you." She resumed her scanning of the sea.

Amused, Archer stroked the beard. It was short and sometimes annoying, but anything was better than being shaved by the barbers in most places here. When he was honest with himself, he admitted that he liked having it. It was another of the things that his family and the firm would not have put up with. Like the archery and fencing.

Well, he had them, too, with a difference. The equipment was primitive: wooden short-bows, bronze- or stone-tipped arrows. And he did no target-shooting, not any more. They hunted to eat. As for the fencing, that wasn't the right word. The sword he wore was not made for fine work. It was bronze, long and heavy, didn't hold an edge very well, and was not pointed. It had taken him weeks to learn to wield it with any dexterity. With swords like that, size and power were trumps in a fight, but the Melaklos could beat him with either hand, small as she was. He had scars and bruises to remind him of that, some of them from the morning's workout. It wasn't always comforting to remember that she was exceptional, made of sprung steel, or to recall the night when she smashed the arm of a drunken mercenary twice her size without breaking the skin.

He looked at her and shook his head. Half a year in this place, and he wasn't used to her. People called her Melaklos as if it were a descriptive term, and referred to her by that fourth pronoun, *ke*, which is used in the trade tongue to refer to something neither masculine nor feminine, but living and therefore not neuter. She called it the neutral. Various peoples applied it to weapons, ships, the sea, fire, the moons, and nearly all mythological figures, gods and monsters alike. The Melaklos was probably a demon of some sort.

Her voice broke across his thoughts. "There."

Where she pointed a small black ship with blue and white diagonally striped sails bobbed just outside the harbor mouth but did not seem to be coming inside.

"What are they doing?" he asked.

"I do not know." She shaded her eyes with both hands. Tension edged her voice.

Worried, Archer shaded his eyes also and watched the ship. Whoever was on her was acting strange. The striped sails came down abruptly, as if slashed.

"They've felled the mast," she said.

In the sun glare Archer could not see much, but he did make out a long irregular shape that glided away from the shadow of the craft. It looked vaguely like a canoe, with insect-leg paddles plying on either side.

"Smoke," breathed the Melaklos. "They have set fire to her and left her."

Incredulous, Archer lifted his gaze to the ship. The air seemed to waver above it. Then he saw the flames, flickering over the black sides like transparent flags. They looked unreal in the bright sunlight. They should have been unreal. Seamen—particularly north-islanders, and that looked like a north-island ship—set far too much store by their vessels to burn them like that. Something was very wrong.

"So," said the Melaklos in a low dangerous voice. She was looking southward along the boardwalk.

Archer turned to see what else had caught her gaze. A small body of foresters turned from the boardwalk onto the southernmost pier, started along it. They moved purposefully, stiffly, bunched together.

The back of Archer's neck prickled. They looked dangerous. He turned to ask the Melaklos about them, but she spoke as he turned.

"Puppets—" Her voice was a strained whisper. She stared past him at the foresters. The skin of her face was stretched tight over the fine bones, her lips curled back in a grin of death.

The look of her chilled Archer. He said sharply, "Melaklos!"

She seemed to freeze for a moment, drew a long breath and turned without speaking to scan the northward docks again. Men were working on the piers, unloading late-arriving shops.

"Go meet the small boat," she said. "There will be trouble."

Trouble? Archer glanced out. The incomers were nearer, so near that he could see that they had no boat. There were about a dozen of them astride what must have been part of their mast, paddling with oar blades. They were approaching the nearest pier, the one the foresters had taken. That must be the trouble. Foresters and the people from the ship.

The Melaklos was speaking again. "There is a woman—tall, black-haired. She knows my name." She started north along the boardwalk.

"Where are *you* going?" he called after her.

"For reinforcements. Go." She increased her pace to a long loping run.

Baffled, Archer looked after her. He didn't think she was deserting. His not to reason why—he turned and started south at a run.

The boardwalk was long. By the time he reached the pier, the mast was pulling alongside a piling. Dockmen lowered a knotted rope from the planking six feet above them.

Archer turned onto the pier.

One of the mast-riders climbed the rope. The stern and bow men clung to the pile lashings, keeping the mast close while the rest balanced it. The climber was pulled over the edge by the dockmen. The rope snaked down again.

The foresters moved. Archer, halfway down the pier, couldn't clearly see what they did. A second rope-climber dropped back onto the mast, spilling his companions. Taken by surprise, they floundered in the water.

Dockmen, apparently protesting, were thrown in after

them. Sailors and Dockworkers alike tried to climb the slippery pilings, gave up and started for shore. The foresters ignored them. They were clustered about a piling-pillar.

Archer was almost upon them. They did not seem to notice. He slowed to a walk, trying to move silently. What were they doing? They were in a semi-circle, he saw now. Someone must be trapped against the post, between them and the water.

A woman's voice came from the semi-circle, clear, biting. "River rats. Bark eaters."

The arc bulged and broke at one point. In the instant before it re-formed, Archer saw her. Tall, black-haired, wielding a long sword. The woman he was to meet.

He had to get her out. He ran at the preoccupied foresters. A charge, a shout, a hard push, and two of them were in the water. Archer burst into the space inside the arc.

The black-haired woman turned, eyes blazing, sword lifted. "So!" she said. "A river rat with teeth!" She lunged at him.

Startled, Archer side-stepped just in time. "I'm with the Melaklos!" he shouted.

She checked in mid-strike. "Melaklos?" Her head went back. Her eyes were gray ice, judging him.

If she didn't believe him, she would try to kill him.

He saw movement out of the corner of his eye. The foresters had come a short step closer. He looked at their eyes for the first time—flat, empty, the eyes of men without souls.

Bronze gleamed in their hands: the long knives that were the river men's chief weapons. They swayed closer, moving as if they were a single organism controlled by a single intelligence.

Abruptly Archer realized just how much trouble he was in. He cursed himself for bursting in like that. There were ten foresters. They could kill him easily. If the woman believed him, the two of them had a fighting chance, especially if the Melaklos brought her reinforcements. If she didn't believe him, he was as good as dead.

She had to believe him.

The foresters swayed forward another step. They were pressed shoulder to shoulder now, a solid wall just out of sword-slash. They moved as one entity, leaderless, their eyes shining.

His sword was in his hand. He didn't remember drawing it.

Less than half a minute ago he had burst through the ring of foresters. In another half minute he could be dead. He had to convince the woman that he was telling the truth, that he knew the Melaklos. How? He had no tokens of her. He could think of only one way.

He edged closer to the frowning woman, pitched his voice low so that the foresters would not hear. Keeping his eyes on them, he tossed out scraps, bits of detail about the Melaklos to show that he knew her.

"She'd come about to your shoulder. She always wears gray, even though it isn't available here. Her eyes would be beautiful if they watched you from this world. I don't think anyone's seen her asleep. You can't tell what she feels or thinks. She never laughs, she never cries, and she—" He broke off.

The woman was laughing.

Startled, Archer looked at her.

Her gray eyes held genuine amusement, her voice was warm. "You do know her."

Reassured, Archer smiled back at her. "I said I did." He had succeeded. She believed him. And she was laughing, surrounded by enemies. He felt a surge of admiration.

The foresters inched forward.

With his first problem gone, Archer wondered why they didn't attack. They must want the woman alive—alive and uninjured.

She said, "We could swim."

Archer glanced at her. Her clothes wouldn't hamper her: she wore a coarse sailor's tunic, dripping from her ride on the mast. They could swim.

No. In the water, a sword would be clumsy, no match for the long knives.

He moved closer to her, so that his shoulder touched the pitch-painted pole at her back. "The Melaklos said she'd get reinforcements," he said in a low voice. "We can wait until they get here—if they get here—or break out now."

He didn't want to wait. It was foolish to stand here and hope she'd reach them in time. He glanced again at the woman.

She said simply, "They expect any break to be made landward. Their weak point is at the seaward side."

She agreed then. He said, "On count. *Ke-bo-sa-trol!*"

Shouting the last word, he charged the arc. She was on his shoulder, also shouting. They bowled over three foresters. A fourth clutched at Archer. Archer slammed the flat of his sword into the man's head, knocking him back.

They were in the clear, wheeling the circle of foresters. Archer grabbed the woman's hand and ran for the boardwalk.

Someone turned onto the pier—two people, the Melaklos, tiny and gray, beside a black-bearded giant.

Archer risked a flying look back. The foresters were just grouping, starting after them in a body.

Someone roared. The woman shouted, "No!"

Archer turned back, glimpsed something flying at him. Desperately he dropped to the planks, twisting away. Something glanced off his skull. Pain exploded in his head.

The black-bearded giant roared again, raised his weapon, a huge brass-bound quarterstaff.

Archer couldn't move, could barely see. Hazily he wondered why the Melaklos wanted someone to kill him.

The giant whirled the staff about his head, brought it down viciously.

Gray flashed at him. He was three times the Melaklos's weight. She could not stagger him, nor did she try. She knocked his arms aside as the staff came down.

It whistled past Archer's ear; the shock of it on the pier numbed his supporting hand. He stared at the dent it left in the ironwood planks, feeling sick. That blow would have smashed his skull like an eggshell.

Through the roaring in his head he heard the Melaklos speaking in the acid tone she used to point out stupid errors in shooting. The giant rumbled uneasily in reply and lumbered away, toward the approaching foresters.

"He's hurt," said the black-haired woman, close to Archer.

He could scarcely hear her through the singing in his head. He looked toward her. For a moment her face swam into focus, watching him anxiously. Then it blurred. He closed his eyes, fighting nausea.

Hands half lifted him, propped him sitting against a piling post. Small competent fingers probed his scalp, sending stabs of pain through his head. He winced, tried to squirm away.

"It is not serious," said the Melaklos.

A lot she knew, Archer thought furiously. He tried to tell her so, but he couldn't get his mouth to work.

"That Lash!" said the black-haired woman angrily.

"He is impetuous," said the Melaklos, as if to explain.

"I'll impel him!" Her tone changed to concern. "Are you sure he's all right? His eyes look strange."

Hers were worried when she came into focus. Through the confusion and pain Archer was dimly grateful to her. The Melaklos was as calm and cool as though he had stubbed a toe, and that irritated him.

They were kneeling on either side of him, the woman

toward the boardwalk. She kept a hand on Archer's shoulder as if to keep him upright.

The Melaklos said, "Your men have swum ashore. Keep them back."

"Back?" The woman was startled. "But the foresters—Lash—they'll be furious."

"No doubt," said the Melaklos dryly.

There was a short silence.

"All right, then," said the woman. She stood up. "All right."

That didn't seem to fit what he had seen of her, Archer thought. The way she had faced the foresters alone, her unexpected laughter. He hadn't thought that she would give in so tamely. The Melaklos must have some power over her.

A hand touched his forehead. He made out the face of the Melaklos herself, looking through him with her distant gaze. Her face tightened, the bones standing out. Something seemed to brush at Archer's mind, like a chill wind in his brain. Then it was gone. Her face relaxed, she sat back.

Had she been messing around inside his head? She could probably do it. He was no longer surprised at the improbable things she did. Still, no distant-eyed sorceress was going to muck about in his head. Angrily he sat up, setting everything spinning again.

She must have seen the anger in his face, for she said quietly, "A liberty, of course. Necessity knows—"

The ringing in his ears drowned her voice. He closed his eyes again, leaning against the post. His head swam.

He remembered suddenly a game that he had played with other children nearly thirty years ago in another world. They would close their eyes and spin about, making themselves dizzy, seeing who could keep his balance longest. Now he felt the same disorientation, the same roller-coaster nausea.

Something cut through the fog in his brain. He jerked his head up, bit back a cry as it hit the post. The pain somehow jarred his senses into focus, so that he saw clearly what happened then.

The woman had cried out, he realized. He looked for her. She stood on the boardwalk at the pier's end, surrounded by angry, dripping wet sailors. They looked like a pack of hounds straining at leash, gazing hungrily down the pier.

Archer turned his head seaward, ignoring the twinges of pain.

The foresters ran toward them in a body. Behind them the giant charged and roared. He swung his staff; a man flew into

48

the dock, flailing. The rest ran faster, but still together, as if they were one animal.

"Careless," murmured the Melaklos. "If careless enough—" She rose to meet them, empty-handed. She stood weaponless in the center of the pier, head half averted.

They would kill her. The thought cleared Archer's head. He couldn't let that happen. He tried to get up, lost his balance and fell back.

Light footsteps ran to him, a hand, caught his shoulder. "No," said the black-haired woman. "She must know—" But she bit her lip and did not look away from the Melaklos.

Clenching his teeth, Archer tried again to get up. His muscles would not respond. He was helpless.

The foresters were close enough now for him to see their set faces, the dead light of their eyes. If they saw the Melaklos, they did not show it. Dead eyes passed her and fixed on the black-haired woman.

Grimly Archer tried to reach his fallen sword, his knife. There would be a fight, and he couldn't move! Beside him, the black-haired woman caught her breath.

The Melaklos raised her head.

The foresters faltered. Then their faces changed.

Archer went cold all over. The change was horrible.

Life leaped into their eyes, and with it terror. They backed away from the Melaklos, spreading apart. For the first time they moved as individuals. They turned to see the giant roaring down on them. With cries of panic they ran aside, leaped into the water.

The Melaklos stepped forward, caught one by the arm. He thrashed in blind fear, trying to pull away from a grip that Archer knew to be like steel.

She spoke to the onrushing giant, "Lash. A prisoner."

Desperate, the forester twisted enough to whip out his long knife. He slashed at the Melakos. She sprang back, releasing him, and he leaped into the water. The giant's staff missed him by inches.

"We can catch one at the shore," he bellowed.

The Melaklos made a sharp gesture. "It is too late to learn anything," she said. She turned back toward Archer and the woman.

She's wearing jewelry, was Archer's first surprised thought.

Metal gleamed on her chest where the forester's knife had ripped her outer tunic.

Either she's a robot or she's wearing jewelry, Archer thought hazily. Neither very likely. He tried to hold onto the surprise and the thought, but his head was beginning to whirl again. It throbbed like a kettledrum.

Jewelry? The Melaklos?

The giant said something in a rumbling roar that faded to silence as darkness took Archer.

Chapter Seven

Autumn Festival, first night of five

There was darkness, and the throbbing ache in his head. Voices far away. A sensation of being lifted, carried. Rhythmic motion that lulled him back into darkness.

Scraps of speech floated by. His name in the deep cool voice of the Melaklos, the tall woman's, "Who is he?" And again—later? He could not tell—the Malaklos, saying, "Deception, yes. It is necessary. Listen to me." She sounded exasperated, he thought drowsily, and drifted back into unconsciousness.

Later, how much later he did not know, there was red light through his eyelids, and familiar air: heavy with smoke, sharp with wine and sweat and perfume, astir with voices. A wine shop. He was in a wine shop. Yes.

Keeping his eyes closed, he took stock of himself. The ache in his head had faded to a dull throb. His left hand hurt where it had hit the pier as he fell. Otherwise, he felt all right.

Someone was speaking in a loud rumble. That would be the giant. Archer opened his eyes just enough to see, wanting to know whom he was with before he said anything.

The giant was seated across from him at a small square table. Archer himself was propped against the wall between the Melaklos (who, as usual, was almost in the corner) and the black-haired woman, who was speaking now in a quick earnest voice, with sketchy movements of her long hands. She spoke to the Melaklos. Archer watched the gray woman.

She silenced the tall woman with a small hand motion, leaned forward and spoke slowly and patiently. Something swung from her neck and hit the table, gleaming in the torchlight.

Archer remembered his last confused thought on the pier, that she was wearing jewelry. He had never seen her with so much as a wire ring. Her cloak clasp was only a thumb-sized oval of beaten bronze.

The medallion that rested against the table was of beaten

bronze also, tilted so that he could not see the pattern hammered onto it. Its long leather cord allowed it to lie almost flat on the stained and battered boards.

Something gleamed silver above it, swinging in the shadow of her ripped outer tunic, against the paler inner one. The second pendant looked like a carved cylinder, tarnished black in its pattern. He could not see it well.

The giant was speaking again, shaking his head impatiently.

Archer realized belatedly that they spoke a language he did not understand. He started to sit up, to ask them to speak the trade tongue.

"*Vershal.*" The word cut harshly across the giant's rumble.

Archer looked at the speaker, and felt a shock. Standing beside the Melaklos, gaze fixed on the silver cylinder, was one of the Silent Men of Sandolan.

The Silent Men were small broad-shouldered sailors with fox-colored hair and amber eyes. They never spoke to anyone, never looked at anyone, except their compatriots. A Sandol alone in a tavern drank his wine silently, ignoring whores and games and brawls. A group of them might exchange a few words, might sing one of their soft eerie songs, but no more. Now this one was speaking to a stranger, speaking loudly.

"By what right do you wear that?" His voice shook, his pointing hand trembled.

The Melaklos turned her head, not surprised. One hand came up, touched the cylinder on its slender silver chain.

"This?" she said.

"Yes." He added something in the harsh tongue of Sandolan.

Archer sat up, alert. Something was wrong here—what? He glanced at the giant and the tall woman. They sat still, watching, worried.

"So," said the Melaklos. She stood up and faced the Sandolan, speaking quickly and quietly in his language. He asked abrupt questions.

Once, his hand gripped the hilt of his seaman's knife. Archer tensed, ready to defend the Melaklos if necessary.

She said one word in a voice like a whiplash. The Silent Man took his hand from the knife. For a long moment they faced each other in silence.

Frustrated, Archer gripped the edge of the table. What were they doing?

Abruptly the Sandolan stepped back and extended both

hands, palms forward. The Melaklos touched palms with him in the gesture of greeting and truce. Without another word he turned and walked away.

"What was that all about?" Archer asked as the Melaklos sat down.

She glanced sidelong at him. "You have awakened. That is good."

He started to ask again, but the black-haired woman forestalled him.

"What do you wear, Melaklos? It looks like—" She broke off, glanced at the giant.

"Only one thing would so disturb a Sandolan," he said soberly.

They both looked at the Melaklos with worry and something else—fear, Archer thought—in their eyes.

He turned back to the Melaklos, to her impassive dust-colored face, the gleam of silver at her throat. The islanders knew, or thought they knew, what she had.

She gazed at each of the three in turn until they looked away. Quietly she said, "You know what it is."

"I—" Archer's voice caught. He cleared his throat and tried again. "I don't know."

She looked at him again. "No." She shrugged one shoulder and lifted the silver chain carefully over her head.

The two islanders moved as if to object, settled back. The Melaklos handed the cylinder to Archer.

It seemed to be a whistle, slightly larger than his little finger. It was carved with a spiral design; turning it, he saw that this was a snake that wound up the cylinder. Tiny marks appeared between its coils—writing, he thought. It was a beautiful thing, and apparently very old, but he couldn't see anything in it to worry an islander and make a Silent Man speak. Puzzled, he looked up at the Melaklos. "What is it?" he asked.

The giant rumbled softly, "It is the Sandolan Talisman."

"*K'kir-aqhel*," said the woman soberly.

Each islander traced a symbol in the air, murmured, "Arila protect."

"It calls the Great Serpent," said the Melaklos, in English.

Great Serpent—where had he heard those words before? Undoubtedly from her. He tried to remember what she had said. "Isn't that the giant sea serpent who's supposed to sleep in the Great Deeps? The one who dreams of everything that happens?"

"Yes."

53

Archer shook his head incredulously. She had told him many tales during the past half year, many of them fantastic. The Great Serpent was certainly that—it dreamed, it spoke to men. Obvious fantasy. But the islanders looked serious, and he remembered the agitation of the Silent Man. They believed it. Did the Melaklos? He could not read her face.

Did he? Or could he? Half a year ago, in New York, he would have said, "No. Impossible." Now he could only say, "Well, maybe." Uncertainty made him angry. Sharply, he said, "This Great Serpent—does it exist?"

"I have seen *ke*—I have spoken with *ke*." She looked straight at him, said, "This is not superstition, or some equivalent of the Loch Ness monster. As to the dreams, I cannot speak. But the Serpent is the oldest living thing in the world Dolesar."

Baffled, Archer looked at the table. He didn't want to believe her. She had been stripping certainties from him since the day when he'd walked into his office and found her waiting for him—waiting with the first impossibility, the panorama egg. It had to stop somewhere.

Impatiently he dismissed the thought. That wasn't important now. Now he wanted to know about the whistle. That was what had upset everyone. It called the Great Serpent, who was important in their mythology. That explained it. All right, then.

But one question still bothered him. He said, "I thought the Great Serpent could not be bound."

The Melaklos smiled her twisted half-smile. "*Sa-il kor*—chosen bondage," she said. "The Serpent bound *keself* to answer the call in the time of Sandolan, when the sea god Arila was young. By no other means can *ke* be called or commanded." She shook her head and was still.

"*Sa-il kor*," repeated the black-haired woman, and again traced the sign in the air.

The Melaklos seemed to wake with a start. "So," she said, and moved her hand. The whistle vanished. She reached for the yellow jar on the table. "Wine, Archer?"

With the break in the serious mood, Archer and the islanders relaxed and picked up their cups. The woman was drinking water, Archer saw, and wondered if it would be rude to ask why.

But, more important, he still didn't know who the two strangers were, or what the foresters had been doing on the pier, or why the ship had been burnt. He lifted his cup in ritual silent salute, swallowed wine, and turned to the Melaklos. "Are we allowed to know each other?" he asked.

She glanced sidelong at him. "They know your name. You are Archer. This"—(indicating the giant)—"is Lash." She pronounced it somewhere between lash-as-in-whip and losh.

Archer tried to repeat it correctly. He looked across the table. The giant didn't look as tall as he had on the pier, but he was tall enough—well over six and a half feet, and powerfully built. His black beard was short and badly trimmed, his hair greased and braided in south-islander sailor fashion. His eyes were startlingly pale, china blue against his weatherburnt face.

"The lady is Nayan," said the Melaklos.

Had there been the suspicion of a pause before the name? Archer thought so. He caught the troubled glance that the woman shot across the table before she turned to him.

"Aach'," she said. She had a north-island drawl.

"Nayan," said Archer. It was accented on the second syllable: nah-YON. He smiled at her. "It's a nice name."

She flushed and looked away.

Archer sipped at his wine, suppressing mild anger. She hadn't flushed at the compliment, he was sure of that. He remembered the pause before the name, her quick glance. Something more—the Melaklos's voice echoing in his head during half-consciousness, saying something about deception. Well, he had found a deception. Nayan was not the woman's name, he was certain. The Melaklos was playing some game with them.

Nayan. It sounded familiar. With a chill, he realized that it resembled "Diane," his wife's name. He looked at the Melaklos suspiciously; had she chosen it for that reason? Surely not. And it might have been the woman's choice. He looked at her.

She was speaking, again in that strange language. Impatiently she tossed back her head, and torchlight caught the beautiful line of her cheekbone and jaw.

She and Diane were about the same age, he thought. The realization surprised him. They didn't look the same age. Why? He poured more wine into his cup and drank it, studying the woman.

Nayan was as tall as Diane, but without her exquisite slimness—the greyhound look. Nayan's hair was black where Diane's was blonde, true black that caught the light in silver rather than gold or blue. She had had time to unbraid and arrange it: silver lizard-shaped clips held it back from her hollow temples.

Her eyes were gray, like Diane's, that stormy gray that would change with her mood and her surroundings. Laughter lines radiated from their corners. Diane called them crowsfeet and hid them, as she hid the darkening of her hair.

The difference between them was in the way they wore their years. Nayan wore hers comfortably, like an old coat. Diane wore hers like—like tight shoes.

Pleased with the simile, he swallowed wine and glanced around the room. When he looked back at the woman, he realized for the first time that she was addressing him.

"I have not yet thanked you for helping me at the docks," she said, and smiled.

He smiled back, said, "But I'm still not sure what was going on. I think it's time I found out."

"I agree," said the woman. She turned to the Melaklos. "He is your companion, so he must be trustworthy. He helped me to evade the foresters. If that is not reason enough, Lash nearly killed him. Surely that at least deserves an explanation."

Lash made an embarrassed noise like distant thunder. "Sorry about the crack on the head," he rumbled. "I thought you were a kidnapper."

"Lash is impetuous," said the Melaklos.

Archer looked at Lash, at the embarrassed twist of his china-blue eyes, and grinned. He liked this seaman, impetuous or not. He leaned over the table, extending his empty hands.

Lash grinned back and touched palms with him. "Good," he said. "Then we're all friends together, eh? And now, shadow-child,"—he scowled at the Melaklos—"what are you doing here?"

"I came to meet you two," she said, and looked across the table at Nayan. "The second moon will rise soon, and we have not heard your story. Will you speak, Lady?"

The tall woman said, "You'll have to stop me if I say too much. I am not adept in deception." Scorn edged her voice.

Archer smiled to himself. So she didn't like to lie. That should make it easier to learn who she was, and what the Melaklos was up to.

Nayan refilled her water cup, drank from it and set it down. Looking at the Melaklos, she began to speak in a quiet voice.

Chapter Eight

Autumn Festival, first night
(cont'd.)

"I have been in the south for two seasons, guesting with the—" Nayan hesitated. The Melaklos moved a hand in assent. "—with the prince of Gurn, on Dragonspaw Gulf. We took ship to return home six days ago."

"Who was with you?" asked Archer.

She did not look away from the Melaklos as she replied, "We were one ship with forty oarsmen, ten crewmen, and six attendants—all my own people, and our own ship."

Archer started to ask, "Who are your people," but he saw the Melaklos's steady gaze on him before the second word was out. Hastily he asked instead, "What happened?"

"We made slow time up the gulf coast. Yesterday, off North Point, we were attacked by two ships. One was of the southern coast. The other—I do not know." She drained her cup.

Archer picked up the wine jar, but she shook her head and reached for the water jug. "I must hold ceremony in the temple," she said.

That explained the water: purification of some sort, like fasting for a festival day. And, Archer thought, it told him that she was a priestess of some sort.

"What happened?" said Lash impatiently.

Nayan swallowed water, still looking at the Melaklos, and went on. "The coaster grappled us at dawn—we had been overnight on the water, wishing to be here for Festival." She grimaced. "A wish bitterly granted." She shook her head and sighed. "We flung them off, of course, and ran before them. They were slow, like all coastal craft, and we thought that they would soon give over."

"Did you lose anyone?" asked Lash.

"Five oarsmen, two of the crew. They didn't shoot at the robed women."

"Women?" Archer was startled. "How many women were there?"

"Twelve rowers, all of the crew, four attendants. Only the attendants were robed, of course."

"None came ashore," said Lash.

She tossed her head back impatiently. "Dead. Dead and in the sea, Arila keep them." She traced her sign in the air again.

This time Archer recognized it. It was the ship of Arila, a straight line down sweeping to a curved one across. The sign of Arila, the sea god, after whom was named the great sprawl of islands that filled the coastal sea from the North of North to the Ice Continent in the south. She was probably a priestess of Arila.

She was continuing, still watching the silent Melaklos. "They pursued us, flanking us coastwards. The other ship matched us seaward. Not wanting to be caught between them, we faced the coaster in early noon. They tried to ram us."

Lash snorted. "Fools."

Nayan shrugged. "The wind was good, and she was clumsy, like all coastal craft. We slipped away under sail. She tried to come about after us, into the wind. We heeled, and she ran broadside onto our bronze beak—"

"Beak?" said Lash. "I didn't know you used them."

"An experiment," she said. "They are effective on oar craft, but I do not think that we will use them on our ships."

Lash grunted and started to ask something else.

Exasperated, Archer struck across him. "What happened?"

She shot him a glance, looked back at the Melaklos. "We had to drop sail and pull back or we would have gone down with them. She sank. We tried to pick up a crewman to find out who they were, but the other ship came in and drove us away with arrows. We shot back and forth until the coaster was down and her men drowned. Then the strange ship fled north."

"Strange?" said Archer. "Did it carry any insignia?"

"None." She shook her head. "And the coaster bore no insignia."

Archer bit his lip and stared at the table. Only one kind of ship usually traveled without signs or banners to identify their ports of origin: pirates. But these didn't sound like pirates. He asked Nayan about it.

"I think not," she said. "The coaster may have been, of course, but not the other. They made no serious attempt to engage us. Though it was not necessary." She shivered, and for a moment the beautiful bones of her face stood out.

Puzzled, Archer leaned forward. "Not necessary? What do you mean?"

She shook her head. "They fled north. We could not catch them." She tapped on the table to emphasize her words. "We could not catch them! That was a calm-craft, a slow-water ship—broad, deep-draughted, over-masted. We were in a lightning-ship of the north. Yet they distanced us as we would distance a swamped coracle."

Lash started to speak, but she went on. "They left death behind."

Archer said, "What do you mean?"

She shivered. "I do not know what it was—some devil's magic. There was death in their arrows. All who were even scratched died within the hour. Others died in the afternoon and in the night. Their bodies rotted before we could sing the death chants and put them into the sea. The ship was like a death house in the south islands, where they keep their dead unburned above the ground."

Archer swallowed hard, fighting nausea. A ship filled with rotting death—horrible. He remembered the ship as they had seen her, slender and black outside the port's mouth, with flames above her like transparent banners. He said, "Is that why you burnt her?"

"Yes." She glanced around. "Nine of us came ashore this afternoon—eight oarsmen and myself. Nine of fifty-seven."

Archer wanted to say something to show that he felt her sorrow, but what could he say?

Lash struck the table, making jars and cups dance, and said, "This strange ship. What did it look like?"

The woman did not turn her head. She had spoken to the Melaklos throughout, Archer thought, and yet the gray woman had not made a sound. She seemed lost in thought, dark eyes on infinity.

Slowly, the tall woman answered Lash. "She was like no ship that I have seen. Broad, deep-draughted, as I said, and so slow-craft. Carvel-built."

"Not north-going, then," said Lash.

"And not wind-running: she carried one mast well forward, over-tall with a fixed square sail."

"Mm." Lash drummed on the table. "Oars?"

"Fifty, in two banks. Double-ruddered, too."

"Slow-maneuvering," muttered Lash.

Archer looked from one to the other of them. He had no idea what they were talking about. He wondered if the

Melaklos did—or if she perhaps knew whose ship it was. He looked at her again.

Her head turned slightly, her eyes met his. They were withdrawn, secret. He had seen her like that before. It would be useless to ask her anything; she would answer in riddles, or not at all. He sighed and looked back at the islanders.

"High-sided, with a high rear deck," Nayan was saying. "Extended keel, but not a high prow."

"Beaked?" rumbled Lash.

"Yes."

"Um." He stared at the table, muttering to himself.

Archer said to Nayan, "Doesn't all that give you a hint as to the ship's origin?"

She shook her head. "It's like patchwork. I only know that it isn't a northern ship—and that it shouldn't have moved as fast as it did."

Lash smote the table again, upsetting the water jug. "That ship. Black? Saffron-colored sails?"

Nayan set the jug upright. "Yes."

"Then I've seen it. It came into harbor this morning. I wondered whose it was."

"This morning?" Nayan's startled gesture nearly sent the jug over again. "Here?"

In kos-Alar—Archer touched his sword. There would be trouble—if it was still here. He said, "Did it leave?"

"Yes—only here a few hours. They picked up supplies and left."

Archer said, "Did you see the crewmen?"

The seaman drained his cup before answering, "I saw the two who came ashore—thought of talking to them, to see who they were."

"Did you?" asked Nayan.

At the same time Archer said, "What did they look like?"

Lash shook his head. "Didn't talk to 'em, and couldn't tell what they looked like—they were all wrapped up in cloaks. Could tell a bit, of course. They looked sort of Sandolanish—short, broad-shouldered. And a shop keeper who traded with them said they had golden eyes."

"No!" cried Nayan. "That ship was not of Sandolan."

"No," agreed Lash.

Archer thought, but what about the Sandolan who had spoken to the Melaklos? There might be some connection there, but what?

"They did go north," said Lash.

Nayan moved her head impatiently. "Half of Arilikan is

north of here. That means nothing." She clenched a hand and struck the table. "The Sandol are allies of—"

The Melaklos halted her with a gesture. She said, "They were not Sandol."

Allies of whom, thought Archer. She had almost slipped there, almost given him a hint of her identity. The Melaklos had stopped her, but if he could talk to her without the Melaklos—there was a chance of finding out what this was all about. If she knew. She seemed bewildered now.

"Not Sandol, then," she said. She nodded jerkily and gulped air. "Then who? Do you know?"

The Melaklos did not answer.

Archer wanted to reach out to the black-haired woman, to say that he was on her side.

She sat very still, looking at the table, shoulders high as if to guard against a blow. She was afraid, afraid because she did not know who or what was pursuing her. And angry, too; he could see that in the trembling of her tight-clenched hands. She shook her head convulsively, looked at the Melaklos. "Who?"

Unable to keep still longer, Archer leaned forward and touched her hand. "I'll stand with you," he said.

She turned her head to him. Her eyes were dark with defiance. "Against whom?" she said. "Against what?"

"The second moon is rising," said the Melaklos quietly.

Nayan closed her eyes for a moment, gathering herself. Then she opened them and stood up. Her voice was clear and steady. "I must go to the temple. My men are there—if they live still."

Lash and Archer had risen with her. She turned to leave.

"Archer," said the Melaklos. "No."

She couldn't order him about. He looked at Nayan.

"Are you initiate?" she asked.

"No."

She shook her head. "Only the initiate may attend tonight."

Stubbornly he said, "You should be protected."

Lash snorted with startled laughter. "Protected? In Festival?"

"She is in no danger," said the Melaklos. "Sit down."

"Please," said Nayan.

He remained standing by the table as she and Lash crossed the room. She had changed from her coarse sailor's tunic to north-island dress: a corded knee-long blue tunic over a full white robe. Among the dirty sailors and gaudy dancing girls, she looked like a sea queen.

When she and Lash were out of sight in the crowded street, Archer turned reluctantly to the table. He and the Melaklos faced each other across the table like antagonists. That, he thought grimly, was about right. He was going to get some answers out of her whether or not she wanted to give them.

Chapter Nine

Autumn Festival: first night (cont'd.)

The Melaklos sat still, back straight, looking into space. She looked entranced. Archer knew that she would not speak until she was addressed.

Archer refilled his cup and sorted out the questions in his head. Most of them centered around the woman called Nayan. First and last, who was she? What was she? A north-islander by her accent, a woman of rank by her bearing and attendance, a woman of intelligence and courage by her actions. Who was she?

Who was pursuing her? Someone of wide-reaching power, to command south-coast pirates and mid-coast foresters—and the strange ship. Whose ship was it; who manned it? The Silent Men? One had spoken to the Melaklos, a thing unheard of. Because of the Talisman? Or for some other reason?

Nayan had said something about the Sandol being allies— apparently allies of her own people. The Melaklos had cut her off before she named them, sliding smoothly in with a reassurance. She was sharp, was little Mera Melaklos. She had a brain like an eel, and a tongue that could turn night to day. After half a year, Archer still wasn't sure whether he hated her.

Hadn't he once written arguments against hate, against all strong emotions? So he had, when he was a lot younger, when "cool" was the keynote, yeah, understatement was the word. Play it cool. Don't get upset, nothing's worth the bother, because there ain't going to be no tomorrow. No, sir. But tomorrow fooled you. It came, and kept coming, tomorrow and tomorrow, until finally you realized that you were frozen into waiting. You decided that if life was a brief candle, you would burn it at both ends. Then you found out, and you envied the ones who kept waiting. You found out that you were too set in your ways, (face it, Archer) too scared to change. So you envied the ones who didn't care.

Happy are those who yet before their death can let their blood run cold.

He looked at the unseeing eyes of the Melaklos and shivered. And yet—and yet she was the one who had helped him break his pattern. She had given him the panorama egg. She had stayed with him for eight months on this world, teaching him, testing him. She was a thief and a market-place story teller, and a sorceress who never used sorcery. She was weaving a tale now—she was gathering threads together. Himself, Nayan, Lash—why had she brought them together, here and now?

What was behind the mask of her distant eyes?

Angry, Archer wrenched away from the puzzle. It was unnerving to wonder about her for long. She was the Melaklos, and that was that. He wasn't concerned with her now, except to ask her questions. And if he didn't start, he might not get the chance to ask them.

Best to begin abruptly, perhaps startle her into revealing something. There was only one question to open with.

He rapped sharply on the table, snapped, "Who is she?"

The Melaklos did not start. Her eyes withdrew from emptiness, focused on him. "She is Nayan," she said quietly.

Archer shook his head. "No. That's not her name, and I know it as well as you do."

"To you, she is Nayan. I do not choose to tell you who she is. I do not choose that you should know."

Anger blurred Archer's thoughts. He thrust it roughly away. "Who are you, to choose what I know or don't know?"

She moved her hands. "I am the Melaklos." It was a simple statement.

"What's that to me?" snarled Archer. He controlled his anger to say, "She's a north-island noblewoman. North-islanders are honest people. She doesn't like to lie. Do you think she'll keep up this masquerade just because you ask her to?"

"Yes."

Archer didn't know whether to laugh or shout at her incredible self-assurance. He reached blindly for his wine cup, choked on the sweet wine. When he stopped coughing, he was calmer. It never helped to lose his temper with her—he had learned that long ago.

She went on as if he had not interrupted, "Nayan is a northerner, yes. She is proud and self-willed. Nevertheless, she will keep silence as I ask it. So will you."

"Me?" Archer had to whisper to keep from shouting. "Why?"

"Because soon—very soon—there will be trouble. More trouble than the pursuit of one island woman. When that comes, security lies in ignorance. The less you know, the safer you are."

Archer tried to interrupt, to question this new puzzle, but she went on.

"So far as you are concerned—so far as she is concerned—you are a traveling stranger named Archer and she a northern noblewoman called Nayan, both known to the Melaklos. You do not know her name or nation; she does not know that you are from another world. Keep it so."

"Not unless you give me a good reason!" Archer burst out. "I think you're playing games."

"That ship—the arrows of death—the puppet foresters: those are no games, Archer."

Exasperated, he said, "But whose are they? Who's behind it?"

"A magician."

"Who?"

"I cannot say." She paused. "He is careless, but powerful."

"Careless?" said Archer. She'd said something about that on the pier. "How, careless?"

"He has twice failed to capture Nayan—both times by foolish tricks. Once by hired pirates, once by—" She stopped abruptly.

Archer remembered her face when she looked at the foresters, with skin tight over the skull, remembered her strained whisper of a word that she had used again. "Puppets," he said. "What did you mean by that?"

"They were puppets today. He controlled them through their minds."

Archer shivered. "Is that why they looked like—like men without souls?"

She cocked her head. "That is well said. Men without souls. So they were—their souls were held away."

"Their eyes changed when they saw you—is that when he stopped controlling them?"

"Yes. He was careless to remain with them so long, or indeed to attempt so many. He could not control them as individuals, but only as a mass."

Archer remembered their actions, how they moved as one, how they were slow to react. A magician, controlling them as puppets. The thought chilled him. He remembered the touch that had brushed against his mind.

"Did you do something inside my head?" he demanded.

For the first time since he had met her, she looked uncomfortable. "I had to correct the injury," she said, and moved a hand. "It was unpardonable."

Archer grinned. She was just a little off balance. If he could disturb her further, she might tell him something important. He said, "Are you the puppet controller?"

"No."

"Can I believe that? You fit the bill: you're a magician."

She sighed and looked straight at him. "I am not a magician. I have some small skill in magic, but I am not a magician. I am a sorcerer."

Archer gave up his impulse to argue. "This magician. You won't say who he is. Do you know?"

"Not yet. I have touched him, but the contact was too brief."

"Touched him? Today?"

"No."

Doubtful, Archer studied her face. He couldn't tell whether she was lying. He picked up the wine jar and half filled his cup, considering. There had been some other trouble with a magician, hadn't there? He said, "Is this the same one who interfered with our arrival?"

"Yes." She seemed abstracted. A torch on the wall behind her sputtered and went out, leaving half her face in shadow like a motley mask. Archer said nothing, waiting. Presently, she roused herself and turned to him. "Give me the egg," she said.

Suspicious, he drew back. "What for?"

She said slowly, not looking at him, "It would perhaps be best that I send you back now."

"No!" He jumped up, knocking the heavy bench over. "I'm not going back yet!"

She did not seem to notice his outburst. Deliberately she picked up her cup, swallowed wine, set it down again. She did not look at him.

Trying to lighten his anger, he said, "Are you kidding? Go home now, just when things are beginning to get interesting? After eight months of sword practice? I'm staying." He hesitated, then added, "I told Nayan I'd stand with her."

She looked at him with her weighing gaze, the one he had faced in his office so long ago. "Very well," she said. "I shall not send you yet. Give me the egg."

Her voice was compelling. He had the egg out of his scrip and half across the table before he knew it. Then he snatched it back. "Why do you want it?" he asked stubbornly.

"I must set the limits of your being gone."

He held onto the egg. "You're tricky, you are. You set the limit for eight and a half months, and I pop back into New York in a few weeks, is that it?"

"No." She tilted the wine jar over her cup and watched the last golden drops run out. "The time of your being gone is not the time of your being here."

"What's that supposed to mean?"

"You have been here for eight months. You have not been gone for eight months. I could send you back to your world within a splintered second of your leaving it, so that in that splinter of a second you would have lived eight months."

Archer shook his head. It wasn't hard to accept, considering some of the things that he had already swallowed, but it sounded confusing.

As if she read the thought, the Melaklos said, "Because of the inevitable disorientation, a time lapse is advisable. Prolonged unconsciousness offers some explanation besides sudden insanity."

Archer laughed shortly and picked up his cup. Insane would be the word for anyone who spent eight months in a dream world and then returned half a second after he'd left. It would drive anyone mad. "Here's to insanity," he said, and drank the little wine he had left. He said, "Then time is relative?"

"Everything is relative. Give me the egg."

"I'm not going back," he repeated.

"I am only going to set the margin in time. I shall not send you back until and unless it is necessary. Give me the egg.

He curled his fingers around the egg, feeling its smooth weight. "How do I know I can trust you?"

"You do not know, and you cannot trust me. Nevertheless, you must." Her dark eyes were steady as she spoke.

Must? She was right. He was here through some sorcery of hers. She could probably send him back if she wanted to. Even if she couldn't send him back without the egg, there were other things she could do: imprison him, cast him into sleep, transform him. He had to stay on her good side, if she had one.

She was waiting, dark eyes glinting in a half-lit face. Silently she extended a hand, palm upward.

Reluctantly, he put the egg into it.

"Two weeks, I think," she said. She closed her eyes, holding the egg between her palms.

Archer watched, scarcely breathing. He had not seen her work with sorcery before.

Her face tightened to the bone, as it had that afternoon when she saw the foresters and again when she brushed his mind. Some trick of light from the single torch cast both her eyes into deep shadow. She looked like a small image of Death. Death in motley.

She gasped. Her face twisted suddenly. Her hands, holding the egg, began to shake.

Afraid, Archer stood up, leaned over the small table. "What's wrong?"

She bared her teeth. Harsh sounds came from her throat, two words that he could distinguish: "Take—egg—"

He pried her hands apart—her fingers were like steel sheathed in ice—and put the egg into his bag.

With it gone, her fragile control snapped. She arched back as if from electricity; her clawed fingers scrabbled at the table top. Her body convulsed with the effort to breathe.

Helplessly he looked around for something to bring her out of it. Water? Lash had spilt it. Wine? It was gone.

Her head went back, the tendons of her neck stood out, pulsing with the effort to draw air.

He could think of only one thing to try. He gripped one arm—the muscles were like stone—and slapped her face, forehand and backhand, savagely.

Air ripped into her throat. She went limp, slumped into her corner as he released her.

Anxiously he watched her, still standing. What had gone wrong? Was she all right?

She spoke at last, her voice rasping. "That was well done, Archer. I thank you."

Embarrassed, he sat down. He had never heard her thank anyone out of sincerity rather than courtesy before. He said, "What happened?"

"I was trapped."

"By the magician?"

"Yes." She opened her eyes and sat up. "He must have been monitoring the egg. He tried to take me to him, to learn who I was. He did not succeed."

"Did you?" said Archer. "Is the egg reset?"

"Yes."

He took it from his pouch, looked into it, put it away immediately. In it was New York, deep in smog. A poor exchange for the clearing and the bright birds. He sighed, knowing that he would not want to look into it again.

The Melaklos was still breathing slowly. She said, "He has erected a sector barrier."

"A what?"

"A sector barrier. No one can travel into, out of, or within the barred time-space sector by magic or sorcery."

Archer said, "To keep other magicians out?"

"Out—or in. I am trapped here now. And so are you. You cannot go home until the barrier is lifted."

Archer went cold, despite his intentions to stay. Remaining voluntarily was one thing; having to stay was another. He had no place to go if things got really sticky. He stared at her, stunned.

He started to ask the Melaklos something, but his voice was drowned by a sudden burst of noise outside. It sounded like Times Square on New Year's Eve, with shouts, whistles, drums, horns. A wave of people crashed into the tavern, shouting for wine.

Archer felt as if he had just awakened from a dream. The wine shop seemed to come to life around him.

"Their ceremonies have ended," said the Melakos quietly. "Festival begins."

"Festival begins," echoed a familiar bellow from the crowd. "Acha, Shadow, come on!"

Archer scanned the crowd, saw Lash ploughing toward them with Nayan in his wake. He carried three gallon-sized wine skins; she had a fourth.

"Here's a good beginning!" he boomed, and threw a skin to Archer and one to the Melaklos. "Share the burden."

"Smile, Melaklos," said Nayan, laughing. Her face was flushed, her eyes bright. She seemed to have forgotten her fears.

"It is Festival," said the Melaklos in an undertone. "There is no danger until Festival is over. No one is solemn in Festival." But she did not smile, and her eyes were somber.

Nayan, pressed against the table by the crowd, grinned down at Archer. Her face was not beautiful, but with that joy in it she was more than beautiful. "I'm crushed," she cried above the noise. "Come on!"

Archer's heart lifted in response to her joy. He stood up, tucking his wine skin under his arm.

"Come on!" roared Lash. "I've got money on the torch races!" He pushed toward the door, hauling the Melaklos after him.

Without knowing how it happened, Archer found himself in the street outside. It was ablaze with torches, filled with people in bright flimsy costumes. Celebration was in the air, heady as wine. It caught Archer up, drove away the magician, the whistle, the barrier—this was Festival.

He half heard a voice near him—"I would speak with you." Turning, he saw the Melakos turn and say, "What would you?"

Nayan and Lash argued, gestured. The roar of the street and the flickering torches made Archer dizzy. He turned again at the sound of the Melaklos's voice.

"Lash!" she called—not loudly, but her voice cut through the racket. As the tall islander turned, she threw his wine skin to him. "I travel other roads. Good night."

"Wait," cried Nayan.

She did not seem to hear, but walked away, talking to a man in a short cloak. As they passed near a street torch, light caught the man's hair: it was coarse, fox-colored. The Silent Man.

Worried, Archer looked after them. She might be in danger if he was still upset about the whistle.

"Come on," cried Lash, pulling him away. "She knows what she's doing."

"She always does," said Archer uncertainly.

"Of course," said Nayan. "She's the Melaklos." She laughed and took Archer's other arm. "Anyway, it's Festival."

Lash said, "And she'll be around tomorrow talking riddles again."

She did not appear the next day, or the next, or the next. No one had news of her. She had vanished without telling anyone where she was going.

Chapter Ten

Autumn Festival—fifth day

Festival was five nights and five days long. For five days no ship was allowed to enter or leave harbor or river docks. For five nights no wagon passed the city gates. Shops were closed, market stalls taken down. All the world was on holiday—except for the keepers of taverns, bath houses, and gaming rooms, who made more money in those five days than in the preceding quarter-year. The brothels flourished. The pickpockets kept busy, too—what pickpocket keeps holidays?

Festival was five nights and days of Saturnalia. By night the streets flared so bright with torches that the difference of daylight was scarcely noticed. The city was mad with celebration. The very air intoxicated, heavy with wine and incense, thunderous with noise. Only in the coldest gray of morning was there relative quiet, when the rubbish carts and the city guard made their rounds in streets still echoing with the night's racket.

Festival was five nights and days of sleeplessness. In that same cold gray dawn one might snatch a few hours of heavy-headed sleep, but it was not restful. A few minutes might be caught in a corner. But no one slept long, and so they reeled through the nights and days in increasing delirium, giddy with wine, silly with sleeplessness, madder with every mad day.

Archer reeled and laughed through the Festival streets, whirled along by the big islander Lash. The sea captain was tireless, catching others up in his orbit until they spun away exhausted and others replaced them, flinging nights and days aside like dust. Archer, caught in this whirlwind, lost all count of time. He could not tell day from night. Only Nayan, laughing and dancing with them, kept the hours. Somehow she always knew when to go to the great temple of Arila and celebrate his rites.

Archer went with her, glad of an hour's break in the madness, and sat silent in the back of the dim chamber while she chanted the litanies in a high clear voice, and the worshipers responded in deep solemn tones. His mind, raw from wine and sleeplessness, kept the scene: the great dim room, the ship models and oars, the grave-faced woman behind the altar, all half-seen in the uncertain light of oil lamps. Their voices stayed with him as well. The Litany of Calm, the Litany of Storm Safety, the Litany of War, the long Litany of Protection—he heard them all, and remembered the solid sound of them when he was back in the raucous noise of Festival.

The beaches were quieter. It was sometimes possible to sleep there, when no one was racing or snake-dancing over the sun-bathers. The narrow sands of the harbor were covered every day with naked bodies, baking in the late sun. Archer said that it looked like a morgue or a waiting room in hell. After the first day they went to the coves, which were north of town and harder to get to, and so less crowded.

Still, it was odd for one to be deserted, Archer thought as he lay in the sun on the fifth day. Usually at least fifty people made the walk from the city to lie here when the afternoon sun had cleared the tall cliffs. Today, on the last day of Festival, storm had threatened in early dawn. Nayan, looking at the clouds with a sailor's eye, had laughed and said that they would withdraw by noon. She was right: they lay piled around the horizon as if waiting for the first moon to rise and end the Festival. And so Nayan and Archer had the cove to themselves. Lash was in the city, prowling the streets with a knot of sailors and dancing girls.

Nayan slept, stretched on her stomach on the pale sand, head pillowed on arms. As high priestess of Arila, she had spent the last night of Festival in sleepless vigil in the temple—no wonder she was tired, Archer thought. They had come here at sunrise, wrapped in cloaks against the chill, and she had slept in the sun above the cliffs.

He sat beside her, hugging his knees, looking over the sea. He'd slept a little during the night, a little more since coming to the cove. For the first time in five days his head was beginning to clear.

As his brain began to function again, one question kept returning: where was the Melaklos? They had asked after her from the forest gate to the piers, but no one remembered her. Not even Lash had heard news of her, and his revels covered the city.

Perhaps the Silent Man had killed her for the silver Talisman. Nayan, coming from the temple one day or night, had said that if the Melaklos carried it by right, no man of Sandolan would harm her. On the other hand, if she had gotten it wrongly, there were—other ways of dealing with her. Nayan shuddered as she said this, and Archer guessed that the other ways somehow involved the Great Serpent.

Where was she? She had gone voluntarily with the Silent Man—that was a good sign. But she had been gone for five days now. She might be dead. She might have gone deliberately—deserted him.

Frightened, he shivered in the hot sunlight. He had felt the same chill when she said that he could not go home. He didn't want to—not yet—but it was terrifying to be trapped in this alien world. Doubly terrifying to be alone in it. She was the only person in this whole strange world who spoke his language. She was the only one who knew who he was, where he was from. The only one who knew anything about him. If she was really gone, he was alone. Absolutely alone.

Shivering, cold in the sun, Archer reached blindly toward Nayan. He touched her bare shoulder, cupped his hand over it, grateful for the living contact. Her skin was hot and slick with the sunlight.

"The sun pours down like honey," he said, and wondered where the words came from. Some forgotten song, perhaps. The sun was like honey today, heavy and golden on the water. The sea was almost blue, the sands almost white—except down by the water, where they were wet and gray. As gray as the clothes of the Melaklos.

Where was she? He had questions to ask her. As his head cleared, it filled with questions about things she had said five nights ago. He hadn't asked her about magicians, or what she was doing gathering them all together, himself and Lash and Nayan. She still hadn't told him who Nayan was.

He was stroking Nayan's back, he realized then. He closed his eyes, driving away his doubts and worries, concentrating on the touch of her. Her skin was warm, smooth, over smooth strong muscles. He savored the sweep of her back, the slow curve from her neck, the dip at the base of her spine, the quick upward turn of her buttocks. He willed everything else away, until he knew nothing except for the drowsiness of the sunlight and the warmth under his hand.

And something more. At first he was only peripherally aware of the excitement that grew in him. Automatically he tried to suppress it. He and Diane hadn't made love for years, not since it had become a game that hurt them both too much to play. For years he had tried to learn to see her without desire.

But this wasn't Diane, stretching under his hand like a sleepy cat. Black hair, not blonde. A fuller, stronger body. Skin the color of dark honey, without white bathing-suit patches.

For the first time he looked at Nayan naked. He had been swimming and sunbathing with her since Festival began, but always in crowds, always as part of a group. Now, alone in an island of sunlight with her, he saw her.

His throat tightened, fire stirred in his groin. Urgently, only half knowing what he did, he pressed her shoulder, half lifted her so that she rolled onto her back.

Now she was beautiful. Heavy dark-gold breasts, sagging a little with their weight, peaked with brown areolas and nipples that hardened under his hands. Her stomach was firm-muscled, taut as a drumhead. Half a dozen lines of silver—*stria gravida*, stretch marks—wandered down her belly, and he traced one with his hand until it was lost in the tangle of black hair at her thighs. He cupped a hand over the delta, feeling the warmth of her, the leap in his groin.

Not yet. He couldn't take her sleeping, unprepared. Not yet. He sat back for a moment, eyes closed, holding that thought through the spinning in his head. Not yet.

He opened his eyes, leaned over her, stroking, caressing.

She stirred and made a sleepy questioning sound. Her legs shifted restlessly, her breath quickened. Her body was taut as a bowstring under his hands.

He bent down to kiss her.

Her eyes opened.

He froze, his face six inches from hers. He wanted to say something, so that she would not be angry, but he couldn't speak through the tightness in his throat. On her shoulder, on her breast, his hands trembled.

The sleep-dark fled from her eyes. They focused on him. She whispered, "Aach'—?"

Still he could not speak. He touched her hair, the line of her cheekbone.

Her gaze shifted down his body, back to his face. For a moment she was still, looking at him. Then with one flowing motion she was in his arms. Her sun-drenched body pressed against his, he was in her and moving with her, and there was nothing else in the world.

Chapter Eleven

Autumn Festival: day five (cont'd.)

"Nayan," said Archer quietly. It was late, and they hadn't yet talked seriously.

She lay on the sand, smiling at him lazily. Her eyes were half lidded, her mouth full and loose.

"It's a nice name," he said, watching her closely.

Her smile faded, her eyes narrowed.

"A nice name," he repeated. "But not your own."

She sat up and looked away, toward the sea and the westering sun. Even in its ruddy light he could see the flush that crept up to the roots of her black hair.

She didn't like deception. And she might confide in him: they had formed a bond today. Or had they? Was this only an afternoon of casual love to her, an expected end for Festival? He thought not—he hoped not.

She might confide in him now. He winced at the cold calculation of the thought, but he had to acknowledge the possibility. And he had to be careful, very careful, not to make her hate him.

"Who are you, Nayan?" he asked lightly. "What are you? A ghost from the sea? Will you vanish tonight, when Festival ends?"

She moved her head sharply, impatiently, and stretched out a hand for her crumpled cloak. She wrapped it about her shoulders without speaking.

The evening chill was coming on, Archer thought. They'd have to start back soon. The sun was beginning to set, turning the sea to molten gold. Festival ended tonight, and something would follow. He didn't know what, but he felt that forces were gathering, waiting for the prohibition against action to be lifted. Before that happened, he wanted to know who this woman was that they seemed to be against.

Abruptly, abandoning the light tone, he said, "You're a noblewoman from a northern island. Your name is not Nayan. The Melaklos confirmed that."

Startled, she turned her head. Her eyes were wide and dark in the heavy light. "She told you?"

"I guessed it. She said I was right."

"Oh," said Nayan in a small voice. She looked out to sea again. The sun traced worry on her face. She said, "Did she tell you more?"

"No," he said reluctantly.

"Then I cannot speak further."

He looked into her face. "Why not?"

"Because—" She gestured helplessly with a long hand. Anger edged her voice as she said, "Who are *you* then, Aach'? Can you tell me that?"

"Of course I—" Archer stopped abruptly. In his head he heard the Melaklos saying, "As far as she is concerned, you are a traveling stranger. . . . She does not know that you are from another world." The cool assurance in that voice made him want to speak, but something caught the words in his throat. He didn't want to tell her that he was from another world, that he might be sent back any time. But he wasn't going to lie and get tangled up in falsehoods.

Baffled, he said roughly, "Who I am isn't important. Who you are is."

Nayan tossed back her hair contemptuously.

Angry, Archer shouted, "Who is the Melaklos, that she has power over you? What is she to you?"

"She is—" Nayan began hotly, and stopped. In a more subdued voice she said, "She has—I do not like to deceive anyone. Yet I was—I am—flattered, at the name she chose for me."

Puzzled, Archer said, "Nayan? Why?"

Her long hands moved abortively. "It is her name—one of our names for her. One who wears a mask, Nayan."

One who wears a mask. Appropriate for an alias. Still more appropriate for the Melaklos, with her dust-colored mask of a face.

Nayan was still speaking, half to herself. "She would appear—we never knew when to expect her. Always she was someone else, and yet herself. A teller of tales, a ship's helmsman, a beggar—but always the Melaklos, and always with new tales to tell. We would—"

"Who's 'we?' " Archer interrupted.

"The—" Her eyes widened, she caught herself. "My people, my family."

She caught herself, but she had slipped. He half suspected that she was talking about the Melaklos to keep him from asking more questions about herself. Well, that was all right for now. She might slip again. And he was curious about the Melaklos. This changer of masks didn't sound like his single-masked fellow traveler.

To start her talking again, he said, "How long have you known the Melaklos?"

"For nearly twenty years. She was on our ship when we returned from the Isle of Magicians."

Startled, Archer said, "The what?"

"The Isle of Magicians," Nayan repeated. "It is customary for the—for certain of my family to go to them in late childhood, so that the magicians can read the stars and the winds for her."

Another slip, another recovery. Keep her going. He said, "Were you the child? How old was the Melaklos then?"

Nayan laughed. "I have known her for nearly twenty years," she said, with a whimsical smile. "In those years, I have come of age, become—what I am, I have married and raised a son and been widowed. In that same time, the Melaklos has aged perhaps ten years, certainly no more. It is difficult to know her age."

"I know," said Archer, remembering some of the things she had said, the occasional ancient look in her eyes.

"She looked twenty at most when she appeared among us," Nayan went on. "We were returning home, and she was on the ship—yet no one saw her board it, although it was guarded."

Just as she had gotten into his office unnoticed, Archer thought.

"She had eyes like the eyes of the magicians," said Nayan, and shivered. "They looked into your soul. Yet she did not frighten me as they did. They were like magicians in the tales—bearded men in long dark robes, very old, with those eyes—those soul-seeing eyes."

"Yes," said Archer softly. He knew that look of the Melaklos. So she had watched him when they met, and again in his office the next day, and numberless times after that—distantly, judiciously, as though she weighed him in some intangible balance.

Nayan said, "She lived with us for a few years, as my teacher. Afterward she would come sometimes and live with us for a while. She talked to me sometimes—she said strange things. Once she spoke of masks; she said that the best mask is a sorcerer's mirror."

Intrigued in spite of himself, Archer said, "What's that?"

She gestured. "I never saw one, but she told me that it can reflect in two ways: a perfect image, or a perfect opposite. She said that the best mask always presents the viewer with his image or his opposite, because then he has to respond to himself and not to the wearer of the mask."

Archer beat the sand softly. This was new, this was fascinating. A mirror—a perfect thing to hide behind. It was simple, it was intriguing. It was also somehow frightening.

Nayan laughed uncertainly. "I was very young when she told me this, and it confused me. It frightened me, too—I kept expecting her face to look like that of the person she spoke to."

"But it does," said Archer, speaking fast with excitement. "It does—surely you've seen it. Yes." He beat on the sand, struck with the realization. "When she talks to someone, she reflects him. Her gestures, her expressions, her voice—no wonder she's so hard to pin down."

Abruptly, he remembered standing in a line in a green-lit drugstore, thinking of the Melaklos and Til Eulenspiegel, Til Owlglass, who showed men themselves. He must have known the mask then without realizing it. Owl-mirror.

Uncomfortably he wondered if she reflected him when she talked to him. Surely he wasn't that cold, that remote. On the other hand, if that was his opposite image, what was he?

"You look embarrassed," said Nayan.

Archer silently cursed the Melaklos. What was she, anyway—an itinerant cutpurse, a teller of strange stories, a wearer of masks, a nayan—a new thought flashed across his mind, a horrible thought. "Look here," he blurted. "You aren't the Melaklos, are you? In some new mask?"

"What?" The sun, now half-hidden behind the rim of the sea, cast strong shadows across her face, like the harlequin-shadows on the Melaklos's face five nights before. She stared at him with eyes bright in shadow.

Then, unexpectedly, she chuckled. "You don't know much about her to ask that—not after today. She's a celibate. Something to do with her sorcery." Nayan chuckled again and shook her head. "No, I'm not the Melaklos."

Archer looked away from her amused gaze, feeling his face burning like a beacon fire. To cover his confusion, he got up and found his cloak. He shivered as the rising breeze chilled his bare skin. Wrapping himself in the cloak, he sat close to Nayan. He said, "You're not the Melaklos, you're not Nayan. Who are you?"

She shook her head. "I cannot tell you."

"Because of the Melaklos?"

"Yes."

Anger made Archer's voice harsh. "Melaklos—Melaklos! She's been gone for five days now. No one knows where she is, or what she's doing. For all we know, she's gone off on some other venture and left us to get out of this one ourselves."

"She'll be back," said Nayan.

"Of course she'll be back! She always comes back, doesn't she, with a new mask?"

"You needn't shout."

"It's enough to make anyone shout!" He took Nayan's shoulders, turned her to face him. "I like you, woman called Nayan. I admire you. And I want to know who you are. If anything happens, I want to know who I'm looking for. Who are you, woman called Nayan?"

"I cannot tell you! The Melaklos—"

"Damn the Melaklos!" He shook her, stopped himself. "She was your teacher for a few years. She's been telling you stories for twenty. Does that make her master of your soul?"

Nayan pulled out of his grasp with one strong twist. She looked toward the fast-vanishing sun. "I owe her much," she said quietly. "My life, my sanity, my—my position. I owe her more."

Angrily, almost whispering to keep from shouting, Archer said, "Do you owe her enough to make you a liar?"

Her face darkened, but she met his gaze steadily. "I owe her that much," she said. "I owe her more."

Archer looked away. He was ashamed of his outburst, but too angry to apologize. He couldn't think of anything to say.

She did not speak either. They huddled together in silence against the chill, lost in their own thoughts. The shadows lengthened, melted together. The sky turned deep blue as the last colors of sunset faded from the clouds. The wind rose, booming along the cliffs.

Suddenly, Nayan lifted her head. "Moonrise," she said.

Puzzled, Archer said, "It's too early."

She shook her head impatiently and stood. "We can't get back in time—" Her voice caught. She moved away, a shadow against the pale sand, to the smaller shadow of their clothes.

Archer got up and followed her. They dressed hastily, in silence. When they were on the narrow path that wound up the bluff, Archer said, "What do you mean, we can't get back in time?"

"Festival ends at moonrise, first moonrise," she said. She was close enough for him to feel her shudder. "When Festival ends, my safety ends."

Roughly, to cover his own fear, Archer said, "They won't come after you the minute the moon rises. Chances are no one knows where you are, anyway. We'll have time to find Lash—and the Melaklos, if she deigns to reappear."

"I've been careless today," said Nayan soberly. "The Melaklos warned me."

"We've both been careless," said Archer savagely. "But I'm not sorry for it. Are you?"

She did not answer, but when they came from the narrow cliff path to the broader footway she walked close beside him, her arm in his. They walked in silence along the dim road that led to kos-Alar.

The ambushing foresters took them just before they crossed the river bridge.

Chapter Twelve

Autumn: first quarter, day 1

"Aacha." The voice in his ear was soft and urgent. "Aach'l"

He opened his eyes and sat up—or tried to. But he was bound hand and foot with coarse ropes, and couldn't move. He pulled at them, but they were tightly tied. "Nayan?" he whispered, peering into the darkness.

"Here," she breathed into his ear. "They're just outside—speak quietly."

"Where are we?"

"I don't know—I've not been conscious long. In a river camp, I think."

Archer's eyes were adjusting to the darkness. They were lying on the ground in what seemed to be a forester's shelter made of interlaced branches. Moonlight filtered through the leaves above them. On the edge of hearing came a sound that could have been the river in a quiet spot, or only a rushing in his ears.

He couldn't clearly recall what had happened. They had been walking up the short slope to the river bridge—he remembered that. The first moon had been just clear of the treetops, a swollen orange hunters' moon. Something had rustled in the undergrowth, something had hit him on the head before he could turn. And now he was in some unknown place with no idea how far they were from the city, or how long they had been gone.

They had been careless, just as Nayan had said. They should have started for the city before sunset, instead of arguing on the beach. Well, it was too late to worry about that. They had to get out of this new mess.

"I'm tied too tightly to get loose," he whispered. "What about you?"

"I've got one hand almost free," Nayan murmured, "and I think they've left me a knife. They must not have searched me—they keep their own women like animals, so they aren't used—" She broke off, breathing raggedly. Archer could hear

81

her moving as she struggled with her ropes. Abruptly she stopped and was still.

A shadow fell across the shelter from behind them. Twisting his head back and up, Archer saw a low entrance with a fire beyond. A man stooped in the entrance, silhouetted against the red light. He called something over his shoulder in the forest tongue, came into the shelter and tested their bonds. He did not seem to find anything amiss with Nayan's, but left without doing anything further.

"Listen," hissed Nayan. "Warn me. I'm almost free."

Archer strained toward the door, blocking out the sounds of Nayan working beside him. Her breath hissed as though from pain, but she did not stop or slacken.

Straining, he heard voices from outside: the voice of a forester speaking the trade tongue in a heavy accent, and another voice that he could not place.

"—Outside the city," the forester was saying. "No problems, and no watchers. The man was with her."

"What man?" said the other. It was a curiously flat voice, without identifiable accent.

The forester said, "One of the two men she was with in Festival. The older, the stranger."

Archer held his breath, listening. They were talking about Nayan and himself—reporting to the flat voice. Their chief, the puppet master, must be in the camp.

Unless the flat voice was that of a puppet. It sounded as soulless as the foresters had looked on the pier five days before.

The flat voice said, "A stranger? Who is he?"

"I don't know," said the forester uneasily.

"Ah!" said Nayan. There was a rustle as she sat up. Strong fingers found Archer's wrist bonds, worked quickly and deftly. "River men never could tie knots," she whispered cheerfully.

"Sh!" said Archer, straining for the conversation at the fire.

The flat voice was saying, "—know who he is. Surely someone knows him."

"No," said the forester, almost whining now. "No one had ever seen him until he showed up just before Festival, with one in gray."

"Gray?" Sharpness broke through the flat tone. "He was with the one in gray?"

"Yes."

Archer's hands were free, Nayan was working at his ankles with a small sharp knife taken from a sheath strapped to her thigh. He rubbed his wrists to get the blood going, still listening.

The flat voice said finally, "Where is the one in gray?"

The forester did not answer immediately.

Archer and Nayan rubbed their ankles, helped each other up. They leaned together as the rubberiness left their legs.

"I want to listen to this," said Archer in a low whisper.

Nayan said only, "I'll make a hole in the back of the shelter."

Archer nodded, touched her shoulder, hobbled to the entrance. There, standing in the shadows to one side, he moved his legs to work the stiffness out of them and peered through at the speakers.

"Where is the one in gray?" repeated the flat voice impatiently. It belonged to a young forester who sat on a section of log close to the fire. His eyes were closed, his face expressionless.

He must be the puppet master's contact, Archer thought. The man must have given up on controlling them en masse and settled for a communicating puppet.

The forester, answering at last, said, I don't know where *ke* is. We couldn't find out!" He was a big man, of a familiar forester type: not a man one would expect to find cringing and almost whining. Yet this he was doing. He seemed terrified. When the flat voice did not come again, he burst out, "*Ke* vanished—early in Festival. No one could find *ke*. The woman and the two men—they were searching, they couldn't—"

"Be quiet," said the flat voice harshly. "You should not have lost the gray one."

The forester went white. "I—we—"

"Don't gabble. I shall send for the woman—"

"You will, will you?" muttered Nayan through her teeth, close at Archer's side.

Startled, he turned on her.

She said, "We can get out now."

Indecisive, Archer glanced toward the back of the shelter, where cold moonlight showed through a gap in the branches. They needed to leave as soon as possible to get a good start, but he wanted to hear the conversation between the puppet master and his deputy.

The forester's voice came clearly into the shelter. "The man. What about him?"

"The man?" The flat voice held an undertone of thoughtfulness. "If he is a companion of the gray one, he could be dangerous. He is almost certainly dangerous—"

"We can kill him," the forester broke in.

"Don't be a fool." Now exasperation tinged the flat voice. "I'll have him when I take the woman. But he may know of the gray one—yes. I'll question him now. Bring him here."

"That's our cue," muttered Archer, turning away hastily. "Exit, pursued by a bear."

"But—to speak now—" the forester was saying.

Archer slipped through the hole after Nayan. If the forester argued, they might gain time. "Which way is the river?" he whispered.

They stood and listened.

"There," said Nayan, pointing to the left.

They started toward it, circling wide around the fire circle. A score of foresters sat in it, watching their leader argue with the puppet master.

"Any minute now," muttered Archer. He and Nayan moved faster through the trees. They came abruptly to the rocky slope that led down to the water. Moonlight cast long shadows along the row of upturned canoes that lay just above the muddy shore.

"I see three guards," said Nayan.

Archer saw them, too. They sat near the boats, talking together at ease. If the alarm wasn't given, he and Nayan might be able to take them by surprise.

They started carefully down the slope, moving as quickly and quietly as possible. Archer stayed alert for any sound from the camp behind them.

They were almost to the shore when the alarm came, shouts from the fire. The three guards below stood and called up the slope in the forest tongue. Answering shouts came. They picked up their bows, scanned the shadows.

"It's now or never," Archer gritted. He gripped Nayan's hand and ran for the boats.

She hissed angrily and yanked her hand away. "That's my knife hand," she said furiously, running beside him. "That was a—" She did not finish the sentence, but launched herself at the nearest guard.

The three turned too late. Archer and Nayan were too close and moving too fast to shoot. The men fumbled for their long knives.

Archer and Nayan bowled them over. One went down with Nayan's small knife in his throat. There was a brief, furious struggle, and the others lay still.

Voices and torches flowed down the slope, loud calls. The pursuit was almost on them. Archer took a knife from one of the foresters, ran for the canoes. If they could somehow sabotage them....

Nayan had the same idea. She was beside him suddenly, with an iron hatchet in her hand. She swung it viciously at the first boat, saying, "Where are the paddles?"

Archer glanced at the approaching pursuit, cast about for paddles. There was no sign of them.

A forester jumped at him, ahead of the main body. Archer leaped aside, tripped him. The rest swarmed down the slope.

They had to go! He turned, ran for the boats. Nayan was almost to the last of them. These were no dugouts, but skin-craft with keels and ribs. With every measured axe blow she smashed a keel and ripped skins.

"Now," panted Archer. "Help me, Nayan!"

Together they got the last light canoe into the water.

"Paddles," said Nayan.

"Must be at camp. Hurry!"

With desperate haste they pushed the craft into the deep water, climbed into it. The foresters yelled angrily from the shore. Arrows whistled over the water like angry insects. Someone threw a torch at them: it hissed and went out a foot from the canoe's side.

The current, deceptively smooth in this part of the river, was already carrying them around the wide bend on which the camp was set. "We'll be all right without paddles," said Archer, hoping that he was right. "They can't follow us unless they swim." He laughed, suddenly relieved.

She echoed his laughter. "The river will take us back to kos-Alar—unless we meet more of them."

Sobered, Archer looked around them. The river was bright with moonlight, broad and smooth around the long slow bends, but trees overhung the edges and cast deep shadows that could hide a fleet of canoes. He looked ahead, down the moonlit path of the water. Nothing moved on it.

After a long silence, Nayan said, "Why did you catch my sword hand?"

Startled, Archer said, "When?"

"When we ran downhill to the boats."

"Oh, yes." He recalled her angry hiss, her furious words. Why had he caught her hand? She had had their only weapon. He hadn't thought of that. It had been automatic to grab her right hand with his left. Why? He didn't know. It seemed a trivial thing, but it puzzled him. He sat brooding about it until he fell into a light doze.

He woke with a start, how much later he wasn't sure. It might have been a few minutes, or several hours. Nayan was drooping in the bow, head bent. Archer looked past her, down the silent river.

Something moved, close to the shadows on one side. Archer's heart stopped, started with a leap. Something was moving on the water. He said softly, "Nayan!"

Her head came up sharply; her eyes flashed, startled in the moonlight. "What is it?"

"Do you see anything?" He indicated the direction.

She turned, shaded her eyes with her hands; there were dark stains on her wrists.

Seeing them, Archer stretched forward and took one. He looked closely at it. The stains were black in the moonlight, dry to his touch, but he knew what they were. They were blood. She must have scraped her wrists raw getting out of the ropes.

She pulled her hand away from him, looking embarrassed. "There's a boat," she whispered.

Then the moonlight hadn't been playing tricks on him. He peered at the darkness along the shore. Where was the boat?

There, gliding in and out of the shadows, as silent as a shadow itself. It was another canoe. Whose? Traders, perhaps, going home after Festival. But only one boat, and at night? It was unlikely. Archer bit his lip, watching the boat come nearer. Without paddles, he and Nayan were almost helpless if attacked. And this might be more of the puppet master's men.

Or it might not. He was starting to jump at shadows—supposing bushes to be bears. It was absurd to suspect everyone of being an enemy. The other boat probably held traders, or perhaps river pirates preparing to wait for home-goers. He and Nayan were not a target for pirates, with their obviously empty and obviously drifting boat.

But the other suddenly glided into the main stream, heading toward them. As it swung into the moonlight, Archer saw that it held two people, one in bow and one, smaller, in stern. They came silently, paddles flashing without noise. Once a sound came from them, carried over the smooth water: a man's deep voice, abruptly cut off.

Apprehensive, Archer glanced at Nayan. She looked back at the oncoming canoe. One hand gripped the long knife she had taken from a forester. Archer found that he was gripping the one he had taken, so hard that his hand hurt.

Who were the newcomers? Possibly they were just curious to see a boat drifting toward the sea. Or they might be the puppet master's men. Should he speak, ask who they were?

They were closer—he could hear the water lapping against their craft, faster than against his own. The bow man rested his paddle athwart the boat. The stern man kept his in the water, but to steer rather than to propel. He swung his craft toward Archer's and Nayan's, seeming to be on a collision course. They swept nearer and nearer, slowing as the current held them back.

Archer couldn't keep silence any longer. He cupped his hands around his mouth. "Good evening, travelers," he called. His voice echoed over the still water. His words hung in the quiet air.

The figure in the stern of the other canoe stirred and spoke at last.

"So there you are," said the Melaklos.

Chapter Thirteen

*Autumn: first quarter, day one—
second quarter, day 16*

Ter-Lashan was only five days north of kos-Alar by sea, but it took them—Archer, Nayan, the Melaklos, and Lash—nearly ten times as long going overland. The Melaklos delayed and prolonged the journey with roundabout ways and back-trackings until only she knew just where they were.

They stayed on the river for four days, with the canoes lashed side by side to form a double craft, stable but not as maneuverable as a single. They beached it above the first white water, divided what was left of the stores that the Melaklos and Lash had brought from kos-Alar, and set off through the forest.

The Melaklos would not answer questions about her absence during Autumn Festival. Of the Silent Man, she said, "He has offered his services to the bearer of the Talisman." Of her activities, she said only, "I have been making preparations."

"For what?" said Archer in exasperation, as they huddled about a tiny fire one night after leaving the river.

She said nothing.

Nayan asked for the hundredth time, "Where are my men?"

"Laying false trails," was the reply, as usual. "You will rejoin them soon."

Archer said, "How did you know where to find us?"

She raised an eyebrow, as if surprised that he should have to ask. "Lash told me where you were spending your days. I found traces of your capture at the river bridge. And I knew where the river men usually camp."

Archer met Nayan's glance, questioning. She shook her head. She trusted the Melaklos.

He wasn't sure he did. The gray one knew too much about things that happened when she wasn't around. She seemed to have eyes everywhere. He wondered if she was responsible for the whole thing—the pursuit of Nayan, the barrier—if there was a barrier—the whole bizarre plot. He couldn't think of a reason for it, but then he had never understood why she'd led him into this world. Maybe he was here just for this unfolding story. Maybe Nayan and Lash were from other worlds, too, and she had gathered them all to act some drama for her. Maybe—

Ridiculous. He was getting too fantastic. Next he'd be wondering whether they were all figments of her imagination. He shuddered and looked at the reassuringly solid islanders.

Lash said stubbornly, "I want to know about the Silent Man."

Nayan said, "I want to know where we're going, and why."

Archer said, "I want to know just what is going on."

But the Melaklos had vanished, as she did every night, and they could only sit and make fruitless speculations until they slept.

After they left the river, they moved slowly, stopping to look at anything that seemed interesting: caves in the stone lands, a ruined city on the edge of the plains, giants' bones in the black Terkan forests. They never spent more than two days near a city. Lash objected to this—two days was barely time for him to get started on a spree. The Melaklos would not stay, however, and it was impossible to argue with her.

When they camped near a city, they kept watch all night. The first time this was done Archer and Nayan nearly argued. The Melaklos had announced that she would take the last watch. Lash volunteered for the first, Nayan for the second.

Archer was never sure why he objected. He just felt obscurely that Nayan's being a watchman was somehow wrong. So he said, "You?"

She smiled at him. "I'll take the third if you prefer."

He said, "But you don't need to watch. Lash and I—"

"So?" said Nayan softly. Her gray eyes narrowed, went dark and stormy. "Do you doubt me?"

Hastily he said, "No, but—it isn't usual for a woman—"

Her eyes widened. "Not usual? What, d'you think I'm a forester or a barbarian tent-girl?" Her expression changed as she thought of something else. She glanced at the Melaklos, looked at Archer again. "Aach'," she said softly. "Why did you catch my knife hand when we ran from the camp?"

Bewildered by the non sequitur, he said, "What's that got to do with the night watch?"

Impatiently, she started to speak.

Lash leaned forward, puzzled.

The Melaklos's dry voice cut across the fire. "Nayan will

take the second watch, Archer the third. Nayan, I would speak with you."

They conversed quietly in Nayan's native language. Although he did not understand it, Archer tried to listen. He was sure that they were talking about him, and his ears burned.

For a few days there was a slight strain between Archer and Nayan. They had realized how little they knew of each other. Still, the strain passed quickly. They always walked together. Lash cast knowing glances at them and made obscure little jokes. The Melaklos did not seem to notice.

Archer found without surprise that he was in love with the black-haired woman. The idea did not disturb him. He had been in love before, or thought he had—a painful thing that he remembered, ten years later, with bewilderment. He had once loved Diane, or assumed that he had. This was something different, something warm and wonderful, something to treasure. And they were comfortable with it: there were no shynesses, no clumsy attempts at concealment.

Only one thing disturbed him. He knew that Nayan was not beautiful and that was wrong. A lover was supposed to think his beloved beautiful whether or not she was. It was her face that puzzled him. It was strong, it was all character. The bones of it had a clean exquisite line that he dimly remembered seeing in films: Katharine Hepburn had the same facial bones. Nayan had beautiful bones, he thought, and then thought that there was something morbid in the idea. That's what was really wrong. Not that she was not beautiful—he treasured that—but that he thought her bones were lovely.

"Get you to my lady's chamber and tell her, let her paint an inch thick, to this favor she must come. Let her laugh at that."

He muttered this one day, watching her as she lay asleep in the sun, her face like a sculpture in honey-colored wood. Her black hair blew about her face, framing it in silver-lit clouds.

The Melaklos spoke unexpectedly, behind him:

" 'My mistress's eyes are nothing like the sun.' "

Startled, Archer turned around. She was perched on a large stone, watching him. He recognized the line—it was from one of the "dark lady" sonnets—but he couldn't remember what came next. He waited for her to continue.

She lifted an eyebrow at him and went on, her deep rich voice rolling the lines out:

" 'Coral is far more red than her lips' red;

If snow be white, why then her breasts are dun;
If hairs be wires, black wires grow on her head.
I have seen roses damask'd, red and white,
But no such roses see I in her cheeks;
And in some perfumes is there more delight
Than in the breath that from my mistress reeks.
I love to hear her speak, yet well I know
That music hath a far more pleasing sound;
I grant I never saw a goddess go;
My mistress, when she walks, treads on the ground:
    And yet, by heaven, I think my love as rare
    As any she belied with false compare.' "

As Archer stared at her, she moved one shoulder, and a half-smile slid over one corner of her mouth. "So," she said, and slipped from the rock, and walked away into the forest.

Archer turned back to Nayan, puzzled. He didn't know what to think of this. Still, it had pulled him out of the beginning of depression. "My mistress's eyes are nothing like the sun." It fit so well with some of his thoughts that when he couldn't remember it, he took courage enough to ask the Melaklos to write it down for him. She copied it, and two more that he wanted and she knew, into the blank pages in the back of his borrowed *King Lear*, with brown-black ink and a quill. Her handwriting was microscopic, but so clear that he could read it easily.

He translated the "mistress's eyes" sonnet into halting prose in the trade tongue for Nayan, thinking that she would like it. She laughed with delight, and said, "He must have been as tired of love songs as I am. Any man who has to compare his beloved's eyes with stars and other things not remotely like them is probably in love with his own imagination."

Archer disagreed, and they argued about it for a few days—there was little else to do while they were in the forests. There was one argument that they kept up everywhere; the question of Nayan's identity. Archer never stopped asking who she was, and she never told him. But even this argument was for daylight only, while they walked in the sunlight and talked together.

The nights were theirs alone. Lash snored across the fire in camp, and roamed taverns in towns, while the Melaklos vanished every night on some errand of her own. Nayan and Archer huddled under one blanket at the edge of the firelit circle, whispering to keep from waking Lash (although he slept like a stone). Their nights were intense, beautiful, until they woke in each other's arms to find the gray morning and the Melaklos just as gray, sitting against a tree and watching the ashes and the dawn.

They didn't know where she went at night. She always slipped away, sometimes before the others settled for sleep, and always reappeared before they awoke. On watch nights she returned when it was time for her turn. They never saw her go, although they watched, and never saw her return. Sometimes they talked about it when she was gone.

"Maybe she sleeps in the trees," Lash offered one night, when they were camped on the edge of the plains. He shivered as a chill gust of wind swept across them. "This is no night to sleep away from fire."

Archer laughed, reminded of something he had long ago noticed about her. He said, "Have you ever seen her asleep?"

"No," said Lash promptly.

Nayan wound a hand into her hair and tugged it, thinking. Finally she looked up with a wry face and said, "No more have I, and I've known her for twenty years."

"Have you?" said Lash.

Archer shook his head. "We traveled together for two seasons before we met you in kos-Alar," he said. "We camped most nights. And in all that time I never saw her asleep. She didn't slip off as she's doing now, but she was always staring at the fire when I went to sleep, and at the ashes when I woke up. I started to wonder if she slept at all."

"What did you do?" said Nayan.

"I tried to outlast her," said Archer, and laughed again at the memory. "One night I managed to stay up—and she did the same. We sat there all night, on opposite sides of the fire, not saying a word, as if it were perfectly normal."

"Nayan grinned. "Poor Aach'."

He groaned. "That's what I was the next day. We started early, as usual, and traveled all day. By night time I was half dead."

"Have you tried again?" said Lash with a grin.

"Never," said Archer fervently.

Nayan, suddenly thoughtful, said, "She must sleep. But why doesn't she let people see her sleeping? Is she afraid?"

Lash snorted. "Afraid? That one?"

But Archer and Nayan looked at each other, wondering. When Archer woke the next morning in false dawn and saw the Melaklos looking over the brown plain, his first thought was, *What is she afraid of?* But neither he, nor Nayan, nor even Lash cared to ask her about it.

From kos-Alar to Ter-Lashan, nearly fifty days on their roundabout way, they did not see her sleep, and they soon stopped wondering about it. They visited the tiny young city called Ker, which the Melaklos said would soon be the most powerful city in the world, more powerful than the great island city, Ytarn of Arilikan itself. Ker was not impressive when they saw it: a few stone huts clustered on a cliff high above the sea, a small huddle of warehouses below. They were there only long enough to see the fire of Itor in the stone square, a small flame whipped by the eternal winds, which the Melaklos said would not go out until the city was destroyed. She would not pass a night within it, so they left quickly.

Ker was north of their destination, but they were still farther north. They visited the stone dwarves in the southernmost spur of the Barebones Mountains, and hunted giant slugs through the caves with them. They went inland as far as the ruins of the plains city called Vlyis, where ghosts of barbarians fight ghosts of foresters at every triple full moon. They skirted the shadows of the Terkan mountains, with their black-barked trees and blue ghost lights, and so came by a circuitous route to Ter-Lashan, the fire city wedged between the black mountains and the shallow sea.

Chapter Fourteen

Autumn: second quarter, day 19

Archer liked Ter-Lashan. It had an unreal quality, an elaborate stone city built in a barren land. So many people of so many races came to it that none predominated—even the permanent dwellers in the counting houses and the tenements came from all the trade lands of the sea. Archer and Nayan spent two long delighted days exploring the city, from the crumbling walls and the curious buildings that were so old that only the Melaklos knew what they had been to the great eight-tiered fountain in the market square, where story tellers sat among the booths on their figured rugs and told tales for coins. Lash had vanished into the tavern quarter, and the Melaklos was undoubtedly around hatching plots and picking pockets—Archer had long ago become reconciled to her ways of getting money. He and Nayan were too busy exploring to worry about their companions. There was too much to see and hear in the incredible city that was Ter-Lashan.

But though they might forget the Melaklos, she did not forget them. She reappeared on the third day in the city. Archer and Nayan were eating midday bread and cheese at the inn where they were staying when she came in and sat at their table with her back to the wall.

Archer thought that she looked tired, if that was possible. Her face seemed tighter drawn over the fragile bones, her dust-colored skin a little grayer and paler than usual.

"I have errands for both of you," she said abruptly, not returning their greetings.

They looked at her without speaking.

She turned to Nayan, spoke in the woman's language in a quick low voice. Nayan protested several times, but the Melaklos overrode her.

Irritated at the Melaklos's apparent lack of confidence, Archer pointedly ignored her until she addressed him directly in English.

"I wish you to carry a message for me."

"Why should I?" he asked, deliberately speaking the trade tongue.

She continued in English, ignoring his question. "The message is for the Silent Man whom we met in kos-Alar. I shall tell you later where to find him. You are to tell him that the Serpent-rider says that all is prepared."

Automatically he repeated, "The Serpent-rider says that all is prepared." Then he hit the table with a fist and said, "But what does it mean? What are you up to?"

"The message must go tonight, after sunset," she said, as if he had not spoken.

"We'll take it, then," he said shortly.

"*You* will take it. Nayan is needed elsewhere."

Suspicious, Archer glanced at Nayan. She was pale under her weather-bronzed skin. She didn't like whatever was going on any more than he did.

He looked back at the Melaklos. She had spoken more formally than usual, though wearily. Whatever she was cooking up was serious enough to tire her. That meant that the magician was probably in it—the one who was trying to kidnap Nayan.

He said, "We're staying together. Someone needs to be with her." He spoke in the trade tongue, so that Nayan could hear.

She looked from him to the Melaklos. Spots of color appeared over her cheekbones; she opened her mouth to speak. Then the Melaklos looked at her, and she subsided.

Frustration tangled Archer's tongue. What was wrong with Nayan? She was a rare woman—intelligent, courageous, strong—but the Melaklos could control her with a glance. There was something wrong in that—the Melaklos must have some hold over her.

The Melaklos spoke before he could sort out his anger. "Meet me at sunset, in the market square," she said. "Wait at the west side of the fountain." She stood up and turned to go.

"Where's Lash?" Nayan asked abruptly.

"Lash is working for me," said the Melaklos, and left before either of them could speak again.

"She's up to something," said Archer, as she vanished through the doorway.

Wearily Nayan pushed a hand through her black hair. "She's always up to something. I wish I knew what she's doing now."

Archer made a decision. Anything was worth a try. He said, "What's your errand? Another riddle message?"

She shook her head. "I cannot tell you."

"She made you promise?"

Nayan nodded, tapping the edge of her cup absently.

Archer clenched and unclenched his hands, uncertain whether to laugh, cry, or curse. The Melaklos blocked him at every turn. He pounded softly on the table in frustration. What the hell was she doing?

Nayan looked at him apprehensively, tossing back her black hair. Her eyes were dark and stormy, as always when she was upset.

Archer met her anxious gaze. He laughed, a short ugly sound. "Curses!" he said. "Foiled again!" And he laughed again, genuinely this time. The Melaklos was tying him in knots, and there was something hugely comical in the idea.

Nayan smiled suddenly. Her eyes were still stormy, but her voice was light and warm as she said, "Well, we've had two days of rest."

"And another half day to go," said Archer, with a boisterousness he did not feel. He stood up and held out his hand. "Let's make the most of it, before she traps us again."

Nayan laughed and tossed back her black hair. She stood and took his hand, and they left the wine shop.

The market square was crowded at sunset, so crowded that they were nearly swept away. The square was full of smells of hot grease and incense, and the calls of merchants and hawkers. There was a feel of distant thunder in the air.

"It is time," said the Melaklos from behind them. They turned, startled. She was holding her gray cloak close about her. She said, "Archer, your man is in the tavern of the Two Red Circles, in the second main square from the docks. He is the only Silent Man there."

"All right," said Archer. "I won't be long—why don't you wait here?" He looked at Nayan as he spoke.

The Melaklos said, "We will meet at your inn. Go there as soon as you have delivered the message."

Nayan moved suddenly. She kissed Archer ardently, whispered, "Hurry." She released him just as suddenly.

He kissed her lightly on the cheek and turned away. As he pushed into the crowd, he heard the Melaklos say, "It is done. You must perform it." Nayan's reply, if she replied, was lost in the noise of the marketplace.

His errand was surprisingly easy. He expected something to happen, though he couldn't have said what, but he reached the tavern without incident. He gave the message to the Silent Man (who said nothing) and made his way back to the inn without meeting anything worse than a drunken mercenary who challenged him to fight. Archer easily knocked him out with the flat of his sword and left him snoring against a wall.

The Melaklos was alone at a table when he reached the inn. He looked up and down the street before entering, but there was no sign of Nayan or of Lash. He realized abruptly that the Melaklos hadn't mentioned Lash.

He bought wine at the counter and took it to the Melaklos's table. She looked up as he sat opposite her. She sat, as always, with her back to the corner.

"Did you deliver the message?" she said.

"Yes. No reply." Archer worked the cork out of his wine jar. "Nayan not back yet?" he asked as he poured wine into his cup.

"No."

Something in her voice disturbed Archer. He said, "Is anything wrong? You sound worried."

She touched her wooden bowl lightly. "The barrier has changed everything," she said, as if explaining something. "I must be more careful with you. I cannot send you out of danger as easily."

Danger. A chill started in Archer's stomach, spread through his body. Where was Nayan? He said evenly, "Is there danger now? To whom?"

"No." She shook her head. "Not now."

He looked toward the door, back at her, fear spreading in his brain. "Has something happened to Nayan?"

"No," she said flatly.

"But shouldn't she be back by now?"

"She is not coming back."

The cup clattered as he set it down. His mind was as clear and cold as ice, his voice steady as he said, "Would you repeat that?"

The Melaklos put both hands flat on the tabletop and looked directly at him. She said, "Nayan is not coming back."

Red fog boiled in Archer's brain, blinded him. Rage maddened him. He was aware of violent movement, of a harsh voice that shouted. Fury mastered him.

Then his head cleared. He was on his feet, shouting—the harsh voice was his own, tearing his throat. The Melaklos was crumpled in her corner, as if she had been flung there.

The room was silent, the customers staring at Archer. The barman was poised for movement, wooden cudgel in hand.

Archer closed his eyes and breathed deeply, driving away the last shreds of the fog. Gradually he suppressed the rage

97

that set his blood pounding, his body shaking. He sat down slowly, watching the crumpled form of the Melaklos. His hands tingled and itched, as if he had touched her.

The other customers turned back to their own pursuits. The barman laid his cudgel aside and waited on more customers. Conversation filled the air again.

The Melaklos stirred, sat up. She shook herself experimentally, like a small dog awaking. With eyebrows raised she looked at Archer.

"I misjudged you," she said. Her voice husked; she put a hand to her throat and coughed. "I did not expect you to lose your temper, much less to half throttle me."

"Where's Nayan?" he said hoarsely.

The Melaklos poured wine into her wooden bowl. Her hands were steady. She said, "Nayan is gone."

Archer's voice was tight with anger held in check. He said, "Gone where?"

She lifted the bowl and drank slowly.

Furious, Archer slapped it away. It bounced on the floor, spilling dark wine across the dead rushes. "Where—is—Nayan?"

The Melaklos sighed and put both hands on the table, side by side like small dusty lizards. "Nayan is gone," she said again. "I have sent her away. I shall not tell you where—not yet."

Archer clenched both hands, staring at the table. She had kissed him in the market square—a farewell kiss, and he had not known. She had gone knowingly, if not willingly. She trusted the Melaklos, absolutely.

The Melaklos said quietly, "I must protect both of you."

Archer looked away from her calm face, wanting to smash it. She was quietly assuming responsibility for them—as if she were a nursemaid and they were children too young to care for themselves. He swore under his breath and beat the table in impotent rage. What could he do about her?

She was still speaking. "When Lash returns from his commission, I will know more. For now, Nayan is going to a place of relative safety. You may rejoin her soon—I cannot say yet."

"I will rejoin her," said Archer thickly. "I don't know what you've done with her. But if you've betrayed her, or sent her into danger—" He stopped and stared hard at her.

She looked straight back at him. Her eyes were dark and steady. She did not speak.

PART TWO

Chapter One

Autumn: fourth quarter, day 16

"This—man!" bellowed the voice from the wine shop. "This creature. This—pah! It would soil the lowest word of language to be given him. He is lower than the sons of Lerkan!"

In the dark street outside, Archer looked inquiringly at the Melaklos. The voice was familiar. He said, "Lash?"

"So it appears." She started for the open door. "Tell him that we have come. I'll fetch wine."

Archer followed her in, pushed his way through the crowd toward the big seaman's voice. Lash had been gone for nearly half a season. During that time, Archer had heard nothing of him—or of Nayan. He could not even ask for news of her, since he did not know who she was. The Melaklos dropped vague hints, but would not answer his questions, and the occasional strangers who brought her news would not speak to him. After more than fifty days of that, he was half insane with frustration and inaction. But now Lash was back, and things would start to happen.

The sailor sat at a long table, hemmed in by dock crowders, drinking hot wine from a huge wooden bowl. Lowering it, he caught Archer's eye.

"Move, you lizards," he bellowed. "Let him through!"

Men gave way reluctantly, and Archer pushed past them to the table. Lash wrapped an arm around Archer's shoulders. "So here you are," he roared. "Where's that shadow-faced companion of yours? Haven't cut her throat yet, have you?"

"She's getting wine," said Archer above the din.

Lash slapped the table. "Good creature!"

He had apparently been drinking for some time. Archer, looking at him, thought that if the Melaklos wanted to talk to him, she had better hurry. After five days of Festival with the big seaman, Archer knew his drinking pattern. The hurricane voice stage was closely followed by a belligerence that would send him roaring into the streets looking for brawls. They had to get him to talk before that happened.

Archer said, "We wondered if you had any news."

101

"News!" Lash spluttered. "News! I was telling these scum-treaders about that—that muck-spawned creature of—that slime-begotten—"

"What has he done?" interposed the Melaklos quietly, from across the table.

Startled, both men turned their heads to her. She had gotten through the crowd without disturbance and was seated on the bench opposite, with an open wine jar and two stone bowls.

She poured steaming wine into a bowl and pushed it across the narrow table to Archer, not taking her eyes from the big man. "What has he done?" she repeated.

"He's set blockades, that's what. Barred northern trade! And now he's starting to block the mainland." Lash snorted and splashed wine into his own bowl, slopping it onto the table. "You'd think we were back in my grandfather's time, in the Kraslo war. Blockades. Smuggling. Bah!" He picked up the bowl and gulped wine.

"Who is he?" said Archer.

Lash started spluttering again. "He's a—a—I hear that he's burning ships, that filth-spawning—he calls himself the Sr of Nym, that—that—" Unable to find words, he waved his arms wildly.

The Melaklos moved sharply. "The Sr of Nym?" she said, and Archer heard a tightness in her calm voice.

"So he's called. It means nothing," rumbled the seaman angrily. "A magician, they say—and I believe it. Magicians!" He turned his head and spat, ignoring listeners who crowded out of his way.

The Sr of Nym. Sr Nym. A magician. Probably the one who was after Nayan. Archer looked at the Melaklos. The name seemed to disturb her.

Her dust-colored face was expressionless. "Lash," she said quietly, "did you go to the Shipyard Isles?"

"Of course," he said belligerently. "That's where you sent me." He scowled at her. "You were right. That's where he's getting his ships."

She picked up her bowl. "Report."

As Lash talked and she questioned, Archer slowly realized that she was using her magician's-mirror mask. As Lash grew more and more upset, she became calmer and colder; as his voice became wilder, hers became even; as he gestured and bounced, she became statue-still. A perfect opposite with one macabre quality: her attitudes, the flat tones of her voice, her sketched gestures, all were caricatures of Lash's own.

Lash started calmly enough, in a rumble like a volcano getting ready to erupt. "We went to Skarol—met no one on the way. The shipyards were deserted. Deserted! They'd been burnt." He hit the table, his voice went up. "Burnt by that—"

She brought a hand down soundlessly, an echo of his gesture. "What else found you?" she asked quietly.

He calmed and went on. "Nothing—there. We tried the neighboring islands, but the herdsmen had gone—gone home, I hope. We sailed around those miserable rocks for fifteen days before we found the Skarol. What was left of them." He clenched a hand and pounded the air.

Heading off the outburst, Archer said, "What was left?"

"Yes." He glared at the smaller man. "Fourteen men—fourteen out of two thousand! They told us what happened. *His* creatures—the tiger men—appeared out of nowhere one day of winter, when the shipyards were closing. They kept the shipwrights working all winter, all spring—kept them building until autumn, this autumn. Made them refuse all other orders. Then, in the autumn, they—those—" He spluttered incoherently.

Her voice was clear, a perfect opposite. "What did they do?"

In a tight voice Lash said, "They took the Skarol—two thousand men, the best shipwrights in the sea—they put them in a ship. An old ship in for caulking. Seam-stripped. Tied them up and set them adrift." There was horror in his voice.

Archer swallowed, feeling sick. A ship with its seams open, bare of the pitch and ropes that kept the water out—it must have gone down like lead. Two thousand men drowned like lizards in weighted net.

The Melaklos spoke in her quiet voice. "Fourteen survived?"

"Yeah." Lash looked at her angrily. "They got out of their ropes, swam to an island—the islands are close together up there, you know. There were thirty of them, but sixteen starved before we found them."

The Melaklos poured wine into her cup, her voice steady as she said, "What else did you learn of the Sr of Nym?"

Lash spoke in an angry growl, watching her unresponsive face. "He appeared out of nowhere, or Nym—wherever that is—about a year ago. He gathered a few ships on a little rock in the north—Kosr it's called, a useless place. No one thought of him, even when these strange ships started appearing. The Skarol made them, but they're no Island ships. And no one knows what his crewmen are. They're of no race I know, and I've been from the Ice Mountains to the North of North, from the Outer Isles to the Poison Desert."

Archer moved restlessly, opened his mouth to speak. The Melaklos shot him a warning glance that silenced him. He wanted to ask if the Sr of Nym's men could be from another world—but Lash wouldn't know about that. It was something to ask the Melaklos, later.

Lash was going on, his voice growing thicker and uglier with every word. "Fleets he had, that—Sr of Nym!" He made the name sound inexpressibly evil. "He started taking islands last spring—slowly, easily, like a child picking *sen*-fruits. No one knew much about it for a while: he started with the small islands. Lots of small islands. Then he took the Tsol islands. He burned the fishing fleets—the gray plague take him for that. And he burned the Tsol forests." He slammed a fist on the table and glared at the Melaklos. "That was in spring—sap-rising spring—and those forests went up like wood two winters dry. That was magic, wasn't it?" He said it as if she had contradicted him.

"He is a magician," she said judicially.

Archer said, "Didn't anyone try to stop him?"

"Saral and Bosl—but they wouldn't unite even against a ship-burner. He took them separately, burned half their ships and sent the rest home to harbor like singed *lervals*. Loban of Bosl—Arila praise!—died in that riot, for battle I'll not call it." He snorted and drank deeply.

In the pause Archer looked at the Melaklos, and what he saw chilled him. She sat looking from distance into distance, and there were shadows behind her eyes.

Lash growled, "He burned the fleets of Sakor and Malan in harbor. Idiot councilors wouldn't agree on commanders, Arila smite them! This democracy is a great hindrance." He swallowed more wine, set the bowl down empty and looked at the Melaklos again. "Then there was Tsiel."

She met his gaze, cool-eyed, cool-voiced. "What of Tsiel?"

"The Tsiel Alliance gathered their fleet—and they've kept in trim since the Kraslo war, even if it was fifty years ago. Two hundred ships with full fighting crews. The best fleet north of Arilikan Itself—Arila's balls, the best fleet on the sea. They met him off the Forest Horn, and what d'you think happens at the height of sun-summer, with a single moon?" He swept his head in an arc, glared at Archer.

Impatient, Archer said, "What?"

Lash hit the table. "A storm sweeps out of a clear sky, and smashes and scatters the Tsiel fleet without touching a ship of this—this Sr of Nym!" He stared at the Melaklos belligerently.

She sat in a pose of thought rather than defiance. Perfect opposite, thought Archer.

It seemed to goad Lash. "Well?" he bellowed. "Isn't that magic?"

She said, "Who commanded the Tsiel fleet?"

He sat back as she relaxed, as if he imitated her now. "Roal of Tsiel—that boy has promise. He got what was left of his fleet safely home. Not that it did him much good."

"Oh?"

"The—that—*he* took Tsiel before they returned. Roal's in prison, or was when I heard of it, and the—that Sr of Nym!— is headquartered on Tsiel."

The Melaklos tapped lightly on the rim of her cup. "That complicates matters."

"Doesn't it?" Lash cast a worried glance at Archer. "He had it well before the Tsiel—"

She cut across him coldly. "Who mans the blockades?"

Archer scarcely heard the reply. He had caught the warning note in her interruption. She didn't want Lash to talk about the Tsiel—that would be the title of the ruler of Tsiel. Why didn't she want him mentioned? Because of possible spies, perhaps. But that glance of Lash's meant that Tsiel had some connection with Archer—or so Archer thought. And that could mean only one thing: Nayan was somehow involved. He had no other interest in the islands. He had to ask about Tsiel. The Melaklos might be willing to talk to him now that things were opening up. He'd have to tackle her—later, though, after she was through with Lash.

Lash had a fresh jar of wine. He drank half a bowl of it, slammed the bowl onto the table. "Blocking trade!" Men gathered up their jars and cups to keep them from spilling. "Burning ships! May the hounds of the Huntress—Arila protect!—devour him alive!"

Every man within hearing hastily traced the Ship of Arila in the air as protection against the Huntress. Archer tried to remember what mythical figure she was, dismissed her angrily. Lash was quickly passing into his final warlike stage.

The Melaklos seemed to realize that. Her next question was spoken crisply, in a tone of command. "What of the other islands?"

Lash drained and refilled his bowl before replying, "The leaders are holding council in Ytarn of Arilikan. Some of them are for raising a fleet, but most of them don't think he'll come south." He snorted. "They'll think that until he burns the council chamber around them."

"What of the Arilikan Fleet?" She snapped the question.

He answered automatically. "The admiral's a man of sense—he's gathering what ships he can. Last I heard, the Gurnal were coming."

"The Gurnal?"

With surprise Archer realized that she was genuinely startled. She obviously hadn't expected that.

Lash chuckled. "Admiral Kyekalan probably pledged them, but Algundor's leading them," he said. "What could lead him to dip his dainty hands in war?" He laughed, shaking his head.

But there was no amusement in the dark eyes of the Melaklos. For this first time since they had come in she looked at Archer, and he saw the shadows behind her eyes again.

She was worried—and this worry had something to do with him. Algundor? He couldn't recall the name. Gurnal? That would mean men of Gurn—and that was a familiar name. Why?

It came into his head suddenly: Nayan's voice, on the night when he first heard her: "—guesting with the prince of Gurn, on Dragonspaw." She had been returning home from Gurn when her ship was attacked. Shadows were gathering again, and he couldn't make them out. But Nayan had just entered the picture again. Archer looked back at the Melaklos, defiant. He wasn't going to remain in ignorance any longer.

Her mouth quirked, as if she read the thought and was amused by it. She looked at Lash calculatingly.

He was drinking again. His china-blue eyes were hot with hate. In a moment he would be on his feet, roaring for a fight.

The Melaklos stood up, looked at Archer again. "I would speak with you," she said quietly.

His heart lifted absurdly. Now for news of Nayan. He left the shop with her.

As they passed into the cool night air, they heard Lash's voice behind them, slurred with wine and rage: "This creature—this son of—of himself, nothing is lower. Burning ships! Pah!"

Chapter Two

Autumn: fourth quarter, day 17

The morning was cold and gray. The stone streets of Ter-Lashan were nearly empty as Archer walked toward the market square. He shivered in spite of the heavy cloak wrapped around him, but he was only vaguely aware of the cold.

He was worried. He was worried about Nayan, and now about the Melaklos as well. She had acted strange last night. She had been uncertain, and that was something that he had not seen before.

She had not told him much about Nayan. Nayan was in Ytarn, the largest city of the Arilikan Islands. The Melaklos had sent her there secretly, with the Silent Man's ship, so that she would be safe for a time. There were other reasons, Archer was sure, but the Melaklos had not mentioned them. She had seemed ready to, and apparently thought better of it.

She would not tell him who Nayan was—but again she seemed unsure, almost ready to speak. She did not explain what, if anything, was Nayan's relationship with the Tsiel leader. She did not mention Algundor, the prince of Gurn, even when Archer asked about him. She made no attempt to explain Lash's disturbing report.

Boiled down, Lash's news was simply that a magician with slave-built ships and mysterious followers was conquering the Arilikan Islands. It was not a pleasing thought. Archer had not been off the mainland, but he had met islanders, and liked them. The north islanders especially were pleasant people, a little hasty sometimes, but honest and enjoyable companions—except of course for the Silent Men of Sandolan.

The Melaklos had told him a little about the Sr of Nym. He was a powerful magician from another time of the world Dolesar—he had to be, for magic at present was a rudimentary art. What he was doing—establishing an empire in another time—was against the laws of something called the Brotherhood, which seemed to be a sort of magical-sorcerous police, or a wizard's guild. She had not explained that very fully, and he had been more interested in Nayan than in the Sr of Nym.

She did not tell him why the Sr of Nym wanted to capture Nayan. It was because of what Nayan was, she said, but she would not tell him what Nayan was.

She had been abstracted. Several times she had checked herself on the edge of revelation. She was obviously worried about Nayan.

That worry chilled Archer more than anything else could have. Nothing had seemed to touch the Melaklos before. This concern was the first feeling she had shown him. That must mean that Nayan was in grave danger.

When the Melaklos had left him the night before after talking abstractedly for half an hour, he had been left with that worry. It had showed all through her false starts and her refusals to enlighten him. It had kept him awake long, staring into the darkness, wondering what Nayan was doing and cursing the Melaklos for hiding her from him.

Now, after a brief heavy sleep, he was looking for the Melaklos so that he could tell her that he was going to Ytarn of Arilikan to find Nayan. He didn't know how he would get there, or how he would find her in a great strange city, but he was resolved. This time the Melaklos would not make him back down. She couldn't.

He made speeches in his head as he walked, working out just what he would say to her. But when he saw her, the words vanished and he was left with his frustration and his rapidly rekindling anger. They had lived in uneasy truce since Nayan's departure, only because the Melaklos was his key to the island woman. Now he was going to end the truce.

She was, as he had expected, in the market square. She was perched on the rim of the great fountain in the center, watching the first stall keepers set up their wares, the fishermen come up with the morning's catch. The sun was just above the hills behind her, so that she was silhouetted against it like a small fantastic bird, as cold and gray as the morning.

She turned her head as Archer came up. Her eyes were tired and dark, the bones of her face prominent beneath the dust-colored skin.

He realized with vague dread that she had looked like that on Nayan's last day in Ter-Lashan, on the evening when Nayan had kissed him good-bye in this very spot.

She did not speak when Archer stopped beside her, but she did not look away. She perched on the basin rim with legs drawn up, feet flat against the under curve of the bowl, hands touching the rim to balance her. She was so still that she might have been carved there, except for her distant shadowed eyes.

"I'm going to Ytarn of Arilikan," he said quietly, watching her.

Her eyes flickered, but she neither moved nor spoke.

He said, "I'm going to find Nayan."

Still she did not respond. The sun was like a round blot of blood behind her.

"The Sr of Nym is moving south," he said. "His agents couldn't catch her, but he probably can."

She stayed motionless, looking at him with eyes darker than darkness.

Uneasy, he looked away. Her silence was making him nervous.

Then he thought that she was probably trying to do just that, and this made him mad. He said brusquely, "I'm going as soon as I find a ship bound for Arilikan Itself."

Only her mouth moved. She said softly, "No."

The truce was over. They were at war again. And she had won her last skirmish two months before, on the night when Nayan disappeared. She would not win again.

He did not say anything. Two could play at the waiting game. He watched her steadily.

"The sector barrier makes it more difficult," she said. "It is not possible to send you quickly to safety."

"You said that two months ago," he said. "It didn't make any difference then, and it doesn't now."

Still watching him, still speaking in her even low voice, she said, "I could send you south to Dragonspaw, of course—he may not get so far. Or inland, although the barbarian lands are uncertain."

He grinned at her deliberately, feeling his lips stretch like dry rubber over his teeth. "I'm going to Ytarn," he repeated. "I'd like some information before I go, but it isn't necessary. You've told me where she is. I'll find her if I have to tear the city down stone by stone."

Something flickered in her eyes—worry? Calculation? She said, "This is not for you to be in. It is large and deadly."

He shook his head. "If you mean the Sr of Nym's empire, I'm not worried about that now. All I'm concerned with is seeing that Nayan is safe."

She said, "It is the same thing. You cannot ensure her safety without confronting him."

Wary, he looked at her without saying anything. She seemed to be taking refuge in cryptic statements again. Unless she really meant that Nayan was so important that the Sr of Nym would sidetrack from his conquests to hunt her.

The Melaklos seemed to make up her mind. She slipped to the stones and stood looking at him from under her eyebrows.

In some clerical corner of his mind he recalled that she never tilted her head back to look anyone squarely in the face—not unless she had a point to make. Just now she was weighing him, weighing words to speak to him. He waited. This was his game now. Let her feel her way.

She said abruptly, "You are a romantic. That is in ways an excellent thing to be. It is also dangerous."

He waited, now wondering what point she wanted to make.

She said carefully, "Only romantics die for ideas." She gestured impatiently, started a new train. "This pleases you. It suits that part of you of which you are still almost ashamed. You have a lady to fight for, and a wicked magician to fight against. It is all very suitable."

Was she being sarcastic? He wished that he could read her face, but it was expressionless except for the tightness that made her bones stand out. He began to feel embarrassed, then angry.

She went on. "It is very nice, but like all fantasy it is very real. This isn't Knights of the Round Table, Archer. This isn't Robin Hood, or Cowboys and Indians. No one bears a charmed life here. This is war, bloody war, and anyone can die."

"I know that," he said coldly.

She continued before he could say more. "Have you seen men killed by the sword in scores? Have you heard the crew of a burning ship? Do you know how long it can take a man to die when he's arrowshot?"

His anger was cold, a dagger of ice poised in his brain. He said, "Do you?"

"Yes, I know," she said, in a low voice that shook almost imperceptibly. "Fifty years ago I closed the eyes of my kinsmen in the Kraslo wars. I see them sometimes in sleep—I remember how thirsty they were. Loss of blood makes you thirsty. They begged for water, and we had no water. They lay on the decks in their blood like dogs, with their tongues swelling out and the flies swarming on their eyes. There is nothing glorious in this, Archer."

"That doesn't matter," he shouted. "You don't understand.

I'm not after glory. I want Nayan. I want her to be safe. If I have to fight the Sr of Nym for her, I'll do it. That's—" He stopped suddenly, staring at her in wild surmise.

Something dropped into place in his head, puzzle pieces fitted together with a snap. He grinned at the Melaklos with savage exultation. "You've trapped yourself," he said. He pointed at her accusingly. "You've trapped yourself in your own scheming. Hoist yourself with your own petard." He laughed shortly.

She waited, suddenly wary.

He said, "This is what you've been heading for ever since we came here. Half a year training, meeting Nayan and Lash—all that time traveling. You've been planning to use me in this, haven't you? Against the Sr of Nym."

She moved her head sharply, as if he had struck her.

Elated, he said, "By all the gods of the sea, you have. I knew you were planning something. And now that it's come, you want to back out. Well, you can't. You planned it too well. I'm in this."

"No," she said, quietly.

"Yes," he said. He advanced on her. She took a step back. He said, "I'm a romantic? Maybe. But this is a fantasy, and it's a fantasy you plotted. You can't get out of it now. You planted the lady in distress and the wicked magician—and me. You can't stop it."

"You're talking nonsense," she said sharply.

He said, "Then it's your nonsense. Maybe you didn't count on my being in love with Nayan. Well, I am, and no magician is going to hurt her!"

"You can't fight a magician with a sword," she said tightly.

"You'll think of something," Archer said brutally. "You're a sorceress, aren't you?"

Her hands curled. She looked straight at him. All of the force of her was in her dark eyes. In a flat voice she said, "You are not going to Ytarn."

He forced himself to meet her eyes. It was not easy. They drained his will. Then he remembered Nayan, and showed his teeth again. "I'm going by the first ship," he said.

They faced each other in the first warmth of morning, tight with anger, breathing hard. The air between them tightened with the battle of their wills.

The Melaklos was the first to turn away. Looking toward the red sun, she drew a long shaking breath. She spoke in a low voice, as if to herself, drawing out the words on a changing line as though she sang them: *"Zieh hin': ich kann dich nicht halten.*" The last words rose, until the last syllable dropped on a low note. It was a song of surrender.

Archer had beaten her, and he was not joyous with it. Something in her robbed him of his triumph—it was as though she had seen this as well, perhaps planned it. He stared at her straight gray back, baffled. He could not think of anything to say.

Lash's shout was a welcome interruption. Archer turned and saw the big man crossing the square, grinning. He had obviously had a good night, Archer thought sourly.

"You're out early," said Lash, waving an arm at the sun. He looked at Archer more closely. "What's happened?" he asked in a soberer voice.

The Melaklos was as impassive as usual. She said, "Archer is—" and stopped.

Archer said, "I'm going to Ytarn of Arilikan. When can I get a ship?"

Lash's face screwed up in thought, puzzlement in his china-blue eyes. Then he shrugged and said, "If you're for Ytarn, you'd better go with me. That's where I'm headed in three days." He peered at Archer. "Didn't she tell you?"

"No," said the Melaklos in a flat harsh voice.

The uncomfortable silence returned. Lash, obviously knowing that there was a strain here, but not knowing why, finally turned to Archer and said, "She's coming, too, you know. We'll be just in time to hear the embassy."

"What embassy?" said the Melaklos sharply.

Lash said, "The Council sent an embassy north—I told you last night, didn't I?"

"You did not." Her voice was grim. "Explain."

Still puzzled, Lash said, "There's not much to explain. They've sent two emissaries to propose terms: if he stays north of the Treaty Island Stirin, they won't bother him. If he comes south of it, they send the Arilikan fleet against him."

Shocked, Archer said, "You mean they'd just *give* him the North Islands?"

Lash shrugged. "He's got most of 'em already. And there weren't many northerners at the Council: the Tsiel Tsieln and a few Sandol, that's all."

"What about Nayan?" said Archer sharply. "She's a northern noble."

"Yes," Lash said quickly, "she's there."

"The case is altered," said the Melaklos in English. The men turned to her. She stood beside the fountain with the

112

sun, now well above the horizon, bright behind her. She said, in the trade tongue, "I must go now."

"Where?" they asked simultaneously.

She ignored the question. "Lash, I have instructions for you." She put a hand in her gray shoulder bag, brought out something wrapped in oil-silk. She gave it to the seaman and talked to him quickly in one of the rhythmic mid-island languages. He nodded and put the small package into his belt pouch. She turned away.

"Wait a minute," said Lash. "If you're going to Arilikan, you'd best go with us. I'm sure we can get through the blockade."

She half turned and shook her head.

"You can't go north," he insisted. "No ship can get through now."

"I shall not take ship," she said, almost impatiently.

"What do you mean?" Archer was alert to her evasive tone.

She fumbled at her throat, held out her closed hand toward them. When she opened it for a moment, they saw the shine of silver. She caught her lower lip between her teeth in a signal for silence, and turned and walked away, toward the sea.

Silver. The whistle—the Sandolan talisman. Archer looked doubtfully at Lash. She must mean that she was going to leave with the help of the Serpent—but how? He dismissed the question impatiently. He was going to Ytarn to find Nayan.

Lash said, "I don't like it. She was supposed to go to Ytarn with me—we were hoping she'd help us with the Council. Where in the names of the twelve gods of Gurn is she going?"

"Never mind about her," said Archer brusquely. "How long will it take us to get to Arilikan?" But he was not as indifferent as he tried to sound, and as they talked he kept glancing westward toward the sky and the glittering sea.

Chapter Three

Autumn: fourth quarter, days 25-26

"What the hell are they doing?" muttered Lash for the hundredth time, peering at their pursuer.

Archer, on the afterdeck beside him, did not answer. The sulphur-sailed ship had been following them since late morning, staying just too far away for them to see the crewmen clearly.

Lash's red-eyed Island ship was six days out of Ter-Lashan on the nine-day journey to Ytarn of Arilikan. Archer had been seasick the first day out, but after that he had enjoyed the voyage. He had never been to sea before, certainly not on a galleyed ship that looked like something out of Roman history.

It was early evening now, the sun just gone behind the waters westward. The late-autumn night came fast. As darkness hid the pursuing ship, everything became silent with that peculiar stillness of water in twilight. Archer leaned on the rail and watched as the first stars blossomed into light. Behind him, the soft sounds of the ship were unnaturally loud.

Footsteps shook the deck. Lash and his chief officer came up beside Archer, stood talking together and watching the shadow of the other ship.

"The men won't like it," said the second in command.

"They don't have to like it," rumbled Lash. "My commissioner'll pay bonus in Ytarn—but only if we get there. We've got to shake that devil ship."

"So, so," said the second in command, and he walked away toward the bow, whistling through his teeth. He was a weather-aged islander with half an ear missing. He said that a Sveln prostitute had bitten it off in ecstasy. He told the story with embellishments at every opportunity.

Archer watched him as he strolled up the galley-walk, gesturing at the oarsmen. They stood and moved about, stretching stiffness from their limbs.

The watch at the bow, relieved of duty, came yawning

back and went below to eat. The night watch ambled up the walk to replace them. Ordinarily only one man watched, but Lash had taken no chances from the beginning of this voyage.

The night helmsman came yawning up. Lash stopped him, muttered a few words. He nodded, still yawning, and went to talk to the chief pilot at the helm.

"What are you planning?" Archer asked curiously.

"Night travel." Lash jerked his head toward the other ship, now invisible in the darkness. "We're going to slip her. Clouds coming up—that'll help. And there won't be a moon until past midnight."

Archer looked at the sky. He could still see a few bright stars, but a thin mist seemed to hide the rest. He said, "If the stars go, how can we stay on course?"

"Helmsman's instinct," said Lash. "Melch can sail this stretch blindfolded. He'll keep us close to line—and we won't go far. Just far enough to lose that—" He nodded toward the invisible enemy.

Archer said, "What if they try to attack us?"

"In the dark?" Lash snorted. "I don't like them, but they're not stupid. You have to have light to fight at sea." The two helmsmen came up to him, and he turned to talk to them.

Lash waited until well after the last light faded before giving the order to move. The oars, muffled at the ports, worked with only faint creaks and splashes. The grinning second in command set the stroke in a soft voice that barely reached through the ship. The clouds had obscured all but the brightest stars, and these seemed to give no light.

Archer leaned on the rail and breathed the cold air, staring into the darkness. Somewhere out there was an island called Arilikan Itself, and on that island was a great city called Ytarn, and somewhere in that city was a storm-eyed woman who was called Nayan. He gripped the rail, angry with impatience. It took so long—he realized with a shock that an airplane could make this nine-day journey in a matter of hours. Even a motor boat would cut it down considerably. He wondered briefly how long it would take to go by serpent. The Melaklos had three day's start. Where was she now?

The night seemed to go on forever. Archer dozed beside the helmsman, lulled by the rhythmic sound and motion of the ship. The helmsman sang under his breath. From somewhere forward, Lash called the change of oarsmen. The clouded sky hung low over them; the sea seemed to pass away behind them only to return again in front, like a treadmill, or a circular sea.

Like the River Ocean circling the earth, Archer thought drowsily. I'll put a girdle round the earth in forty minutes. Or was that the Midgard Serpent, who was coiled about the world? The Melaklos was riding the Midgard Serpent, riding to Ytarn to take Nayan away. She saw Archer and smiled, leaning down to speak to him. "Wake up, Archer," she said, in a voice like rushing wind. "Wake up and see—they come."

With a start he woke up. A gust of cold wind from astern made him turn.

The ship loomed out of the night, sails like pallid ghosts above her. Archer stumbled to his feet, opened his mouth to give the alarm. Then she struck them.

The lighter island ship rocked with the glancing blow. Oarsmen, thrown from their benches, struggled with each other to get up. The oars, released, swung crazily over the benches.

Lash came pounding along the galley walk. "What is it?"

Archer, thrown against the rail by the collision, shouted back, "They've caught us. The—"

The helmsman yanked him into the galley without warning. Confused, he looked back to see why.

The other ship matched their pace with unnatural ease, now that the wind was gone. Amidships, something moved against her pale sails, something huge and black that leaned down, down, and fell with a crash to the rear deck of the islander.

Boarding bridge, thought Archer automatically. A light structure of wood and leather, one end mounted and hinged on the other ship, the other holding a metal spike now buried in the islander's planks.

"Axes!" shouted Lash, appearing out of the night. "Boarders!"

Dark figures swarmed over the bridge. Archer drew his sword and vaulted after Lash onto the rear deck.

What followed was like the worst of nightmares. Silent shapeless enemies came out of the dark at him. He struck at them, but they were as numberless as ants. They made no sound. The islanders cursed and shouted and Archer shouted with them, to avoid being taken for an enemy.

The axe-men came, four of them. Islanders ringed them and fought the strangers back while they worked.

Archer stood beside the helmsman, in a line at the deck's edge, keeping the silent men from the rest of the ship. Like shadows they leaped and retreated, bearing bright death. Archer shouted and hit at them, fighting panic. Was there no end to them?

Fire lanced into his side. He swung savagely at the attacker, felt the shock of blade against bone. The man made a small startled sound and fell.

They could be hurt. They could be killed. They were mortal and material. Panic left Archer. Ignoring the pain in his side, he fought carefully, watching.

"Can they see in the dark?" Lash bellowed from somewhere in the fight's center. "Serpent-eyed silent-tongued—Tyef! Prepare!"

Someone broke from the struggle, ran for the galley, calling, "Let me through."

It was Tyef, the grinning second in command. Archer and the helmsman let him pass, reclosed against the enemy.

Archer thought abruptly that he could see better. The air seemed to be growing lighter. The attackers had form; he could see the gleam of their eyes. The nightmare feeling drained away as the light grew. Exhilaration made his blood race.

Snapping and creaking sounds came from the boarding bridge. The axe-men must have cut it nearly through. A wind was rising, the ships strained against each other. The ghostly sails of the stranger bellied, collapsed.

"Tyef!" shouted Lash.

The grinning second appeared from below the decks with a long torch in one hand, a net of clay jars in the other. "Clear me," he cried to Archer.

Archer cut him a path through the fight, swinging his sword like a machete. The second came close behind. The torchlight caught the attackers.

Tiger men Lash had called them, and Archer could see the resemblance. They were spare broad-shouldered men with tigerish golden faces. Their eyes were golden also, with slit pupils like a cat's eyes, or a snake's. Archer felt cold at the sight. He slashed at them, forcing them aside.

The ship lurched, spilling him to the deck. The bridge creaked and groaned. Islanders and tiger men struggled to their feet.

"Drive them onto the bridge," Lash called. He was still up, and the second in command stood with him.

The islanders surged forward to obey Lash. Archer had just time to see what the island captain and his second were doing before the renewed struggle caught him up.

Tyef's clay jars were loosely filled with oil-soaked rags—primitive Molotov cocktails, which Archer had helped make. Now the second in command was lighting them and Lash

117

threw them onto the pallid-sailed ship. They didn't explode, but they burst on impact, and flames began to creep along the black decking. A ship so heavily pitched would go up like a torch, Archer thought.

The tiger men saw, and some tried to get back. Others turned and attacked the islanders more fiercely than before. Archer set his teeth and drove at them, helping to force them back and onto the swaying bridge.

Some were over, hauling up water to throw on the slow-moving fires. More were on the bridge, fleeing for their ship. A few remained on the island ship, fighting. The wind rose again, filling the enemy's sails. For a moment she strained forward, lurched against the link that bound her to the island ship. Then the bridge parted with a snap.

The island ship rolled, sending men slipping sideways. The other moved away, sails set, toward the widening line of dawn.

There were nine tiger men on the island ship, and they fought like madmen. One knocked Archer into the galley. His head hit a bench, making it ring like a kettledrum. He watched almost without interest as four of the men were killed. The other five broke away from the islanders and leaped overboard.

That was it, Archer thought hazily. A little nightmare. A fight with shadows, and what did it get anyone? There didn't seem to be any sense in it.

"Acha."

Lash's voice, rasping, its power gone.

The second in command, appeared at the galley rail. "He wants you," he said.

Archer mounted to the deck, and stopped short. The light was stronger. He could see the battlefield. It was dark and slippery with blood. Men were already at work, tossing the bodies of tiger men overboard after cutting off their hands so that their ghosts could not attack islanders. The bodies of their own dead would be chanted over, the ceremonies duly performed, so that they could sleep well in Arila's submarine halls.

A crewman sluiced a bucket of water across the deck. It rolled like a crimson tidal wave. Archer looked away, feeling sick.

"Acha."

Lash's voice, weaker. Archer turned from the rail.

He was slumped against the rail by the tiller, naked and

mottled with blood. The second in command worked over him with rags and unguents.

"Talk," said Lash as Archer squatted beside him. "—Melaklos—message—" He breathed in deep uneven gulps, painfully.

Something froze in Archer's stomach. He said, "You're hurt—better not talk."

Lash shook his head. "Now." He coughed, spraying tiny flecks of blood. "—Melaklos—message—Tsiel—"

Quickly, Archer said, "A message from the Melaklos to the Tsiel Tsieln?"

Lash nodded. "—Your—errand—" he said, and grinned unexpectedly. "—Told me—if you stayed—" He coughed again.

An errand for him to run for the Melaklos? If he stayed. He said urgently, "What's the message? What is it?"

Lash tried to lift his hand, but it only moved feebly. He rolled his head sideways, to the pile of rags that was his clothes. "—Bag—scroll—" The second in command wrapped a long rag about him, binding a pad to his side.

Archer found the bag, a small drawstring sack. He opened it, took out the scroll. It was tiny, wound on a single red stick. Dark brush strokes showed through the thin paper. He said, "This goes to the Tsiel? Where do I find him?"

"—Stel tree—"

Puzzled, Archer repeated, "Stel tree?"

"—Wine—" Again Lash coughed. Blood trickled from the corner of his mouth. "Ytarn," he said clearly.

Archer fitted it together fast. "A wine shop called the Stel Tree, in Ytarn. I'll find it." He looked at the seaman, worried at the pallor of his face, the ragged breathing. "You'd better not talk any more."

"—More—the Tsiel—" He choked. His body tightened. "Father Arila!" The cry forced through some blockage in his throat. "Let me tell him!" He choked again, coughed, great racking coughs that seemed to tear his throat.

Archer touched his shoulder. "It'll keep. It's all right."

Lash's head rolled toward him, eyes glazing. Through a rush of blood he whispered, "—Tsiel—the Tsiel—" His eyes held Archer's. His mouth worked. Then he shuddered and went limp. Beyond him, the first red rim of the sun burned like blood above the sea.

Chapter Four

Autumn: fourth quarter, day 30 (last day)

The streets grew narrower and more twisting. The tall wooden tenement houses leaned together above Archer's head. The rough stone alleys were slippery and noisome with filth and garbage. The sun was scarcely set, but in these knife-cut ways it was almost pitch dark. Hardly a likely place to find a ruler, even a ruler in exile.

Archer turned another corner and looked down another twisting tunnel. He sighed and started down it, wishing that his feet didn't hurt, and wondering if all seven of his guides had misled him. They had said that this was the way to the Stel Tree.

The island ship, under Tyef's command, had arrived in Ytarn harbor in mid-afternoon. The docks were crowded, but they had found a berth. In the confusion at the piers Archer had slipped past the customs inspectors. For several hours—he wasn't sure how many—he had been walking, and asking directions, and walking more. Ytarn of Arilikan seemed to be all one mazy alley that led nowhere.

He turned another corner, and was on the edge of one of the tiny squares that occasionally appeared. Five alleyways met at this one. Archer looked at them one by one. Which way now? He leaned against the wall beside him, tired and hungry and hopeless. He had no way of knowing which alley to take.

Light flashed across the square. He looked for it. It was gone almost immediately, but he had seen what it was from: a door had appeared for a moment in one of the dark walls. And painted beside it was a crude image of a tree with long dark leaves and clusters of golden berries: a stel tree. He had found it.

Cautiously he crossed the square. Obviously they were keeping the shop a secret—who? He wondered. There was a furtive air to it. Most taverns did not close their doors.

It was not locked, however: it opened as soon as he touched it. He slipped inside and closed the door after him.

The dozen or so people in the big square room looked at him and then away, as any group might look at a newcomer. But he thought that there was more than idle curiosity in their glances. They were on the alert for someone. He looked over the group—and saw the one person who did not look away from him. It was Nayan.

Archer forgot his errand, forgot the Melaklos and dead Lash. He went to Nayan's table without taking his eyes from her. She waited for him silently. He sat down across from her.

"Good evening, Aach'," she said gravely.

A jar boy appeared beside them with wine and water and a wooden bowl for Archer.

Nayan poured the wine. Her hands shook a little. Archer studied her. She was paler than he recalled, and gaunt with worry. There were lines of tension in her face. She wore white: the color of mourning, he thought. Her gray eyes were dark and tired.

He realized that she was watching him curiously. He picked up his bowl and lifted it toward her, swallowed wine. It burned in his throat.

Nayan said, "I didn't know you were coming to Ytarn." Her voice was tight.

He said quietly, "You've been having trouble here, haven't you?"

Her smile was bitter. "Is it so obvious?" She looked around the quiet room. "I haven't left this place for ten days—not since I was led into an ambush by a man who has served me for twenty years."

Archer waited.

She looked at him again. "I had six men left. Two died in that encounter, but we won. The traitor couldn't tell us much afterward."

"What happened to him?"

"He died." Her voice was cold. "Sometimes I wonder if I can trust anyone. I'm almost afraid of Festival."

Startled, Archer said, "Festival?"

"Winter Festival. It begins tomorrow. And I'll have to leave my hiding hole and go to the temple, Melaklos or no Melaklos."

"Is she here?" Archer half hoped that she was.

Nayan shrugged and drank wine. "She was here three days ago. I don't know where she is now. She didn't say you were coming."

Archer shrugged. He didn't want to tell Nayan about that

strange clash of wills in Ter-Lashan. Remembering why he was there, he said, "I'm on an errand for her. I've got a message for a man named Tsiel. Do you—" He stopped, feeling her stiffen.

Her head went back as if from a blow. "Tsiel," she said flatly.

Surprised at her reaction, he said, "Yes. I was told—"

"So." She took a deep shaking breath and looked away. "Another trick. I should have known."

"Known what?" Worried, Archer leaned across the table to touch her hand. "Nayan—"

"You!" Something snapped in her. She was on her feet, eyes blazing. "And you were a companion of the Melaklos. His hand reacheth far, that—" She broke off, turned away.

His hand? Archer began to understand. He stood, caught Nayan's wrist. "The message is from the Melaklos, not from the—from him. Nayan, if this Tsiel is your enemy—"

"Don't lie to me, Aach'. You of all people." She faced him again, her eyes bright with tears. Her voice shook. "Don't lie to me."

Desperately he said, "I'm not lying. She sent us to find a man named Tsiel, here at the Stel Tree. Lash—"

"No!" She tried to pull away. Her voice, out of control, was high and mad. "There hasn't been a man named Tsiel for forty years, and she knows it!"

Stunned, he relaxed his grasp. She twisted free and ran for the curtained stairway at the back of the room.

He followed. At the foot of the stairs, a tall islander with a spear stepped from behind the curtain and blocked his way. "Go," he said.

"I've got to talk to Nayan," said Archer.

"There are no maskers. Go."

Archer tried to push past him. The man prodded him with the spear. Another spearman came from the curtain.

Slowly Archer backed away. He couldn't fight both of them. And people were stirring behind him. He turned.

The other customers were standing, watching him. The tavern keeper's hand rested near a rack of throwing knives.

Archer left. He had no choice. Retreat made him furious, and he stood outside, cursing in English and Dolesar.

Why had she reacted like that? Why?

If the Tsiel Tsieln was her enemy, why was she staying where he was supposed to be? Was he her enemy? Maybe that was what Lash had tried to say, when death had silenced him.

122

Puzzle pieces that wouldn't fit together. Lash's dying words. Nayan's fury. The Melaklos's reluctance to have Lash speak of the Tsiel, back in Ter-Lashan. Nayan's enemy?

Or her ally? Archer started to walk away down the twisting alleys, turning this thought. Her ally, or friend. She was in mourning—for him? If he had died, she might expect the Melaklos to know. If so, then anyone looking for him from the Melaklos was a liar. It was a thin chain of reasoning, but it might be true.

Or it might be some perverse joke of the Melaklos.

Archer considered that. No. It didn't sound right. There was no sense in it as a joke.

"There hasn't been a man named Tsiel for forty years."

Something stirred in his mind, another answer. It hovered on the edge of thought, tantalizing. He stopped and pounded a stone corner-marker softly, trying to grasp the thought. What was it?

"Your name Archa?"

The voice at his shoulder startled him. He turned sharply. "Who are you?"

The speaker, a dark shape in the dark street, sidled toward him with a trench-coat-and-slouch-hat air. "I'm from the Tsiel Tsieln," he whispered. "We've been waiting for you."

Chapter Five

Winter Festival—day one

Archer spoke fast, with one eye on the approaching spearmen. "Isn't it customary to at least question a possible traitor? You could listen, if nothing more."

Nayan turned her head from the altar lamps that she was lighting. Lines of strain showed in her face. "All right," she said wearily. "In justice, you should have a hearing. But be brief—the ceremony must begin in fifteen minutes."

"Last night—" Archer began. He turned his head as the spearmen came up through the dark temple.

Nayan gestured, and they retreated to a bench against the wall, just out of earshot.

Archer said, "Last night, after you—after I left, I saw the Tsiel Tsieln. He said that, although your family and his are enemies, he wishes to offer alliance until the Sr of Nym is defeated."

Nayan bit her lip and turned to light altar lamps again. The candle in her hand shook. She said tightly, "Go on."

Puzzled, Archer looked away from her. His mind was strangely blank. He said hesitantly, "I think that's all."

She glanced at him, looked away. "Tell me, Aach'," she said evenly. "What does the Tsiel look like?"

Words came into his head, and he grabbed at them gratefully. "He looks pretty ordinary—about my height, black hair, blue eyes. He has a scar on the inside of his left wrist—a ragged line about a hand span long."

Something was wrong with that, he thought. He couldn't recall ever seeing a man with that scar.

"But—that—" whispered Nayan, with horror. She gripped the altar table with one hand, staring at Archer. Her other hand trembled violently; the rush light threw wild shadows behind her. She closed her eyes and shuddered. When they opened, she was in control of herself again. She turned away, pinching out the rush light. "Does he wish to meet me?" she asked coldly.

Again he knew the answer, but couldn't remember hearing

it. It was as though someone were inside his head, dictating. Even as he had the thought, it was gone as if snuffed out. He said, "Yes, the Tsiel wants to meet you. On neutral ground, with no one else except me present."

"Where?"

"Here," he said. "After the ceremony. You're to send your men away with the other worshipers—they can stay outside, if you wish—and he'll come alone."

"I see," she said slowly. She looked past him into the great dim room.

Archer turned and looked too, not sure why he did so. Eyes light-blinded by the altar lamps, he could see only shadows of the worshipers. There were not many: this was a minor temple, used only at Festival now.

"Very well," said Nayan tonelessly. "Now go. The ceremony begins." Her hands were clenched as though she held some great emotion in check.

Savage satisfaction filled Archer's head, so remote that it seemed to belong to someone else. He made his way to the back of the shadowy room and sat against the wall to think.

He was apprehensive. He was beginning to be afraid.

He could not remember meeting the Tsiel Tsieln, much less talking to him. After leaving the Stel Tree, he had followed the furtive little man to a huge empty room, much like the temple chamber. Here his guide, a thin-shouldered pot-bellied man, had left him to await the Tsiel. There had been tall torches burning before a dais with a cushioned couch on it. Smoking torches—the smoke had the cloying harshness of cheap incense. Archer's head had gotten heavier and heavier, until finally he must have slept.

Returning to awareness, he had found himself heading for this small temple, knowing what his errand was, but not remembering who had told him of it. He had known what words to say to Nayan, but he did not recall hearing them before.

The incense must have drugged him, he thought. His thoughts were slow, pushing against some barrier in his head. He concentrated, thinking carefully.

Drugged or hypnotized, or both—that had to be the answer. Someone had entranced him and told him what to say. Anger flared in him at this violation of his mind. He hardly noticed that it was immediately suppressed.

Who had done this? The Tsiel Tsieln, apparently. Yet he was not quite sure. The Melaklos, perhaps? Or the Sr of Nym? The Tsiel was the obvious answer—why was he un-

125

sure? Last night. The furtive little man had interrupted him just as he was about to find an answer to the mystery of the Tsiel. There had been words in it: the Melaklos, the Melaklos and Lash talking in Ter-Lashan, Lash's dying words, an angry cry from Nayan. They all fit to form some answer, something that he had almost touched last night. What?

He looked around the temple, as if the answer waited there. The worshipers were shapeless shadows against the flickering light from the altar lamps. Nayan stood behind the altar table, dressed in white, clear against the shadows behind her. She chanted in a clear voice, and the worshipers rumbled the responses. She stood very straight, head high, hands held out in the gesture of protection. Once, her head turned and she looked straight at Archer.

Then he knew. Everything fit into place. He started to get up, to warn her.

He could not move. He could not even lift his hand. Panicking, he fought inside his unresponsive body.

So you guessed, said a voice in his head. *Too bad*.

Get out of my mind, Archer thought at it savagely.

Be quiet.

White fire lanced through Archer's thoughts. Everything dwindled and disappeared.

"They're waiting outside. When will he be here?"

Nayan's voice came to Archer through a rush of white noise. As the noise faded, he heard another voice answering.

"He should be here in half an hour, Nayan. He's at ceremony in the Great Temple."

Hazily Archer thought, *that voice is familiar*. Then as he woke up fully, he knew why. It was his own voice. But he was not using it.

He tried to stay still, so that the interloper would not know that he was conscious. He could see and hear. He—or his body—was standing by the altar table, facing Nayan. Her face was haggard in the uneven light, her eyes huge and dark.

The interloper moved abruptly. "I'll close the door," he said with Archer's voice.

"Why?" she said sharply.

"To make sure there are no interruptions." The interloper smiled with Archer's face and walked down the dark room.

Archer raged impotently in his head.

Keep calm, Acha, came the cold thought of the invader. *You can't do anything*.

Oh, can't I, thought Archer furiously.

The interloper closed the heavy wooden doors and slid home the stiff bolt. *No. You can't,* he thought. *You don't know how.*

He was right, Archer thought despairingly.

Cold amusement came from the interloper. He started back toward the altar and Nayan.

Archer tried to shout, to warn her, but he couldn't speak. He could not control anything except his thoughts.

There had to be some way to fight an invader in your head, he thought desperately. There must be some way to get rid of him.

Nayan, still behind the table, watched as they returned. Her face was unreadable in the uncertain light.

The interloper stood close to her and spoke in a low earnest voice. "Nayan, I know that he's not really the Tsiel. But we've got to let him damn himself. It's the Melaklos's plan."

She nodded without speaking.

The interloper took her hand and stroked it, looking at her. "You didn't really think I'd betray you?" he asked softly.

She shook her head, still without saying anything.

Archer struggled futilely for some hand-hold, something to grasp that could help him out of his helplessness.

"It'll be a while before they get here," said the interloper, still more softly. He moved closer to Nayan, put an arm across her shoulders.

Get away from her, Archer shouted at him.

Nayan froze at his touch. In a flat voice she said, "They?"

"The Melaklos is coming after him."

Archer scarcely heard the reply. Nayan's voice—he reached for it, willing her to speak again. He was sure that he could touch it, catch it as a rope to pull him back.

She said nothing, and he concentrated on other senses. He clung to the feel of the dusty air, the oil smell of the lamps, the sight of the shadows of Nayan's face. How he knew he couldn't tell, but he did know that he was gaining ground. He was regaining control.

The interloper kissed Nayan. She did not respond. "I love you, Nayan," he whispered.

She did not move.

Get away from her, Archer thought furiously. This invader was trying to seduce her—in Archer's guise. The thought made him sick. He tried again to warn Nayan, but he still couldn't speak.

The interloper turned his head sharply. Archer saw what

had alerted him—a flicker of movement, or was it? in the shadows. They watched, but nothing stirred.

The interloper was concentrating, off-guard. Archer lunged past him, shouted, "Tsiel! It's a trap. Get away."

Nayan twisted out of his arms, sprang for the door.

The interloper caught her within two steps of it. They struggled silently in the darkness. Inside his head, Archer struggled also.

The interloper, caught between them, flung Nayan away from him. She staggered, caught herself against a bench.

"Talk," said Archer desperately. "Keep—" He lost the voice.

All right, said the interloper grimly. *I didn't want to destroy you. You might have been useful.*

Don't be sure you can, said Archer.

Don't be a fool. You don't know how to fight me.

He was right, Archer thought, but that didn't matter. This was his own ground—that had to count for something.

He saw Nayan suddenly, standing beside a bench, half her face lit by the altar lamps. Her lips moved. He reached for her voice. She was chanting one of the litanies of Arila. He gripped it, climbed it like a rope.

The interloper pulled at him.

His senses slipped away. He clung to Nayan's face and voice, thrashing and kicking.

Slowly, relentlessly, the interloper peeled him away, like a man pulling a starfish arm by arm from a rock.

Frightened and angry, Archer hit at him, but there was nothing to hit. He could not see anything. He could scarcely hear Nayan's voice.

Something stirred in his mind, an alien thought so faint that he could hardly hear it. *Help*, it said, as if to identify itself. Archer caught at it blindly.

Power flowed into him, power and knowledge. He knew how to fight the interloper. He pulled the invader away from his muscles, away from his senses.

Surprise yammered at him—the interloper's surprise. *Archer?* The thought was doubtful.

Get out, Archer said savagely.

Amazing, thought the interloper. *I didn't realize*—and he was gone.

Unbelieving, Archer stretched and shook himself. He was completely in control again. He laughed exultantly.

Nayan, still chanting, watched him.

He walked over to her, stopping when she flinched back. "It's all right," he said. "He's gone."

She had stopped chanting as he approached. She said, "Is it really you—Aach', not the puppet master?"

"Of course," he said. He laughed again. "I could be lying."

"The Melaklos will know," she said, her lips barely moving.

"The Melaklos." Archer reached inside his mind. That tiny alien thought was gone, but he was sure he knew whose it was. He said, "Where is the Melaklos?"

"I don't know."

"And why didn't she tell me who you are?"

Nayan's head moved sharply; she bit her lip and looked at him.

He reached for her shoulders, but withdrew his hands when she shrank back. Gently he said, "You are the Tsiel Tsieln, aren't you?"

Chapter Six

Winter Festival—day one

Something moved in the shadows by the door. The bolt groaned as it was drawn back. Archer and Nayan, glad of the break in the tension, turned toward the door.

It opened, letting in the chill night air and the torchlight from the squares. The opener turned to the two by the altar.

"So," she said quietly. "Well done, Archer."

"Melaklos," said Nayan quickly. "It is Aach'?"

She came up to the altar before replying. She wore a black cloak over her pale gray garments—no wonder they hadn't seen her in the shadows, Archer thought.

She looked at him gravely, looked at Nayan. "He is Archer."

Abruptly, because he was cross, Archer said, "Why didn't you tell me she was the Tsiel?"

The Melaklos moved one hand. "You were safer not knowing, if you decided not to remain active. Lash would have told you when you arrived."

"Lash is dead," said Archer harshly.

"Yes." There was no surprise, no emotion at all, in her voice. She turned to Tsiel/Nayan. "The Council meets at second nightwatch."

The black-haired woman frowned. "I was not informed."

The Melaklos shrugged with one shoulder. "I doubt that they made any great effort to find you."

Tsiel/Nayan shook her head. "Tonight is Festival firstnight. It must be an important meeting."

"The Gurnal have arrived," said the Melaklos quietly. "Algundor leads them."

Archer looked from her to Nayan. Algundor, the prince of Gurn—they had mentioned him before. Nayan had been coming from Gurn when she was attacked near kos-Alar, where Archer had met her. Lash had spoken scornfully of him there and later in Ter-Lashan. Algundor, the "palehanded princeling." It was odd, the way he kept popping up.

"Algundor?" Tsiel/Nayan's voice was dry. "Coming with

gilded masts and perfumed purple sails, no doubt. Is Admiral Kyekalan with him?"

"Yes."

The Island woman nodded.

This was a side of her that Archer had not seen before—she was cold and competent, weighing what the Melaklos told her. She was a ruler, he told himself. She was the leader of one of the two most powerful islands in the north. Looking at her, at the set of her shoulders, at the light in her gray eyes, he thought suddenly that she must be a good leader.

She was saying, "This may goad the Council to move. They've been marking time, waiting for their embassy to return."

"It has returned," said the Melaklos.

Something in her tone made Archer look at her, alert.

She quirked her mouth. One hand emerged from her black cloak, moved sharply. Something clattered onto the altar table, rocked gleaming in the torchlight. It was a broad collar of bronze, the ends bent into tabs and secured by a screw.

Tsiel recoiled from it. "They are dead, then?" she asked.

"Dead."

Gingerly Archer touched the shining collar. "Garotte?" he said.

She nodded. "The Deadly Collar. Not a northern execution device—it can kill slowly."

Harshly, Tsiel said, "We don't care for such refinements. Death is not a toy. Put it away!"

North-islanders were superstitious about death, Archer remembered. Our oldest shipmate, one of their songs called it. They did not fear it as the southerners did, but death had his place in everything they did. Nayan had told him a lot about that while they traveled to Ter-Lashan. Nayan—he had to remember that she was the Tsiel, probably the most powerful woman in the Islands. It was a disconcerting thought.

"Second nightwatch." Her voice claimed his attention. "It is that now. I must go."

"I'll come with you," said Archer quickly. He wanted to know what the Council was planning to do next.

She looked at him, at the Melaklos, questioning.

"Archer—" began the Melaklos.

He turned his head and smiled at her deliberately, to show her that he would not be commanded.

She looked at him for a long moment, not speaking, not

changing expression. Then she said carefully, "Archer, I would speak with you. Immediately. It is important. Will you drink wine with me?"

She hadn't commanded him, but there was an urgency in her voice more compelling than any command could be. He said slowly, "All right, but after I take Nayan—Tsiel, I mean—to the Council chamber."

"That—" The Melaklos stopped abruptly. She took a deep breath, let it out slowly. "As you will," she said. "I shall wait two squares west of the chamber building." She turned quickly and left the temple, holding her black cloak close about her.

Worried, Archer watched her go. Her manner had been strange. It could be irritation or anger at his rebellion, but he didn't think so. Something was troubling the Melaklos, troubling her enough to disturb her inhuman calm. He didn't—

"I don't like that," said Tsiel, echoing Archer's thoughts.

Startled, he turned his head.

She met his eyes. "Something's wrong," she said. "I've never seen her like that before—abrupt, uncertain." She looked toward the door again, tossing back her black hair. "Find out what it is, will you, Aach'?"

The wine shop to which the Melaklos took Archer was small and dim, and full without being crowded—a thing unknown during Festival. The Melaklos managed as usual to find a seat in a corner. Archer sat beside her with his back to the wall, wanting to be able to see the shop's patrons.

"They're a rough-looking lot," he said in an undertone. "This looks like a hangout in a gangster film."

She glanced at him sharply. "Perceptive," she said. "We are in the heart of the Thieves Market." She poured wine into his cup and pushed it toward him. Setting down the jar, she said, "You have questions. Ask them."

About to point out that this tête-à-tête was her idea, he hesitated. After all, he did have questions. And he sensed that she wanted something steadying—like answering questions. He said the first thing that came into his head. "Was that you who—"

She interrupted, in English. "Who helped you against the puppet master? Yes." She bit her lip. "Archer. You should know. He has left a—a contact inside your head. I cannot get it out."

Alarmed, Archer said, "You mean he can read my mind?"

"No." She looked down at her hands. "He can see with

your eyes, hear with your ears—he can sense with all of your senses."

Archer stared at her. The idea was revolting. It was frightening. He said slowly, "Then I'd better stay away from the Council—" He didn't go on. This couldn't separate him from Nayan so soon after he had found her.

The Melaklos said, "No. Go to the Council—he knows all that passes there. I speak for your warning and protection. Use your judgment about what you see and hear. Remember that he will know of most of it anyway. But do not discuss me with anyone—not even with Nayan."

"Is he listening now?" said Archer worried.

"It does not matter. He does not understand English." She dismissed him with a gesture, drank thirstily from her wooden bowl.

After a pause, Archer said, "What's been happening to Nayan? She looks hunted."

"Her people have been dying," said the Melaklos. "He has killed five of her spearmen and induced another to betray her. The Silent Man who brought her here for me is dead. He is trying to wear her down."

Archer remembered the shadows in Nayan's eyes, the harsh edge in her voice. Looking down, he saw that his hands were clenched and trembling. If he ever caught the Sr of Nym—

The Melaklos was speaking, half to herself. "We gave him time when he did not want it, going roundabout from kos-Alar to Ter-Lashan. He wanted her urgently then. Now—now he is known, and there will be war. Time is his ally now."

Archer watched her, only half comprehending her words. She was not speaking to him—she spoke as though trying to convince herself of something. She was afraid, he thought suddenly. Nothing had gone amiss yet, but she was coming to some delicate and dangerous stage in her plan. So delicate and so dangerous that she was afraid.

That frightened him. She had never shown any feeling stronger than mild exasperation. Now the fear seemed to hang about her like a cloud. He sat still, unable to move.

She moved abruptly, breaking the spell. She looked at him with empty dark eyes. "Tonight was to be the climax of his persecution of Nayan," she said. "When you appeared, it gave him a perfect opportunity. He was going to strike at her personally, at herself."

Archer waited, not wanting to hear what came next, but knowing that he must.

"He never intended her to think that you were yourself," said the Melaklos. "To violate her with the body of her lover—that was a terrible idea, Archer."

Choked with hate, Archer could not speak.

"She told me about your coming when I met her this morning," said the Melaklos in the same quiet even voice. "I did not know then what his plan was. We could only wait—you did well, Archer."

"You helped," he said gruffly.

She looked at the table, embarrassment on her face. He had seen her embarrassed once before—when she admitted having touched his mind, in kos-Alar. At least she seemed to have scruples about invading people's minds.

The Sr of Nym, now, the Sr of Nym had no such scruples. The puppet master—Archer shivered. He would never forget the horror of that mastery, the helpless rage. And now the Sr of Nym had a listening post in his, Archer's, head. The knowledge made him sick. He pushed it to the back of his mind. There were other things to worry about now. The Melaklos's fear. The Tsiel—Nayan. He couldn't think of her as the Tsiel.

He said, "What does he want with Nayan? How can she help him?"

The Melaklos, staring at her curled hands, did not seem to hear.

He repeated the question, loudly.

Her head snapped up. "What is it?" she said sharply.

Alerted by her manner, Archer said, "What's wrong with you?"

"Nothing," she said shortly.

Worried, Archer tried to read her eyes. They were empty. He said deliberately, "You're nervous, irritable. You don't take in what people say. *What's wrong?*"

She banged her hands onto the tabletop. "I am devising an escape from the society of idiots. Apparently it cannot be done."

"You really are worried," he said.

Impatiently she picked up her bowl, tilted it. It was empty.

Afraid now, Archer stared at her unreadable face. She stared at the bowl as though it threatened her.

"What's wrong?" said Archer gently.

She did not look at him, did not look away from the empty bowl. She shivered.

Archer forced himself to smile. He picked up the wine jar

and filled her cup. "Come fill the cup," he said lightly. "Drink that and tell me what's wrong."

"In vino veritas," said the Melaklos. A corner of her mouth lifted mirthlessly. "In wine is truth." She looked at the bowl without touching it.

Archer waited. Nothing he could say would influence her now. If she chose not to tell him what was bothering her, he could do nothing.

She glanced at him. "I am going to fight the Sr of Nym," she said quietly.

He didn't understand. "So is everyone else," he said. "I'm going with the fleet—if the Council ever sends it."

"They will send it," she said. "Tonight they will decide, and you will sail the day after Festival ends."

"You?" said Archer. "What about you?"

"I must go before the fleet." She curled both hands on the wooden tabletop. "If he can be distracted when the fleets meet, he will not be able to direct the battle. Otherwise—" She shrugged.

Otherwise, Archer thought, the islanders don't have a chance. He remembered Lash, telling of the storm that blew out of a clear sky and destroyed the Tsiel fleet. Yes, if the Sr of Nym was in charge there would be no chance for the Islanders.

But that didn't explain the Melaklos's fear—unless she was afraid of dying. No. He didn't think that death would frighten her. But there had to be something.

A movement of her hand caught his eye. Her eyes were dark, unseeing.

Suppressing his concern, Archer said, "If you beat him, that solves the whole thing, doesn't it? Why didn't you try this before?"

She picked up the cup, set it down again. "I cannot defeat him."

She needed to be encouraged. With a heartiness he did not feel, Archer said, "Well, if you think you'll lose, you probably will. Defeatism—"

She interrupted, speaking slowly. "You do not understand, Archer. I *know* that I cannot defeat him. He is a powerful magician, and I am a very minor sorceress."

Archer started to say something, but she overrode him.

"I know that I cannot defeat him. But when I stand to him and power meets power, then I will believe that I can win, I will believe that I *will* win. I shall believe in spite of knowledge. And when I have lost, I shall be crushed."

Archer stared at her. If she was telling the truth—and he was sure that she was—then she was going to walk right into something that could destroy her. He didn't completely understand what she meant by believing that she would win, but—from some corner of his memory a phrase drifted into his mind, a tag-line. He caught at it.

Faith is believing in something you know ain't so.

Belief against knowledge, that's what she had said. She was going to face the Sr of Nym with absolute faith in herself. What would happen to her if she lost?

He said inanely, "Losing wouldn't kill you, would it?"

"There are worse things than death, Archer," she said quietly. "Itor grant that you may never know them."

Startled, he said, "Itor? I've never heard you call on a god before."

She flushed and looked away, and that, too, was new and upsetting.

"Drink your wine," he said at last, at a loss for anything else to say. "It'll be cold outside, and it's good wine."

She stood up. Then, very deliberately, she picked up her full bowl of wine and hurled it against the stone wall.

Chapter Seven

Winter Festival: day one (cont'd.)

Archer's head started to hurt as they were passing the dusty vineyards outside the city. He ignored the pain at first, but it grew to a throbbing that blinded him and took away his balance.

The Melaklos caught him as he stumbled. "What is it?" she said, and then, "Yes. So. It will pass."

"What is it?" Archer managed to say. He squeezed his eyes shut and clutched his head with both hands.

"Come on." She half carried him between two rows of clipped vines, to the top of a narrow twisting path.

Halfway down, Archer's head cleared. He stopped and looked back up the path, not sure how he had gotten so far without mishap.

"Come," said the Melaklos impatiently.

Obediently Archer followed. The path was so deeply worn in places that it was a gully, so narrow that Archer could scarcely get one foot into the bottom of it.

They came out at last onto a narrow strip of coarse sand and stone. White in the moonlight, the sea hissed and boiled around rocks before them.

"All right," said the Melaklos. She held her hand toward Archer; silver gleamed in it.

Recognizing the silver cylinder, Archer said, "The Great Serpent?"

"Yes. There is not much time." She looked toward the sea. "He cannot hear us now—that is why your head hurt. He was attempting to keep contact."

"I don't understand," said Archer quietly. He didn't want to risk upsetting her, in her uncertain mood.

Still looking over the sea, she said, "Magic and sorcery do not work near the Great Serpent. That is why I have brought you here."

Archer waited.

Beyond the rough rocks, the cove they faced was calm and

dark. The shore dropped sharply, Archer remembered. He had heard of this little inlet near the vineyards. This was Deadman's Cove. No ships could land in it—but perhaps a sea-serpent could.

The Melaklos seemed to come to some decision. She faced Archer, her face deep-shadowed by the two moons. "He gets his men from another world," she said. "There is no break in the barrier, but there must be a portal—a gateway opening only between that world and this. If my—my colleagues have detected it, there will be a guard waiting for him." She stopped, watching Archer doubtfully.

"Go on," he said impatiently.

"The portal must be on the island of Tsiel. If I can find it, I may be able to close it." She shook her head. "If—there are—" She broke off, turning toward the sea and raising the whistle to her lips.

Hastily Archer said, "Wait a minute. If you've got something to tell me, say it."

"The chances are small," she said uncertainly.

Archer had never seen such hesitation in her before. He said cheerfully, "I've heard you say that every chance is worth the taking."

She looked at him again, then she nodded abruptly.

"Here," she said. She put something cold and flat in his hand. "When you are away from the Serpent, do not look at it. The Sr of Nym must not know that you have it."

Archer looked at it closely. It was a bronze medallion on a leather cord, with a curving triangular pattern beaten into it. "What is it?" he asked.

She was looking out to sea again. "A talisman of my clan," she said. Before he could say anything, she raised the silver cylinder to her lips again and blew.

Pain stabbed through Archer's temples. The whistle's note rose, and the pain rose with it, until the pitch passed out of hearing. The pain faded, leaving only a throbbing in his head. Archer passed a hand over his forehead, wiping away cold sweat.

The Melaklos stood still, alert. She said rapidly, "Any member of my clan or any sorcerer of any time of Dolesar will know that you are my companion while you wear the medallion."

Puzzled, Archer said, "There aren't any more sorcerers here, are there?"

She gestured impatiently. "That does not matter. A chance

is worth taking." She glanced at him. "If the portal is closed, he cannot get more of his tiger men."

"But what can I do about it?" cried Archer, bewildered. "I'm no sorcerer."

She shook her head impatiently and blew the whistle again.

When the sound died away, it was quiet in the cove except for the angry mutter of the water. The Melaklos stood tensed, straining toward the dark waters.

Archer peered into the darkness. The water beyond the rocks was black, broken by points of silver where the moons reflected in it. Something was beginning to obscure the silver points, something dark rising from the water. Something huge, shining, moving with a slow sound toward the shore. A shadow moved across the white water.

Archer could not move, could not speak. Something terrible was rising from the sea. He felt the cold power that emanated from it.

Eyes opened suddenly. Eyes in the air six feet higher than his head. Yellow eyes, huge, shining, with black slit pupils like a cat's eyes. The shadow of a head behind them swung slowly closer.

Fear froze Archer. His heart stopped, then pounded painfully.

A voice seemed to come out of the ground, so deep and slow that Archer could scarcely make out the words.

"Who wakes me from sleep?"

"Only I," said Melaklos. Her voice was slow and calm. "Again I ask your aid, Old One."

"So." The dark head swung above her now. Still paralyzed, Archer saw the serpent: darkly shining scales, the great triangular skull, the batrachian eye ridges. Twenty feet of shimmering body lay on the beach, but it disappeared into the water with no perceptible tapering.

The serpent was—huge, Archer thought confusedly. In his terror, he could understand why the Islanders were so grave when they spoke of the Sandolan Protector. The deeps held something more terrible than he had dreamed.

"A stranger," the voice rumbled. The head swung toward him, the great mouth opened. Moonlight caught on sabre-curved fangs and the long triple-forked tongue.

"My companion," said the Melaklos. She gestured impatiently. "I must go to Tsiel, Old One."

"Tsiel." The voice was thoughtful. "Is that magician still there?"

"Yes."

"So." The great head swung lower, lower, until it rested on the sand. The Melaklos vaulted onto the neck, just behind the flaring of the triangular jaw. Scales rippled and shimmered in the moonlight as the serpent slipped backward into the water.

The Melaklos's voice came urgently from the shadows. "Keep council, Archer. Do not forget the Sr of Nym."

Released by her voice from the paralysis that held him, Archer called hesitantly, "Good luck, Melaklos."

There was no reply. The water muttered about the rocks; beyond them, the black waters were unbroken. The Melaklos and the Great Serpent were gone.

Suddenly Archer began to shiver. He had never been so terrified and so alone in his life.

Chapter Eight

Winter Festival: day one to Winter: day fourteen

Tall guards stood outside the Council Chamber. They stared stonily at Archer until one of Tsiel's spearmen came and identified him. Then they stood aside and let him pass.

The spearman cleared a path for him through masses of chattering men. Archer heard snatches of talk about ships, winter storms, alliances. He came suddenly into the council chamber. This was a big square room, hung with coarse draperies and lit with scented torches. Four long tables set in a hollow square took up most of the floor space. At least a hundred men sat at them. The men were an odd mixture: narrow-eyed merchants, bored aristocrats, impatient seamen. There were perhaps half a dozen women at the tables.

Tsiel/Nayan looked up as Archer slipped onto the bench beside her, displacing a yawning minor official. "What's happened?" she asked in a whisper. "You look like you've seen the heart of hell."

Archer shook his head. He couldn't discuss it with her. "Who's that talking?" he whispered.

Tsiel tossed back her black hair. "That is Algundor, the prince of Gurn. The young ass is playing politics." Her color was high, her eyes bright with anger.

Curiously Archer studied the speaker. Algundor was a tall thin young man with a smooth voice. He gestured with long pale hands. Unpleasant, Archer thought. The sort of thing you'd find growing in a cellar or under a rock.

Just as Archer turned to ask Tsiel what they were debating, the pallid princeling stopped speaking and bowed across the square to her. He sat down, smiling. Beside him, a powerful man with a dark brown beard glanced at Algundor, and then at Tsiel.

Admiral Kyekalan, leader of the Gurn fleet, Archer thought. If it was he, he didn't seem impressed by his leader's arguments.

"My lords in council—" Tsiel was on her feet, head high, voice ringing clear. "My lords, I submit that the prince

Algundor speaks of things that have no place at this meeting. We are here to decide whether to send the fleet against the Sr of Nym, not to discuss the petty politics of a swamp-water prince."

Algundor smiled lazily across the tables. "Marriage alliance will benefit you most, Tsiel," he said. "The land Tsiel will need rebuilding—"

"Time to speak of rebuilding Tsiel when Tsiel is free," she said.

He continued as though she had not spoken. "My domain is rich. Together we can restore Tsiel to its rightful glory."

Her hands clenched on the tabletop. "This is no time to speak of glory," she said evenly.

She sounded dangerous, Archer thought. What were they talking about? Marriage alliance, Algundor had said. Meaning that he married Tsiel and ruled both their lands? Archer suppressed a lip-curl of disgust.

Algundor bowed to the Island woman. "We will speak of alliance, then," he said. "I have the best fleet in southern waters at my command."

Blackmail, thought Archer angrily. My cue. He said aloud, "At your command?"

Red patches appeared on Algundor's bloodless cheeks. He said flatly, "My fleet arrived yesterday. If there is no alliance—as demanded—between Tsiel and Gurn, then it will return to Dragonspaw with the first tide after Festival ends."

I was right, thought Archer savagely.

The council stirred. Men muttered to each other, shouted at Algundor. A fat middle-aged merchant next to Archer beat the table and cried softly, "A quarter of the Fleet. A goddam quarter of the goddam Fleet."

"My lords!" Tsiel, still standing, called over the uproar. "My lords in council!"

Archer shouted, "Order! Order!" as loudly as he could.

The confusion subsided. Heads turned toward the north-island woman. She said, "Do you believe that he controls the Gurnin fleet?"

"I hold the keys to the Treasury," he drawled. "Surely that is enough."

She shook her head. "The ships are fully equipped and supplied. They are led by a man who can see beyond his nose—a man who was captain under Lak, the counsellor of Sanan. Tell me, princeling—can you risk Kyekalan's taking them north without you?"

White to the lips, Algundor glanced venomously at the bearded man beside him.

Recalling everything that he had heard about the Gurnal, Archer stood up and said loudly, "The Gurnin fleet is pledged to Arilikan. He cannot in honor withdraw it."

"I did not pledge it," shouted Algundor.

A touch. Archer goaded him again. "But you are responsible for it."

Algundor glared at him. "This does not touch my honor."

Tsiel said, "It does." Her voice was a whip-crack. "You are responsible for your fleet, for the fate of every man in it, for the acts of every man in it. You are responsible for the pledge of the fleet commander."

"Then I suppose you're responsible for the defeat of the Tsiel fleet," he sneered.

Her face went white, but her eyes fixed on him. "Yes, I am responsible. I am the Tsiel Tsieln. I trained my son to command. I left him in charge of my rule."

"And he has done well," said an islander.

She inclined her head toward him. "I thank you, Kora of Bukol." She raised her voice, looking around the assembly. "Algundor has given an ultimatum: unless there is marriage alliance between us, his ships will not sail. I tell you now, my lords in council, that I was in Gurn for a season, discussing alliance. I decided that it would not be good. I have not changed my mind."

The lords in council did not look happy, Archer thought, at the prospect of losing a quarter of their fleet. But no one wanted to be the first to argue with the black-haired northern ruler. No wonder, Archer thought admiringly. She was incredible.

She faced Algundor squarely, and her voice was clear and cold. "Hear me, prince of Gurn. There is a proverb in the north: a ruler should marry once for the state, once for herself. I took as consort a man of my blood. He is dead now, but we had a child. My son is of age, though young. Hear me, Prince of Gurn. Hear me, my lords in council. When Tsiel is won back—and it will be won back—I shall abdicate. My son will rebuild Tsiel."

Algundor stared at Tsiel, eyes hard, white cheeks flushed. The councillors buzzed among themselves. The islander who had supported Tsiel, Kora of Bukol, got up and made his way around the table toward her. Only one man did not move: the bearded man beside Algundor. He had to be

Kyekalan, Archer thought. He wondered what the admiral planned to do.

"I am sincere," said Tsiel, turning to speak to Kora of Bukol. "True, my son is young—but I was no older than he when I took the throne. He is old enough to rule—and there will be much to rebuild."

"I understand," said Kora. "I understand also the reasons you have not spoken. Still, was it wise to say this?"

"It is too late now," she said. "I have spoken it." She looked around at the shouting, gesticulating councillors. "Better to celebrate Festival than to remain in this idiots' nest," she said to Archer.

Grinning, he stood up. She was a remarkable woman, he thought. Standing there unafraid with the whole council against her. He said, "This may be our last Festival. Let's make the most of it." He took her hand. "They can't send the fleet until it's over, anyway."

"They won't have it decided even then," said Tsiel/Nayan acidly.

But the council did decide. On the fourth night of Festival, Kora of Bukol pointed out that Admiral Kyekalan had been preparing his ships to sail north despite Algundor's threats. On the fifth and last night, Kyekalan himself (who had not before spoken in council) stood up and quietly announced that the Gurnin fleet was ready to leave.

The Arilikan Fleet sailed on the second day of winter, two days after the end of Festival. As a result of hasty compromises, Tsiel went in Algundor's purple-sailed ship, with Archer as her only attendant. Her two spearmen were assigned to Kyekalan's flagship.

Kyekalan and Sotar, the *Arilikan Itself* admiral, were the joint commanders. The two wings traveled in loose formation, each fanned back from its flagship. Algundor's two shiploads of aristocrats trailed along the right flank, Kyekalan's division.

Tsiel, Archer, Algundor, and the ship's dozen aristocratic passengers slept in tiny cubicles in the stern. Tsiel was not actually a prisoner, but after the first two days she showed little interest in exploring the ship. She and Archer spent most of their time on the projecting rear deck, a Roman-like stage deck, talking and waiting. Every night at sunset Tsiel untied another knot in the string calendar she carried, and calculated their speed and position by the stars.

"There should be storms," she said. "There always are at this time of year, and uncertain winds."

"Maybe it's a good year," Archer said.

She shook her head and looked at the sky. "It's unnatural," she said. "We're having a steady favoring wind. There hasn't been the ghost of a storm. It isn't natural."

Archer met her eyes. Was she thinking the same thing, he wondered: that the Sr of Nym was so eager for the sea battle that he was making good weather for the enemy fleet.

Unless, of course, it was the Melaklos. Archer wondered where she was. She'd gotten a six and a half day start on the fleet. She might even be on the island of Tsiel by now. She might be dead. She had been almost insane on that last night in Ytarn.

He didn't tell Tsiel where she had gone, or how. He suspected that she knew something about it, and he hinted about the serpent—talking about their first meeting in kos-Alar, and the stranger who spoke to the Melaklos. He dared do nothing more with the eavesdropper in his head.

The eavesdropper put a damper on his feelings for Nayan, too. He kissed her sometimes—as much to irritate Algundor as for anything else. But he did nothing more. He had not slept with her since they had met again. He couldn't, not while he knew that the Sr of Nym could see and hear and feel everything that he did. He was relieved that Nayan/Tsiel did not approach him. It hurt his vanity a little, but he preferred that to failure.

With good wind behind them and the sea smooth before them, the Arilikan Fleet made good time. The rowers had little work to do. As the ships came closer to Stirin, the Treaty Island, boundary between north and south, men prepared for battle. They did not know where the Sr of Nym's fleet was, but it must be near now. They passed Stirin without incident.

"The Forest Horn tomorrow," said Tsiel that night, untying another knot in her string calendar. "If I commanded his fleet, that's where I'd wait. It's only five days south of Tsiel."

"Three days," said Algundor. They looked up and saw him grinning from the deck ladder. His bloodless grin broadened as he looked at Tsiel. "Three days," he repeated.

"Three days through the wall," she said. "No helmsman alive could get this perfumed hulk through the Wall."

Algundor laughed, an unpleasant high-pitched laugh, almost a giggle. "No helmsman alive, my dear?"

Involuntarily, Archer turned his head to look at the helmsman. Algundor's pilot was a strange silent man, wrapped and cowled in colorless cloth. He spoke only to Algundor, never left his post, never noticed anyone or anything except the movements of the gilded tiller. As Archer watched, the folds of the colorless robes stirred and a draped hand reached out, moved the tiller. The hood lifted toward Archer, turned away. He could see nothing within the shadow.

Tsiel/Nayan's hand was on his arm, her voice clear in the cold air. "I'm tired, Aach'. It's time we were asleep."

Algundor stood aside to let them pass down the ladder. His pale eyes shone strangely. Archer thought with a shiver, *He looks mad.*

Chapter Nine

Winter: first quarter, day fifteen

"This is where your fleet was destroyed, isn't it?" Archer asked Nayan/Tsiel the next day, as they stood on the foredeck watching the Forest Horn grow out of the sea.

"So I was told," she said. "A storm out of a clear sky—and the sky is clear now." She tilted her head back to look at it, a pale blue late-morning sky.

The Forest Horn was high, flat-topped and straight-sided. Its knife-cut walls curved away from the ships: it was scimitar shaped, Tsiel said, and beyond it was the Wall. Trees blew atop the flat island, but their sound did not carry over the water. The ships drew close together, lowered their sails. The deep channel at the island's base caught them as the oars were unshipped.

The strong water swept them along the curve of the shore. They swung in a wide arc, heeled into the Horn Bay—and saw the fleet of the Sr of Nym.

The windless water was black with his ships. Their sulphur sails hung motionless in the pale sunlight. They rocked on the water, waiting.

The ships of Arilikan, out of the channel current, spread to meet them. Commands rang over the bright water. Ship-soldiers brought up their weapons, stood ready.

Archer, at the bow rail on Algundor's ship, stared at the silent fleet. Were they all empty—a flock of decoys left by the Sr of Nym, some sort of trap? Or was this—

Tsiel/Nayan gripped his arm with sudden steel fingers.

"Those are my ships," she said through clenched teeth. "Ships of Tsiel, in the fleet of that—" She broke off, released Archer and gripped the rail.

Puzzled, he saw the ships she meant. They were moving, snaking past the sulphur-sailed ships. They were small, slender black ships with sails diagonally striped in blue and white.

"I wonder who mans them?" said Algundor behind Archer.

Archer ignored him, scanning the line of the Arilikan fleet.

They were in the front rank. On other ships, bowmen lined up at the rails. Torches flared transparent in the daylight. Only on Algundor's ship no preparations had been made.

Tsiel screamed.

Startled, Archer whirled, saw the slender black ships nearer now. A wind seemed to come from them, an icy wind that carried them and yet did not stir the sails of the Arilikan fleet. The small ships came nearer, and Archer saw what Tsiel had seen. He swore loudly, harshly. The ships were manned by the dead.

Oarsmen, sailors, officers, moving about their duties. Eyes eaten away, or turned up, leprous white. Flesh blue with decay, hanging in tatters where the fish had nibbled to the white bone. Long teeth gleaming in the mirthless grin of death.

Archer closed his eyes, fighting fear, fighting nausea. They couldn't be real. The ships were an illusion, a trick to frighten the Islanders. They had to be an illusion.

He opened his eyes. A man waved at him, tattered flesh swaying in the wind that was not a wind. The ships ran among the fleet now. A sick-sweet smell came from them.

The Arilikan fleet was in panic. Men shouted and gibbered, ran from the death ships. An oarsman on Algundor's ship leaped shrieking over the side. He landed on one of the death ships, shrieked again, and vanished.

He had fallen through. They were illusions. Archer went to Tsiel. She had to know that they were a trick.

She crouched by the rail, eyes wide with horror. "Arila, Father Arila," she sobbed against the gilded wood.

"Tsiel." He said it urgently, in her ear. "They're shadows—a trick."

"They are our dead, our kinsmen," she said. "We cannot fight them."

"You won't have to if this keeps up," he said grimly. "Look." He waved an arm at the Arilikan fleet. The ships, unguided, were moving randomly. They would collide and destroy each other if the shipsmen weren't brought to sanity.

Tsiel shook her head and shrank against the rail.

Archer looked back. Algundor stood behind him, face chalk-white, eyes dark with fear. Beyond him, at the tiller, the shrouded helmsman sat unmoved. He was not afraid—this was no time to wonder about him. The black ships bobbed among them now, the crewmen grinning. Archer turned back to Tsiel/Nayan.

She was standing now, eyes wide, but not with fear. She said in a trembling voice, "Father Arila, protect us."

An image flashed into Archer's head: a large dark room, altar lamps, Nayan behind the altar chanting, shadowed worshipers responding. It was worth a try.

He caught Nayan's arm fiercely. "Wake them up!" he said. "Give the Litany of Protection."

"Protection," she said uncertainly. "Protection. Yes." She took a deep breath and closed her eyes. When she opened them, they were clear and calm. She did not look at her ghostly ships. She walked to the broad rail at the rear of the deck, stepped onto it. Archer stood beside her, supporting her, watching the men of the fleet.

She raised her arms. Her voice was clear. "Silence, ye unsanctified. Silence, all ye people."

The men nearest fell silent. It was the opening formula for the Litanies.

She began the Litany of Protection in a ringing voice. "Thou who makest the seas to flow."

Automatically, the hearers responded: "Arila protect us."

"Thou who makest the winds to rise."

"Arila protect us."

More heads turned, more voices came.

"Thou who shapest the oar."

"Arila protect us."

The responses gathered strength, rolled over the water. Archer joined them, feeling the solid sound that bound the ships together.

... "Thou who spreadest the sail."

"Arila protect us."

"Thou who holdest the helm."

"Arila protect us."

(The death ships were gone, Archer realized suddenly. The responses rang like thunder over the sea.)

"God of seas, protect us."

"Arila protect us."

"God of storms, protect us."

"Arila protect us."

"Island god, protect us."

"Arila protect us."

(Archer caught a glimpse of movement, turned his head. Dark figures stirred on the sulphur-sailed ships. He nudged Nayan. She turned her head, turned back, without breaking the chant.)

"God of ships, protect us."

"Arila protect us."

"Arila protect us."

"Arila protect us."

The Litany of Protection was over, but Tsiel gave the spell that gave the men no time to weaken. She threw back her head and gave the long eerie cry that opens the Litany of War.

"His voice is the thunder, his eye is the lightning," she chanted.

"Arila, god of battle," they responded.

"He shaketh the mast-high spear."

"Arila, god of battle."

Her voice came faster, stronger. She caught up the responses, making them quicker. She sang the Litany, they stood and shouted the responses. Archer shouted with them, caught by the excitement she created. The chant lifted, lifted —the last response hung quivering in the air.

She swooped it up, turning, sweeping her arms toward the yellow-sailed ships. "The enemy!" she called.

They shouted. The rowers bent, the ships leaped forward, over the gray water, toward the shadows of the bay, toward the fleet of the Sr of Nym.

Beside Tsiel/Nayan at the bow, Archer gripped the rail and shouted. Tsiel tossed back her hair. "God of storms, guide our spears," she said savagely. Then she turned her head. "Archer—"

He had noticed it at the same time. They were not advancing; Algundor's gilded ship was slipping back through the fleet, swinging away on another line.

Suspicious, Archer turned to look for Algundor just as the princeling stopped talking to the muffled helmsman and climbed into the galley.

"Where are we going?" Tsiel demanded as he mounted to the foredeck.

He grinned at her, but his pale hands shook. "Look. Tell me."

She swung away from him, tight-lipped. "This track? You're mad."

"What is it?" said Archer.

She jerked her head to the right. "That. The Wall."

The wall was just that, a sheer expanse of rock rising from the sea. They were swinging in a wide arc toward it.

Puzzled, Archer said, "But where is he going?"

"Through it—if he can." She pointed toward a thin black line that ran down the wall. "That's the passage. My grandmother took it once at this time of year. She had one of the north's best ships, and she was desperate. She almost didn't make it. As for this—this perfumed pleasure-barge—" She broke off and snorted.

Algundor laughed. "The stories say that Arila split the wall with one blow of his axe, when Sukrol tried to block his way."

Tsiel turned on her heel and strode toward the ladder.

He caught her arm, shouted, "Guards!" Two spearmen came, bowed. "Keep them here," Algundor ordered. He giggled. "Just watch, Lady Tsiel."

She hissed and swung away from him. Archer followed her to the rail.

"Is it really that bad?" he asked in a low voice.

She nodded.

The black line in the wall expanded, became a narrow crack. Tsiel watched it closely, occasionally glancing back at the muffled helmsman. "At least he seems to know what he's doing," she muttered. "He's trying to ride the center current. If those offshore crosses catch us—ah!" She bit her lip. "We're in the track."

Archer looked toward the fleets. He could not tell what was happening: they were a confused mass of ships, no more. But two of them—two of them were coming after Algundor's ship, two sulphur-sailed ships.

They matched pace with the south-island ship, ran alongside her.

"They'll be in the crosses," said Tsiel. "Fools."

Archer looked ahead. The passage opened suddenly before him. White water boiled about the narrow mouth.

"Get the oars up, you idiot," Tsiel shouted to Algundor. "If this pig of a southerner can make it, we may survive—if you get those salt-cursed oars up."

Algundor looked at the helmsman, gave the command. The oars were raised and pulled in. The oarsmen sat still, pale-faced.

Archer felt strangely calm. He didn't think that they would die in the wall passage—someone had been taking too good care of them to permit that. No, they wouldn't die here.

Then the ship lurched, hesitated, and plunged into the narrow passage. The water boiled through too swiftly for rowers, even if there had been room for oars. The water boomed, deafening in that narrow space. Looking up, Archer saw dimly a strip of dark blue with a few glints of silver—stars, he thought calmly.

Tsiel shouted something. Archer turned to look back with her. Their pursuers had caught the crosscurrents. One wallowed outside, jolting against the rocks. The other was flung into the passage.

She came after the island ship, flung from side to side as a *ler*-cat shakes a lizard. Even in the deafening boom of the water Archer could hear the crash as she struck the stone walls.

Light burst around them. They were through the passage, in the open sea. The pursuer crashed against the wall, lurched out into the treacherous crosscurrents. She turned sluggishly twice, riding low in the water, then sank like a lump of gold.

Chapter Ten

Winter: first quarter, day fifteen (cont'd.)

"So," said Tsiel quietly, looking at the white water where the pursuing ship had gone down.

Archer saw Algundor standing beside the helmsman. It was strange that this bloodless creature should have the courage to be a traitor. But there was no other explanation, not now. The pale-handed princeling was taking Tsiel to the Sr of Nym. Archer took a step toward the ladder, fists clenched. The spearmen moved, lowered their weapons.

Frustrated, he swung away and gripped the rail until his knuckles were white, trying to control his rage. The pale-handed princeling!

"Three days," said Tsiel quietly. "In three days I shall be home—a prisoner in my land." Her voice shook.

Almost pleading, Archer said, "There couldn't be an honest explanation."

She did not answer.

Algundor came down the galley-walk and climbed to the foredeck, grinning. "Well done, wasn't it, Lady?" he asked. His tone was light, but Archer saw that his long hands were shaking. Algundor, prince of Gurn and traitor, was afraid.

Tsiel said evenly, "Where are we going?"

The lipless grin widened. "You'll know in three days, Lady. Relax. Enjoy the journey."

Furious, Archer started toward him. Spearmen or no spearmen, he was going to smash that pallid grin.

Tsiel's touch on his arm stopped him. She was looking straight at Algundor, and when her voice came, it was harsh and horrible.

"*E vir lamara—*" She raised her hands toward the prince of Gurn, took a step forward. "*Khalovela sontral—*"

Algundor went white. He backed a step, licking his dry lips.

"*Sorke vashlor an velak—*" The voice was deep, guttural, inexpressibly evil. "*—astrol kan k'erol so chran—*"

The spearmen clambered over the deck wall, dropped into the galley.

Archer backed away from Tsiel, his head singing with the hatred in her voice.

"—*Khalovela sontral—s'tersa Arilan astor lan—*"

Be this man accursed—in the name of Arila—

Algundor went whiter still. He tried to shout her down, but her curse-voice overrode him, heavy, monotonous.

"—*khalovela sontral—*"

Desperately he flung himself at her, tried to cover her mouth.

Archer felt his own mouth stretch in a mirthless grin. He took two steps forward, dragged the tall man back. He hit him once across the face and flung him down against the deck wall.

"—*s' Arila van—estra vornan—khalovela sontral.*" The horrible voice stopped. Tsiel lowered her hands and looked calmly at the prince of Gurn.

He struggled to his feet, not looking at her. Blood ran down his face from his mouth, where Archer had split his lip. He pressed a hand to it and fumbled for the ladder-head.

"Remember," said Tsiel, quietly. "Remember that you have been cursed by a high priestess of Arila. Never forget that, son of Lerkan."

He started to lift his eyes, then turned and hurried down the ladder.

"What did that accomplish?" said Archer in a low voice, when they were seated at the rail and looking over the sea.

"Nothing," she said savagely. "I cursed him, and I'm glad of it. I've never cursed anyone before. It probably won't do more than relieve us of his company for the rest of the voyage."

"That's something, at least," said Archer. He stretched. Her curse had relieved her tension, and his own. And now he wanted the answer to a question that had been bothering him for months. He said, "Why is he taking you to the Sr of Nym?"

"He doubtless expects to be well paid," said Tsiel/Nayan dryly.

Archer shook his head. "Why does the Sr of Nym want you?"

"Sanction," she said bitterly. "As my husband—"

Astonished, he interrupted. "Husband? Does everyone in the Islands want to marry you?"

"Well?" she said icily.

Hastily he said, "Oh, it's not surprising. I'd like to marry you myself."

She grinned crookedly, and kissed him on the nose.

"But I love you," he went on. "His reasons are political, aren't they?" He leaned against the rail. "If he's a legitimate ruler, those south-islanders will manage to avoid trouble. So if he marries you and becomes king—"

"What?" she stared at him. "He can't be the ruler of Tsiel any more than you can, or anyone else not born to it. My consort would have no official power."

Archer frowned. "But wasn't your first husband the king?"

"No." She tossed back her black hair. "There hasn't been a male Tsiel since my grandmother's uncle died, forty years ago. The rule passes in the female line. A man can inherit it, but his children don't unless he marries a woman of the clan. If a woman inherits, then her children will succeed no matter whom she marries." She looked away and added, "My son will be the next Tsiel—unless the Sr of Nym has killed him."

Embarrassed, Archer couldn't think of anything to say to her.

She spoke finally. "I know what would happen if the Sr of Nym married me. I would be a puppet—completely under his control."

Horrified, Archer shuddered. He remembered too clearly the infuriating helplessness of being a puppet.

"My people would obey me," she said quietly. "He would have a legitimate position—not high, but enough to keep him safe. The Melaklos and I have spoken of it."

"The Melaklos." Archer recalled her abruptly, her odd nervous manner on that last night in Ytarn. Where was she now? On Tsiel? Had she faced the Sr of Nym yet, or found the portal to the world from which he got his men? It would be good to talk about her to Tsiel. It might soothe his worries and fears. But she had warned him not to discuss her with anyone. The Sr of Nym was still inside his head, listening. Or was he? Archer wished that he could be sure of anything the Melaklos told him. She was as elusive and untrustworthy as the season-change winds.

He shivered, reached for Nayan. He held her close against his side: something warm and substantial that he could trust.

Chapter Eleven

Winter: first quarter, day eighteen

Three days later, Archer was awakened by the sound of Tsiel shouting for Algundor. He wrapped himself in his fur robe and padded out of his compartment into the galley. Tsiel stood glaring at the afterdeck. As Archer joined her, Algundor approached and made an elaborate bow.

"Where do you intend to land?" Tsiel said sharply.

He grinned. "That should be obvious to such an accomplished seaman."

"Algundor, you're a fool."

Algundor giggled.

Startled, Archer looked at him narrowly. The princeling's face was as pale as his white furs. As they had come north and the weather had grown colder, Algundor had become more and more nervous, until now he looked on the edge of hysteria.

And now Tsiel was mad at him—why? Archer said, "What's he done now?"

"He's heading for the South Harbor—for the Sorovel-Tsieln."

"Is it dangerous?"

"It is deadly."

Algundor giggled again. "Remember the Wall, Lady. You said that the best helmsman alive couldn't pass that."

"So I did." Her voice was tight. "And now I say this: the Sorovel-Tsieln looks less impressive, but the Wall is landsman's work compared to it."

Algundor shook his head, grinning.

He had had that look of secret laughter at the Wall, Archer remembered—when Tsiel said "the best helmsman alive." Now he laughed at the same phrase. Archer stared up at the muffled helmsman, a horrible suspicion forming in his mind.

"The best helmsman alive," repeated Algundor.

"The best helmsman that ever lived couldn't take Sorovel-Tsieln in winter with a three-moon tide," said Tsiel. "Kiern himself couldn't have done it."

Algundor doubled up with hysterical laughter.

Archer looked at him, at the unmoving helmsman. He had wondered who the man was—a criminal, a *sof*-priest, the Sr of Nym himself, even the Melaklos in a new mask. But now—now he had to know.

He was up the ladder in two bounds and at the pilot's side. He seized the hood, tore it back. The pilot raised his face to him.

Tsiel, coming up beside him, bit back a cry. The head turned toward her.

Archer stood paralyzed. He had been half expecting it, but it terrified him all the same: this time it wasn't an illusion.

"Not an illusion," he muttered hoarsely.

The pilot's face turned back to him, the sightless face of a mummy, skin blackened and shrunk tight to the skull, lips shrivelled away from yellow teeth.

Algundor's voice came shrill from the galley below. "You've met my helmsman? Greet him with honor, Lady: that is Kiern."

"Kiern," she said in a dazed whisper. "Kiern has been dead for three hundred years."

The horror in her voice broke Archer's paralysis. He looked at her set face, at the dead helmsman. Kiern terrified him as the death ships had not. They had been illusion. But this?

Tsiel's pale face decided him. Gathering his courage, he leaned forward and pulled the hood roughly back over the helmsman's head. Tsiel's breath caught. She turned and went down the ladder, and he followed.

She walked directly up to Algundor. "Have you seen him, Princeling? No? You should." She started along the galley-walk to the bows. Over her shoulder she said, "I repeat: Kiern himself could not land in Sorovel-Tsieln today."

It was cold on the exposed foredeck. Since they had passed the Wall, the weather had become icy, and there were clouds and storms far away. Apparently whoever had been controlling the weather south of the Forest Horn was having trouble with it now.

Still, it hadn't hindered them. They would arrive at Tsiel as scheduled. Whether they would land was another jar of wine altogether, Archer thought grimly.

Coming to the rail beside Nayan/Tsiel, he looked out and saw that the island she was named after was surprisingly small and rocky. He had been expecting something as large and impressive as Arilikan Itself, perhaps. Instead, there was this little pile of crooked stones.

Looking at Tsiel/Nayan, he saw that her eyes were bright with tears. A sad homecoming, he thought. He said, "How long?"

"A few hours." She closed her eyes for a moment. "A few hours. That's all." She opened her eyes and looked at him. "Still, death will be better than being the puppet of the Sr of Nym."

Surprised, Archer had never expected to hear defeat in her voice.

On the other hand, why not? What could they do?

Seeking hope, he said, "That helmsman did get us through the Wall, after all. Maybe he can get into the harbor."

She shook her head. She said, "I couldn't do it, and I know the shore. He doesn't." She spat into the water and added, "Algundor is a fool. Like my husband."

Uneasily, Archer said, "Your husband?"

She looked at him and laughed. "My husband was like a saga hero. I married him for political reasons—but he should have been a sea captain. Perhaps then he would have had more respect for the winds of winter." She gestured toward the island.

"What did he do?"

"He wagered that he could land in Sorovel-Tsieln in early winter. He was a good pilot, although he did little traveling." She looked at Archer with clear gray eyes. "He was killed—he, and the twenty men with him. They didn't quite make it through the Jaws."

"Jaws?"

"You'll see." She turned back to the rail, and the rocky little island.

Worried, Archer sat huddled on the deck to keep warm and to think. She had never spoken of her husband before—perhaps there was nothing to say about him. ". . . A saga hero. . . ." There was a touch of scorn in her voice as she said it. She was not a woman to love a saga hero. She was, he thought suddenly, a remarkable woman.

A remarkable woman who was not going to be killed by some hysterical princeling's idiocy. Archer pulled his fur cloak closer and shivered. There had to be a way out. . . .

"Tsiel," he said abruptly.

She turned her head.

"If we could take over the helm—could you land us in another harbor?"

After a short pause, she said, "The only other harbor is at the city, and *he'll* have that. I don't intend to sail right into his hands." She turned back to the growing island.

Archer bit his lip. She didn't seem to want to live. He said, "What about swimming? If—"

"You're serious." She turned fully around and stared at him. "You really want to land here."

"Don't you?"

She tossed back her hair. "I've been thinking about it. I keep thinking that I would rather be dead than a puppet."

Archer shook his head. "No, you don't," he said firmly. "You're a fighter. You won't just give up."

She laughed shortly. "All right. But what can we do? We might swim—but that water is like ice. Chances are that we'd take cramp and go down immediately."

Archer was glad that there was something there that could be worked on. In the galley one of the crewmen was giving wine to the working rowers, squirting it into their mouths from a wine skin. Archer stared at the skin. Something stirred in his memory.

Tsiel glanced at him curiously when he left the deck and returned with an armload of wine skins and a coil of rope. "What's that for?" she said.

He shook his head and grinned at her. Let her guess—he was sure she would. He dropped his burden, sat down beside it. He picked up a skin and began to blow into it.

She watched. After a while her mouth twitched. She said, "You look like a scarlet puffer-cat."

Gasping for breath, he said, "Then help."

She sat beside him. "Floats," she said, picking up a wine skin. "Aach', you're a marvel."

They blew up only one of the skins apiece, but it was hard work.

"We're coming in," gasped Tsiel. She tied off the mouth of her float, helped Archer fasten ropes around it for handholds. "I hope this works."

"So do I," said Archer grimly. He looked up.

They had entered a shallow bay in the island's side, running like a funnel toward a small mouth. That must be the harbor, he thought. He could see the island itself more clearly now. There were trees among the stones, twisted trees that clung to tilted boulders and crooked witches' fingers at the gray sky. Scarlet-leafed *alor* vines gave an odd festive note to the bleak shore.

"You'd better get rid of that fur," said Tsiel. "It'll drag you down."

She had taken off her woolen trousers and hooded jacket. She slit open an empty wine skin, knelt and rolled her outer clothes into a tight bundle. Despite the cold, she did not shiver in her thin wool tunic.

Grimacing, Archer forced himself to take off his own heavy clothes. The fur cloak would have to stay behind. The jacket and trousers—Tsiel packed with her own into the split skin. She added their knives, and wound rope around the bundle to keep it shut. "So," she said with satisfaction.

"So," mimicked Archer.

Algundor said behind them, "What is this, Lady?"

She glanced over the rail. "Sorovel-Tsieln."

"That's not what I—" He broke off, stepped to the rail. "It looks smooth enough."

Archer looked ahead. The broad pass into the harbor did look smooth. He looked at Tsiel.

"Half-tide," she said. "Look there."

Archer looked where she pointed. Lines of turbulence extended from each side of the harbor mouth, the water dimpling and swirling in complex patterns. "The Jaws?" Archer asked.

"Yes." She turned to Algundor. "You'd better slacken speed and come around. He's too far starboard."

Algundor laughed. "He's in the channel."

Tsiel snorted and turned away. She and Archer tied the floats to their belts, stood at the port rail. Archer blew on his fingers, which felt like icicles in the wind.

Algundor came up behind them, laughing shrilly. "He's the best helmsman that ever lived. We'll—"

"Now," shouted Tsiel. She vaulted the rail, launching herself as far from the ship as possible.

Archer followed. Algundor's clutching hand just brushed his shoulder.

The water hit him like a huge cushion. He went down until he thought he would never stop, thrashing and twisting. Then he slowed, went up. He burst from the water, gasping, and clung to his buoy. The air burned his face.

Tsiel was close by, only her head above the chill water. "Pull your knees up," she said through chattering teeth. "They're only a few feet under."

Archer obeyed. He was shivering too much to speak. He looked around for the ship.

She seemed to be standing still on the other side of the

Jaws. Then he realized that she had struck the rocks. She shuddered, slid back, leaped forward. Timbers snapped. She would batter herself to death on the hidden Jaws. ...

Water caught Archer, spun him, lifted him. He clung to the float, closing his eyes. He was dizzy. Finally the spinning stopped. He bobbed like a cork.

Cramp seized him. He doubled up, swallowed salt water. He fought to stay with his float. Far away, someone was calling his name. The sea turned over and went black.

Chapter Twelve

Winter: first quarter, day twenty

"That's the Hall," said Tsiel/Nayan in a low voice.

Archer sneezed violently and peered down the rock-strewn slope, trying to focus on the dark shapes below. He and Tsiel lay among the boulders near the top, looking down on her home—now the headquarters of the Sr of Nym.

Squinting, he could see the Hall: a long low windowless building, built of wood with a stone foundation. The other side, facing the sea, would be stone as well, he thought. Radiating from the Hall like the spokes of half a wheel were six longer, lower structures, all of wood. Between them and the Hall lay a great black square.

"What's that?" Archer asked.

Tsiel shook her head. "Something of his—it does not belong there." She shivered. "It looks like a hole into emptiness."

Or into—what? Something stirred in Archer's head, something the Melaklos had said. He almost had it—

He sneezed again, and swore. After losing consciousness in the sea, he had awakened in a deserted fisher-hut with a colossal cold. He didn't know how Tsiel had gotten him out of the water and up the rocky hillside beyond the pebble beach. She had built a fire in the hut. They had dried, and dressed, and left. Archer didn't clearly remember crossing the island. Tsiel had been indignant about the neglect of the winter harvest, whatever that was. They had passed a herd of animals that looked like distorted oxen, and she had been angry about that. Apparently the Sr of Nym was neglecting the island. They had traveled for several days, or maybe it just seemed like it. Anyway, now they were looking down at the Hall, the capital (so to speak) of the island.

Having reoriented himself—the cold still made him hazy—Archer sneezed again. He said, "Well, we can't sneak in. At least, I can't. I'd probably sneeze at just the wrong moment."

"We should have talked about it," said Tsiel. "We were so

busy getting here that we forgot to decide what to do when we arrived."

Something moved—Archer glimpsed it. He turned his head, looked carefully. "Nayan," he said quietly, "I think the decision's been made for us."

Nayan turned her head, and her eyes widened at the sight of the approaching tiger men.

There were twenty of them, obviously a patrol, seeming to know just where to find their quarry. Of course, Archer thought. He can see what I'm seeing. I can't hide from him.

The tiger men spoke in a language that neither Archer nor Tsiel understood, but the gestures with their spears were plain enough. The two got up and started down the hill in the midst of the guards.

Tsiel said in a low voice, "I know that Hall, Aach', no one better. If we can break away when we get close, there's a hiding place—"

"Don't tell me where," Archer said savagely. "When we're close enough, break for it. I'll cover for you."

Seeing her look of bewilderment, he added, "I'll explain later." He didn't want to tell her about the Sr of Nym's listening post—not yet. He had shrunk from telling her on the voyage, knowing that she would draw back from him, flinch when he touched her. He couldn't stand the thought of that.

She looked at him searchingly. "You must have a reason," she said slowly. "Is this—ah!" She jerked away from a prodding spear.

Archer turned on the prodder, caught the spear shaft and yanked. The tiger man stumbled forward, caught his balance. The others checked their stride, turned toward Archer.

Tsiel seized the opportunity. She was ten yards away before they started after her. She ran fast, dodging among the rocks, black hair streaming and snapping behind her.

Archer tore after her, keeping abreast of the leading tiger men so that he could trip them up if necessary. The going was bad; the tiger men fell, bounded to their feet. Archer kept his by some miracle. Tsiel was as sure-footed as a mountain goat.

They passed onto the hard-packed ground around the outbuildings, Tsiel well in the lead. She curved into an avenue between two of them. Archer, twenty feet behind her, saw her quick swaying stop, saw the cause. More tiger men appeared, gathering in the space between the buildings.

Tsiel darted forward, ducked under an arm, kicked a

guard; she was in the clear. In the clear and running straight for the black square.

Ludicrously clear in Archer's head came the voice of the Melaklos, rapid, hesitant, speaking on the beach in Arilikan. Telling him about the tiger men, about—

"Nayan!" he shouted. "Look out!" He burst through the blocking tiger men, calling frantically.

She did not hear, or did not heed. The tiger men came after Archer. He wove away from them, caught Tsiel on the edge of the square. They were going too fast to stop. They stumbled forward and fell

and fell

and fell....

Tantalus, according to the Greeks, was condemned for his sins to suffer eternal thirst while standing in a pool of water. Lovely water, cool, clear. But whenever he bent to drink and ease his terrible thirst, the water sank and vanished, to return as he stood up again.

If the Grecian hell had been lightless, Archer decided, they would have put Tantalus into a huge echoing cavern where he could hear the sound of water dripping, but could not tell where it came from. Archer sneezed, waking echoes.

"Shh," said Tsiel, at his shoulder.

"I can't help it," he snarled. He felt terrible. His eyes ached from trying to see through the pitch darkness of the caves. His throat burned with sickness and thirst. He had stopped feeling hungry, although his stomach still twinged or growled occasionally to remind him that it was there.

"It can't be much farther," said Tsiel.

"You've been saying that for—" He bit the words back. There was no sense in yelling at her. But the tap-tap-tap of water was driving him mad. Speaking through it, he said, "How long have we been here?"

"I don't know," she said wearily. Her head moved against his shoulder. "There doesn't seem to be any time here."

Archer resettled against the stone wall. "The Melaklos doesn't think that time exists at all," he said lightly.

"She doesn't have to live in it," said Tsiel tartly.

Archer said nothing. Tsiel's breathing became slower and deeper until it settled into the rhythm of sleep. Archer, wide awake, stared at the darkness and tried to ignore the sound of falling water. When they were rested, they would try again to find it.

The sound of the water echoed through the cavern,

seeming to come from everywhere. If they could just find it—Archer licked his cracked lips. He listened for movement in the shadows, half hoping that the tiger men would find them again.

The Sr of Nym's men had not followed them onto the black square. He and Tsiel had fallen forever, it seemed, only gradually realizing that they had stopped in some great darkness. They were looking for a way out when the tiger men came with spears and torches and took them prisoner.

These were not the Sr of Nym's tiger men. Seeing them, Archer knew that he had guessed correctly about the black square: it was the portal to the world where the magician got his troops.

The tiger men marched them in silence through long corridors of stone, some rough tunnels, some carefully carved halls. When the light appeared, they moved faster. The light was a dim firefly glow that floated after them at a constance distance. Parties sent to investigate found nothing: it vanished as they approached. As they became more uneasy about their pursuer, they became less careful about their prisoners.

It was ludicrously easy to escape. The light danced nearer during a rest period, the tiger men watched it uneasily. The one set to guard Archer and Tsiel watched also. He didn't even twitch when Tsiel slipped his dagger from its sheath.

They took his water skin and his food bag and slipped back down the tunnel, leaving him lying in a heap just within the torchlight, an expression of surprise on his dead face. Tsiel still carried his dagger; Archer took his spear. Armed, with supplies (though not much), they set out to retrace their way to the cave they had landed in. There should be, Archer said, a portal there to Dolesar.

They walked for days, or years. The food bag emptied despite their care, the water skin was finally dry. When they stumbled into the cavern filled with echoes of water, they were exhausted.

They had moved along the walls, trying to find the source of the sound. It seemed that they had been around the cavern several times without luck. Now they sat side by side against the wall, Tsiel sleeping, Archer listening to the water and thinking of Tantalos.

Tsiel woke with a convulsive shudder. They did not speak, but got to their feet simultaneously and started out again. Archer walked close to the wall, questing along it with one hand. Tsiel held the other, inching toward the center of the cavern, on the chance that there was a fountain within the chamber itself.

They came upon a passage quite soon this time. Archer, feeling the gap in the wall, stopped.

"What is it?" said Tsiel from the darkness.

"Passage, I think." He moved into it, exploring. "It's larger than the one we came in by. Smoother walls."

"What about the sound?" Her voice was startlingly close.

He listened, then said, "What do you think?"

She listened for a long time to the baffling echoes. At last she said, "I think this is it."

They crept down the passage, one along each wall, holding hands across the center. Twice they passed smaller branch corridors, but one turned abruptly down into silence, and the other ended in a blank wall. The broader passage they followed had no perceptible slope.

Archer rounded a turn in the passage. The tapping of water was suddenly loud in his ears. "Must be just ahead," he muttered.

"Is that light ahead?" said Tsiel.

He saw a faint pallid glimmer up there, or so he thought, so ghostly that he could barely see it. And the water sound was certainly louder. Eagerly he grasped Tsiel's hand and strode forward.

The floor was gone. He stepped into air, threw himself back desperately. Tsiel stumbled against him, squatted beside him.

"What happened?"

"Hole in the floor."

They explored what they could of it. Archer could not touch the bottom or the far side with the tiger-guard's extended spear, not even while hanging precariously over the edge with Tsiel anchoring his legs. The gap went across the passage. Apparently there had once been a bridge against the left wall, but all that was left of it was a crumbling pillar and a ledge, about a foot wide, that extended as far as he could reach with the spear.

Their choices were obvious: stay there, go back, try the ledge. Staying was out of the question: they had no food or water, and nothing to wait for. Going back was little better. They needed water badly. They had to have it, and they knew that there was none for a long way behind them. There was really only one choice: they had to try the ledge.

Chapter Thirteen

Timelost

Tsiel had salvaged the rope from the wine-skin floats. She unwound it from about her and they tied it around their waists, leaving ten feet of slack between them.

"The ledge seems solid enough," said Archer, "but we'd better go one at a time. It may not hold both of us." He started back toward the gap.

"If you'll belay your rope on the pillar, I'll start," said Tsiel.

Surprised, Archer turned toward her voice. "What?"

"I'd better go first," she said quietly.

He snorted. "Don't be silly. Come on."

Her voice brought him up short. She said, "I'm lighter than you are."

"So?"

"I am also faster and more sure-footed. I have a better chance of escaping if the ledge gives way."

Angry suddenly, he curled his hands. "You're being silly," he said evenly.

She moved sharply. Her voice was weary. "You're still sick, Archer. Your balance is bad. You've been stumbling all day."

"I've done all right so far, haven't I?" he said hotly. He tried to block out the sound of the water. What was wrong with her? She was being unreasonable. He said, "You can't go first."

"Why not?"

"Because—" He stopped. Why not? It was obvious to him that he should lead the way, but he couldn't think why. Blustering to cover his agitation, he said, "It isn't done."

She sighed and moved again, her clothes rustling. When she spoke, her voice came from lower in the darkness: she must be sitting on the floor. She said, "Aach', why did you catch my knife hand when we ran from the *kos*? Why didn't you want me to take night watch in the forests?"

167

Baffled, he stared toward her. What was she getting at? He recalled the incidents, but what did they have to do with her present stubbornness?

She sighed and said patiently, "I am the Tsiel Tsieln, and have been for ten years. I am a north-island woman. I am not used to men who treat me as—well, as a useful inferior."

Startled, he started to speak, but she was not finished.

She said, "I spoke to the Melaklos. She said that this—this attitude has been customary among your people for many generations. Custom is rock. I did not like to speak against it. But now you are endangering us."

Archer sat down slowly. His anger fled, leaving only astonishment. He had never thought of Tsiel/Nayan as an inferior—not consciously, at least. On the other hand, he *had* objected automatically to her standing guard—objected because women simply didn't stand night guard. Maybe she had a point. But he'd never dreamed she felt as she did.

He peered toward her, wishing that he could see her face. The image that formed in his mind was not of her, but of another woman: a thin blonde woman whose name he recalled with difficulty. Diane. His wife. Diane, coming home flushed and angry in the few months when she attended NOW meetings. Diane, who had grown up beautiful and bored and useless.

He wasn't facing Diane, with her awkward rage. This was Tsiel, the leader of the strongest northern island. This was Nayan, the woman he had fallen in love with so long ago. And she wasn't angry: her voice was puzzled. She was trying to understand something that he didn't understand himself, something that he had never seen in himself.

Uncertainly, slowly, he said, "Nayan, I'm sorry if I—"

"I don't want apologies," she interrupted. "I just want you to see. You've taken the lead always, except when I had the knowledge you lacked, but I didn't mind that. Now—now it's different. I have the best chance of crossing the ledge. I thought you'd see that."

I did see it, he thought suddenly. *That's why I was so angry at her insistance. I don't want to relinquish authority.*

Authority? He caught the word. What authority had he over Tsiel/Nayan? None. Not even the authority of a lover. He winced. He wondered what she thought of him now. He felt painfully vulnerable.

He stared back for several minutes before the light registered on his brain. Then he drew in his breath and shot out a hand for Tsiel. "The light," he said urgently. "It's following us."

It floated up the way they had come, a green firefly light, coming nearer and nearer.

"Ghostlight," whispered Tsiel.

The light dipped and rose as if in answer.

Archer sprang to his feet and went to the ledge as quickly as he dared, Tsiel beside him. He wound his end of the rope twice about the broken pillar two feet from the wall. "You're on belay," he whispered.

She touched his shoulder and moved away.

Minutes dragged by. Tsiel's breath, hissing through her teeth, became fainter and fainter. The firefly glow came on without growing larger. Gradually the slack in the rope was taken up.

When it was straight in his hands, he called softly, "Are you across?"

"Not quite," she said unsteadily. "It's quite solid, except for one place about six feet out where there's a gap."

"All right. Hold on." He carefully unwound the rope from the pillar, stepped to the wall, and inched his way onto the ledge.

The ledge wasn't all that narrow, about a foot, but the wall above it bellied out, forcing Archer into what felt like a back-bend over a bottomless pit. He spread his hands, pressed them to the wall, made himself breathe deeply and evenly.

He sidled along the ledge, hugging the cold stone wall. Inch by inch he moved. He found the gap unexpectedly, stopped. He swung his right foot out and groped for the far side. His head swam suddenly and he swayed. He closed his eyes tight and clung to the rock. His heart pounded hard enough to shake the caves.

"Aach'." Nayan's voice, quiet, calming. "I'm across. When there's enough slack, I'll make fast here."

Her voice gave him the hold he needed. He was clear-headed, balanced. He found the far side of the break easily, swung his left foot over. The ledge was narrower on this side. He felt as though he were hanging on by his toes. He inched on, breathing carefully, telling himself that it couldn't last forever.

It didn't. Not quite. He was wondering if it would when Nayan spoke again, her voice closer. "You're on belay, Aach'. Watch the last few feet, it's—"

The ledge collapsed. Panicking, Archer grabbed in all directions. One hand brushed the wall. Then he came up with a jerk on the end of the rope. His right shoulder smashed against the wall.

"—shaky," finished Nayan/Tsiel from above.

"Now she tells me," Archer growled to himself. The first panic had fled instantly. Now fear chattered in the back of his mind, but he could ignore it and think. He groped at the wall for a handhold, but it was smooth as glass. With every motion he swung and turned, and the rope creaked. It was already cutting him in two.

"Aach'?" Tsiel called softly.

"Keep me anchored," he said. "I'm coming up."

He hadn't climbed a rope for years, but he'd climb this one. He twisted, caught it, started the climb hand over hand. He had to favor his injured shoulder, but he could climb all right.

He reached the top, got a hand over the edge, the other hand. He hung there, breathing hard, trying to gather the strength to pull himself up.

Then Tsiel was there, touching him. She reached down, caught his belt, pulled. Together they hauled him over the edge. For a moment he lay gasping. Then the reaction set in and he started to shake.

After a while Tsiel said, "The light's gone."

Archer sat up and stretched. "Never mind, he can't get across now." He stood. A sound filled his ears, the most beautiful sound he had ever heard: the sound of water dripping. He headed for it beside Tsiel/Nayan.

They came suddenly into lighter air: a larger space, a cavern. The sound of water filled it. Hand in hand they stalked the sound across the floor.

Archer's foot was suddenly cold. It took him a moment to realize that he must have stepped into the water. He turned to tell Tsiel, but her hand tore out of his and she cried out. He heard a splash; cold water drenched him.

"Nayan?" he said tentatively.

"I—I think so," she gasped.

She was all right, then, and they had found the water. Lightheaded, he chuckled. "That was a trifle impetuous, my dear."

"Oh?" She pulled him in. He swallowed water, came up spluttering.

"Impetuous, hah!" she said. "I'll give you impetuous."

He scarcely heard her. This was water, really water. Cool, wet, wonderful. Tantalos, you poor bastard, eat your heart out.

It was morning when Archer awoke. He blinked at pale light coming through a hole in the roof far above him. Where was he? The Melaklos would tell him. He sat up and looked around.

The Melaklos was not there. He was alone in a huge domed cavern with glassy red walls and a broken fountain in the center.

No, not alone: something stirred against his side. He looked down at a black-haired woman curled up beside him. She opened gray eyes and blinked at him sleepily, and he remembered.

"You're Nayan."

"I am?" She sat up and shook her head. "I guess I am." She looked around, up at the ceiling. "It's been forever since I've seen light."

Archer stood and stretched. "Light," he said happily. "Sunlight. There is something in this world besides caves, after all."

"The walls are too smooth to climb," said Tsiel wistfully.

She was right, Archer saw. The walls were slick, like red stone warped and folded and coated with glass. The hole at the top was irregular, almost round, and the light—it had to be noon light, Archer realized abruptly—the light fell on the broken fountain like a spotlight.

Casually Archer walked to the fountain and studied it. It was simple: a broken statuary group in the middle of a shallow round basin set flush with the floor, and tiled in black. The water was fresh and clear—he wondered how it circulated. It ran silently from broken spouts in the fountain, and dripped from somewhere on the arched ceiling.

The eight statues had once been mermaids on a rock, elbows linked, in a circle facing outward. Their bodies, broad-shouldered, small-breasted, fish-tailed from the hips, were still covered with tiny carved scales. Only one still had a head, and that was worn to a featureless stump. Archer shuddered when he saw it and walked on around the basin.

What was this beautiful thing doing in this deserted cave? It was a lovely piece of work, a labor of time. A vine ran about the rock, shooting out delicate tendrils and tiny star-shaped flowers. The dripping water, dividing over some of these, had worn deep grooves in the rock. They had been here for a long time.

Archer felt cold suddenly. Someone has lived in these dark caves once, someone skillful enough to build a drainage system that outlasted them, sensitive enough to carve the statues. Who were they? Where were they?

Something glimmered gray against the black of the basin. Archer leaned over to look at it.

A mermaid's head laughed at him, a flower-crowned head with the high broad features of the tiger men. He stared at her, his blood quickening in response to the bubbling mirth on her face. He laughed, kept laughing.

Tsiel came over, looked at Archer, looked at the mermaid's head and laughed. They leaned on each other at the fountain-side, looking down at the head of the merry mermaid, and their laughter ran echoing up the roof like the laughter of those who had stood, ages ago, beside the mermaid fountain.

Chapter Fourteen

Timelost

"We have to find the light," said Tsiel soberly.

"We have to find food," said Archer.

They faced each other at the mouth of the passage leading out of the fountain chamber. They were rested; the water skin was full. They couldn't stay in the red room to starve. Still they lingered, reluctant to go into the dark again.

"There's sure to be a way out soon," said Archer firmly. "We're near the surface. We'll just have to go up whenever we can."

They turned their backs on the sunlight and marched into the passage.

The full light faded quickly, but the ghost of it lingered, gleaming in Tsiel's eyes when she turned her head. The corridor ran straight and, Archer thought, gradually upward. Somewhere above them were the surface and the sun.

As the light faded, Archer became more and more aware that he was hungry. His stomach was not satisfied with water. He ignored it, looking ahead along the passages for the least glimmer of light.

They did not find the sunlight.

When they were not moving they slept, and when they were not sleeping they moved. The darkness became absolute again. As hope faded, despair grew, and the laughter of the mermaid fountain was, in retrospect, the cruel laughter of mockery. The water ran low and was gone.

They had long ceased speaking. They crawled along invisible tunnels until one or both collapsed, they slept where they fell, and woke up and crept on. They drank greedily when they found water, icy rills that crossed the path, subterranean lakes into which they blundered unaware.

The first of these captivated Archer. Images and words from his forgotten past crowded into his mind. He shouted across the lake. Echoes roared back over the still water. Something splashed, a fish jumping perhaps. Perhaps something else. Archer clutched Tsiel's arm. He knew who was following them, the green glow.

"It's Gollum," he whispered. "It's—yes. He wants it back."

"Wants what?" she mumbled.

He couldn't remember. He felt in the pouch hanging at his belt. "The egg," he whispered. "He wants the egg." He cupped his hands at his mouth and shouted over the water, "You can't have it!" The echoes pounded back at him. He shrank away. "Come on," he muttered, pulling at Tsiel's arm. "He wants to play at riddles in the dark, but he can't have it."

"He can't have it," she repeated and called over the lake, a long eerie wail. The echoes screamed back like a legion of banshees, deafening them.

Terrified, Archer pulled Tsiel away. They crawled back in panic.

Movement was a terrible necessity, long after they had forgotten why. They crawled on burning hands and knees, lurching against each other, breath rattling in torn throats. Hearing was painfully acute. Once, Archer heard something scuttling. He lunged at it, caught it. It was small and dry and leathery, and it squealed until he wrung its neck. They tore it apart and ate it hastily, shaking.

"Rats and mice and such small deer have been Tom's food for seven long year," Archer chanted, while beside him in the darkness Nayan cackled hysterically. That was the beginning of the final madness.

Hunger passed from pain to the ache of constant torment, too painful to be ignored, too familiar to surprise. The universe, stars and seas and singing winds, shrank to darkness, stone, hunger, the terrible necessity of movement.

Sometimes Archer saw the green firefly glow, or thought he saw it, and hugged the floor until it was gone. Odd music seemed to drift down some corridors: reedy music, thin, eerie, somehow familiar. He did not really notice that they followed it.

Once, he came out of mindlessness to hear voices about him, shouting, laughing, crying grotesquely. "Poor Tom that eats the swimming frog—" One voice stopped, his own surely, but who was it who spoke beside him in darkness?

He groped and found her rocking back and forth, crooning in a high cracked voice, laughing like a Halloween witch. He shouted at her, caught her shoulders and shook her until she must fly apart in his hands. Her shoulders were dry as parchment stretched over dry bone. With a shudder he envisioned her, a drawing he had seen, skeletal, her heavy breasts shrivelled to long mummy-sacks: the breasts of Death's Paramour. He drew back.

"Aach'." Her voice rasped, dry, horrible. Her hand came questing for him; he recoiled from her bony touch. "Aach', how long have we been mad?"

He felt her trembling in the darkness. He shrank again from her searching hand. Then he knew that she was wrong, that they were not mad, that everything was all right because they were dead.

Exultant, laughing, he gathered her into his fleshless arms, kissed her lipless mouth. The reedy music was all around them now, the dance of death. How long had they lain there, skeletons dusty in darkness—dry bones. In darkness, in death, in—

"In the midst of death we are in love." He chuckled like dry leaves rustling, and gathered her closer, rocking and crooning:

> " 'Young soul, put off your flesh and come
> With me into the quiet tomb,
>   Our bed is lovely, dark, and sweet;
> The earth will swing us as she goes
> Beneath our coverlid of snows
>   And the warm leaden sheet;
> Dear and dear is their poisoned note,
> The little snakes of silver throat,
> In mossy skulls that nest and lie,
> Ever singing, "Die, oh! die.' "

She was moving in his arms, trying to wriggle away.

"No," he said softly. "Our bones will mingle here. When they are dust and we are dust, no one will know us apart."

"Aach'!" She pulled free. "We aren't dead."

"Dead as Giants' Bones," he said exultantly, catching her hands. "Dead as Kurilan's Eyes."

She tried to pull her hands away. "Listen," she said urgently. "Listen to the music."

He shook his head, but the piping would not be ignored. A dance in discordant minor, like some familiar mockery. He had heard it before. Where?

An image flashed into his head, an image from a world so far away that he had almost forgotten it. Green: trees, grass. Himself exhausted, lying in the shade, watching a small

175

person in gray who sat cross-legged among tree roots, playing fitfully on a wooden pipe. A name came to him.

"Melaklos," he said aloud. The name and the music filled his head. "Melaklos!" He had to find them. He started to crawl away, barely aware that Nayan came with him.

They lurched around a corner side by side. Light reflected on stone ahead of them, flickering red and yellow light. The thin piping was palpable as the stone. They hurried forward, not heeding the pain of bruised and bleeding knees.

At a tight corner, Archer edged into the lead. He crawled around it, head down. The floor vanished. He pitched forward with Nayan on top of him.

The piping stopped. In the deafening silence someone said dryly, "So there you are."

Archer struggled onto his elbows. A small fire burned before him, dazzling his dark-dilated eyes. Something moved beside the fire, came toward him. He blinked away the tears that blurred his vision.

Not the Melaklos. A small person, child-sized, dressed in dark brown.

Archer gave up. "A Hobbit," he said. His voice cracked. "A goddam Hobbit."

"I am not familiar with the name," said the brown one.

Archer shook his head and rested his forehead on the cool stone. "Imaginary creature," he said in a muffled voice.

"So am I," said the other equably.

That was too much. Archer slumped to the floor and let the darkness have him.

The brown person had fed them some sort of stew, and they had slept. Now Archer and Tsiel sat against the wall and watched the stranger as he packed bowls and jars and a brass pot into a worn pouch that should have been too small to hold them, but was not.

At first glance he was a child, at second a dwarf. He was small and large-headed, with the proportions of a seven-year-old boy and the face of an ancient child. He had ragged dark hair and large dark eyes, and there was something familiar in his face. An oddly alien face, fine-boned, dust-colored, with a distinctive shape and tilt to the eyes. Archer had seen only one face like it.

"You're a Melaklos," he said, half accusingly.

Some expression—anger? fear?—flashed across the other's face. "So I have been told," he said. He had the Melaklos's dry musical voice, too, baritone where hers was contralto.

"What's your name?" asked Tsiel.

"I have no name." He began to lace the top of his traveling bag. "I am called the Owlet. You are the Tsiel Tsieln, and you—" He looked at Archer—"are named Archer." He turned back to his task, adding over his shoulder, "You carry a talisman of the—of the clan."

Archer put a hand to the bronze medallion. He had forgotten it, forgotten most of the Melaklos's hasty words on that dark shore. Recalling them now, he said, "Then you're guarding the portal?"

"I am going to close it, with your help."

"But we're not magicians," cried Tsiel.

"That is unnecessary." He finished tying the pouch and laid it aside, sat tailor-fashion looking at Archer and Tsiel.

"How can we help?" said Archer curiously.

"By going back through," said the Owlet. "I'll send you back. You will be the instruments, so to speak, of the closing."

They waited, silent, watching him.

"I've been trying to find you since you came here," he said severely. "When you blocked me at the bridge to the Mermaid Cavern, I had to take the long way around. We have lost time."

"You had the green light, then," said Tsiel.

He nodded. "The Kial are coming also," he said. "You have been in the Forbidden Caves, which they will not enter, but you're out of them now."

Uneasily Archer looked around. They were in a sunken crossway: five corridors dropped into the small area. The Kial—who must have been the tiger men—might come from anywhere.

Tsiel said, "If you can close the portal, why didn't you do it before?"

"I am outside the barrier," he said, as if it were an obvious objection.

Curious, Archer said, "What does that have to do with it?"

The Owlet looked from one to the other of them. Then he cupped his hands together. When he opened them, he held a smoky bubble three inches across. "This represents the sector barrier," he said, like a lecturer. "No one can pass through it."

He blew at the bubble. A small bump appeared and grew. "That is the portal. You have come through it and moved about, always carrying the barrier with you." A thin tube spiralled out from the bump. "Men of the Kial have gone

177

through the portal into Dolesar, but they are outside the barrier." More small threads appeared, leading into the bubble. "I could go as they do, but I could not do anything by sorcery. So I shall use you. Send you back quickly and with enough power to destroy the portal." He popped a tiny breath at the outward tendril. It shrank, the bump popped back into place. The bubble was whole and undistorted.

Archer said slowly, "If I understand you, shouldn't that bring the tiger men back here?"

"It should."

Archer looked at Tsiel. She spoke his thought. "Then he won't have his greatest crews. Only renegades and mercenaries."

"And magic," said the Owlet dryly. He turned his head sharply. "They are near now."

Archer listened, but could hear nothing. Tsiel shook her head when he looked at her.

The little brown man raked the fire together with bare hands. As he scraped from the edges to the center, it seemed to grow brighter and hotter, as if he were condensing it. Finally he picked up what was left and sat back on his heels. He held a ball of fire the size of a baseball, too bright for Archer to look directly at it. The Owlet stood and slung his small pouch over his shoulder. "Stand together," he said. "Otherwise you may be blown anywhere."

"What about you?" said Archer.

"Action produces reaction," said the Owlet. "I'll stop somewhere and sometime."

"I hear them," said Tsiel suddenly. "Archer?"

He listened. Booted feet and excited voices, hurrying. "They must see the light," he said.

"Stand together," said the Owlet.

They obeyed. He stood facing them with the ball of light in his hands, staring at it. The air in the room tightened. Things slowed down. The Owlet's face was set like stone.

Tiger men burst from a corridor in slow motion. They swam toward the three.

Archer could not move. Something pressed around him like a cocoon. The cave seemed more and more distant.

The Owlet moved like a sleepwalker. He raised the blinding sphere above his head, dashed it to the stone floor. Everything exploded in fire.

Chapter Fifteen

Winter: first quarter, day twenty

The audience chamber was all of stone, with a flat-vaulted ceiling and a floor intricately inlaid. The room was cold, being open to the sea on one side: a flight of stairs ran the length of one wall, leading up six feet to a terrace overlooking the harbor. The feathery tops of rock-clinging *verilan* trees brushed the low terrace wall.

On this terrace a man appeared suddenly, black against the pallid sky. He bounded down the steps toward Archer, who waited alone in this cold room in Tsiel's halls.

"So there you are," said the newcomer cheerfully.

Flash Gordon, was Archer's first thought. Young, blond, cocky. He wore a dark blue tunic and short cape, laced boots. He couldn't have been much more than twenty.

"I'm sorry the journey was bad," the young man went on. "I should have watched Algundor to see that he didn't try that harbor."

"Look here," said Archer desperately. "Who are you?"

The young man laughed. "I'm the Sr of Nym."

Archer looked at him, trying to find something that would make it believable. He was an open-faced youth, pleasant, intelligent. A Nordic hero for high-school girls to drool over: Flash Gordon, Siegfried, the team captain. Not a master magician building an empire in blood.

The Sr of Nym was still talking, "You closed that portal well—we'll talk about that later. A nice job. My guards say that you just seemed to flicker, and then the portal was gone and so were the Kial." He grinned at Archer. "I'll admit that I wasn't sure what you were until then."

Archer opened his mouth, shut it. So the young idiot thought he was a magician? Okay. It might be useful. "I greet you," he said, then added, "Where is Tsiel? Your guards took her somewhere else."

"She's all right," said the magician indifferently. "She's in her rooms. I'll talk to her when she's rested. I just wanted to meet you." He gestured to Archer to follow him and walked to a corner where a small table was set beside a burning brazier. He sat down and gestured to one of the guards at the room's door. The guard bowed and went out.

Archer sat opposite the Sr of Nym. He was worried about Tsiel, alone in a house of enemies. Still, there was no immediate danger to her: the Sr of Nym had taken too much trouble to get her here to hurt her now. Silence was his watchword, Archer thought. He would be quiet and listen. The Sr of Nym was a person who might talk too much, might give clues for his own destruction.

The magician regarded him with his head tilted slightly. "You puzzle me," he said. "Even when I manipulated you, I didn't suspect that you were a brother in craft. Even now—there's no power trace about you. I didn't think it could be hidden."

Archer smiled tightly and said nothing. Let the young fool convince himself that he was right.

The guard returned with a small wine jar and two silver cups. He set them on the table and retreated at a signal from the magician.

The Sr of Nym touched the cork, and it popped into the air. Showing off, Archer thought. The magician poured pale green-gold wine into the cups, pushed one toward Archer.

"Drink with me, brother," he said, grinning. "We can work together."

Deliberately, Archer withdrew his hand from his cup. He said, "We'd have to discuss that."

The Sr of Nym shrugged and set down his cup untasted. "There's little to discuss. You've sent most of my men home and closed the portal. I need more men. You carry a shielded portal. You are my prisoner. Surely we can agree."

Puzzled, Archer looked at the table. A shielded portal? Of course: the panorama egg. This magician wanted to recruit men from *his* world. An image popped into Archer's head: a fat, self-important little man wearing a leather-strip kilt and carrying a bronze-headed spear. A man named—Whistlin? Something like that. Archer suppressed laughter at the picture.

The Sr of Nym said, "Fortunately my ships got back just before you closed the portal. I've got a fleet; all I need are men." He looked hopefully at Archer, like a young clerk seeking approval.

Angry, Archer didn't like this idea of taking people away from their worlds and using them as pawns. And yet—and yet there was something immeasurably absurd in the idea of

New York City's space-age citizens manning bronze-age galley ships.

"Well?" said the Sr of Nym, after a silence. "Will you drink to our alliance?"

Archer pushed his cup away slowly. He was pleased to see the magician redden. "I will not drink wine with you," said Archer formally. "I must have time to consider. Also, I must speak with the Lady Tsiel."

"Tsiel?" The magician's blue eyes narrowed. He looked thoughtful. "Tsiel—of course. Tomorrow. For now, you'll have to stay in a cell. I'm sorry. You'll find an old friend there. I should have suspected your true nature when I saw you with her."

That could only be one person. Archer said, "The Melaklos? How is she?"

The Sr of Nym shrugged. "As well as can be expected, under the circumstances."

Something cold seemed to hit Archer in the stomach. He said, "What circumstances?"

"You're a wizard." The Sr of Nym shrugged again. "You know what happens to the loser of a duel."

The cell had one barred window in the west wall, toward the sea. Because it was so late, only a little dim light came through it. Archer stood still by the door after the guards locked him in, letting his eyes grow accustomed to the gloom.

The room was about twenty feet square, all of stone. Remembering the stairs they had come down to reach it, Archer decided that it was cut from the bluff on which the Hall stood. There was no furniture. As his vision cleared, the first thing he saw on the stone was what looked like a heap of rags against the wall under the window.

Archer crossed the floor quickly, knelt beside the mass. He touched it gingerly: it was a person, huddled and covered with dusty cloth. He pulled at the cloth, trying to uncover the still form. If it was the Melaklos—if she was dead—

"Who are you?"

Archer's heart jolted at the voice. He turned around.

The speaker came toward him: a boy, seventeen at most, tall and gaunt, with black hair. He looked sleepy, but alert and suspicious. His face was familiar: long-nosed, highboned, with deep temples and steady gray eyes.

Archer said, "You're Tsiel's son."

Impatiently, the boy repeated, "Who are you?"

"My name's Archer." He hesitated, embarrassed. He

couldn't say, I'm your mother's lover. He said, "I'm a friend of your mother's. I came here with her."

The boy's eyes widened. He caught Archer's arm in a crushing grip. "Here? Is she here?"

"We got here today," said Archer.

"How?" said the boy fiercely.

Not sure whether to tell him, Archer hesitated. The boy's grip tightened. He had bony powerful hands. Archer looked at his strained face and said quietly, "Kidnapped. By Algundor, the prince of Gurn."

The boy swore in the harsh northern tongue.

"He's dead," said Archer.

"Dead and damned," said the boy savagely. He released Archer and squatted beside him. Abruptly he said, "How do I know you're not lying?"

Indignant, Archer started to reply, but he could think of nothing that would help. He said, "The Melaklos can vouch for me."

The boy laughed. He indicated the covered body by the wall. "She won't vouch for anyone."

Cold with fear, Archer turned back to her and managed to pull away the worn cloak that covered her. She was curled into a tight ball, face hidden by folded arms. Her muscles were set like stone, cold to the touch. He felt for the pulse in her wrist, found nothing. The pulse at her ear was there, so faint that it might have been the blood beating in his fingertips.

She was alive, at least. Relieved, he tried to shake her. She did not move. He shouted in her ear. There was no response.

Tsiel's son said, "She was like that when they brought her in, five days ago."

Urgently Archer said, "Have you tried to wake her?"

"Yes." The boy looked at her with unreadable eyes. "If you pinch her earlobe hard enough with your nails, she'll go limp for a while."

Archer tried it. She slumped suddenly into the floor.

The boy said something else, but Archer didn't hear him. He looked at her thoughtfully. Pain? It might wake her up. It was worth a try.

He tried to pull her into a sitting position, but she was as limp as a rag doll. He took both her tiny wrists in one hand, pulled until her back was just clear of the floor. He shouted again; she did not react.

He set his teeth and slapped her, forehand and backhand,

as hard as he could. She gave completely with the blows, head lolling.

The boy clutched his arm. "Look out. She'll—"

"She's got to wake up," said Archer through his teeth. He hit her again. On the back-hand, his knuckles caught her high on the cheekbone. Her head moved, not with the blow. She was responding.

"But that's—" began the boy.

Archer hit her with all his strength.

Something flung him across the room. He hit the wall and slid to the floor.

"Are you all right?"

He heard the boy's voice through a haze of pain. He tried to reply, but couldn't. He struggled to a sitting position, clutching the wall.

The boy knelt beside him, gray eyes worried. "I tried to warn you," he said. "She did that to me once: I was out for hours."

Archer shook his head to clear it. "She did that?" he asked.

"She must have."

Determined, Archer got to his feet. If she was conscious enough to fight back, she could be awakened. He crossed the dim cell unsteadily. Tsiel's son came with him.

She was half-curled into her fetal position, with her face upturned. A thin bar of blood showed black on her cheekbone where he had hit it.

He knelt beside her again, pulled her roughly up so that she sat slumped against the wall. He shouted in her ear.

She turned her head away, made a noise in her throat.

He squeezed her shoulders. Something pushed against his hands, forcing them back painfully. He loosened his grip, and the pressure ceased. Her defense mechanism, whatever it was, was good. He couldn't hurt her—physically, at least.

Frustrated, he shouted at her, "Melaklos! Wake up!"

Brokenly she whispered, "Let me sleep."

"Look at me." He made his voice compelling. "Melaklos, look at me."

Her head rolled back. The eyes were squeezed shut.

He bit his lip. Maybe he could shock her out of it. Brutally he said in English, "So you lost after all."

For a moment she did not respond. The she said, "Yes," in a flat, lifeless voice.

Loudly, still in English, he said, "What happened?"

Her chin lifted. "Archer?" She sounded bewildered, but the language must have reached her.

He said, "That's right. Open your eyes."

They opened.

He felt sick at the sight of them. She had always had the look of a watcher from some distant world, seeing more than others saw. Now her eyes were the blind eyes of the dead.

Tsiel's son turned away, traced the Shield of Kirn in the air between himself and her. It is not safe to look into the eyes of the unconsecrated dead.

Angrily, Archer said, "What happened to you?"

She rolled her head slowly from side to side. "I cannot—"

"You can!" he said savagely. He shook her. "You will."

Her blind head turned toward him. He had to force himself to look at her beautiful dead eyes. Slowly she said, "There is little to tell. North came I with the Old One, the Sleeper. In Sorovel-Tsieln I landed, and gave to the Dreamer the talisman of Sandol, so that *he* would not have it. In the caves of Tsiel slept I, gathering power against the day of the meeting of ships."

This is what the voices of the damned would sound like, Archer thought. No weeping and wailing and gnashing of teeth. Just this hopeless toneless voice going on and on.

"On the day, I entered the Hall," she said. "I faced him—I engaged him as he directed his ships. I forced him from them, so that they were leaderless. He laughed that I should dare him, but he could not return to them. At last he threw me into sleep. There was I—there should I be. Who has awakened me?" She moved her head and shoulders as though fighting something. "I cannot awaken to defeat!"

"This is not defeat!" Archer gripped her shoulder insistently. "Defeat is not yet. He has lost most of his men."

She turned her head away. "Let me sleep."

"No." He took her head between his hands, turned the sightless face to his. "There is work to do," he said. "The portal is closed."

She froze. "The portal. Closed."

"Yes." He made his voice deep, forceful. "We can still fight him. Wake up! Look at me."

She looked at him. Her eyes had the dark surprised look of someone just awakened.

"Archer—" she said. Her voice was faint, but no longer lifeless. "Roal—"

Tsiel's son reached to touch her shoulder.

Her eyes returned to Archer, puzzled, as though she could not quite recall him. She said in a questioning tone, "Archer—?" Then her eyes closed and she slumped sideways.

184

Archer reached to shake her; stopped. He looked at her face, listened to her breathing.

"Is she back in trance?" whispered Tsiel's son Roal.

Relieved, Archer shook his head. "She's asleep." He pulled her away from the wall so that she would not be cramped and spread her cloak over her.

Roal said, "She knew you—I guess you're all right. But what did she talk about? That is, if you don't mind *him* hearing. He's got eavesdroppers everywhere."

"Eavesdroppers." Archer stared at Roal and went cold. The Sr of Nym had an eavesdropper in his, Archer's, head. He must know who had really closed the portal. He must know that Archer was not a magician. In that case, he was plotting something at which Archer could not even guess.

Chapter Sixteen

*Winter: first quarter,
day twenty-one*

Their guard, a red-headed north-mainlander, fed them gruel and watered wine at dawn. An hour later, he took Archer to see Tsiel.

The guard took him through a few short corridors and locked him into a tiny antechamber with one wooden door and an archway hung with heavy blue curtains. These stirred, and a frightened girl of about fifteen looked out.

"I'd like to see the Lady Tsiel," said Archer. "I'm Archer."

The girl withdrew abruptly. She reappeared almost at once and beckoned him through the curtains.

Tsiel came to him quickly, hands held out. He took them and kissed her. He could not speak; his throat ached.

She said something in her own language. The girl vanished through another curtained arch.

"Come sit down," Tsiel whispered.

He followed her to the broad cushion-strewn stone seat beneath the window. She looked unfamiliar in her long white robe and blue over-tunic, with her hair braided with silver, and gold about her arms and waist. The hollowness of her cheeks and the haunted look in her eyes were the only signs he saw of the troubles she had been through.

"I've seen your son, Roal," Archer said. "I'm imprisoned with him."

"How is he?" Her voice was calm, but her eyes were wide.

"He's all right." Archer hesitated. He should say more, but what?

She said, "That is well."

There was a silence which she broke with fury. "I spoke with *him*—with the Sr of Nym. He is starving my people. He did not allow the winter harvest, he's destroyed the fishing fleet, and now he has all of my people shut up in the Winter City." She curled her hands and looked at Archer. Her eyes flamed. "He's got to be stopped!"

Grimly, Archer said, "He has. Nayan—did he talk about his plans."

She laughed shortly. "He spoke of little else. The Arilikan Fleet is on its way—it should arrive tomorrow. As soon as it docks, he will gather the Island leaders for a marriage feast."

Archer looked away from her bitter face. Hate tightened his muscles. He said, "Will they accept this?"

"Why wouldn't they? He'll offer treaty and trade terms—and they lost nothing in the battle. He recalled his ships before the fighting had really started."

"I know," said Archer. "The Melaklos told me."

"The Melaklos?" Tsiel caught his arm. "Is she here?"

"She's here. She fought him."

Tsiel caught her breath. "How is she, then?"

Hating every word he said, Archer told her, "She's insane. She lost, and it just—" He gestured helplessly. It was a terrible thing to tell her, but he had no choice.

She seemed to fight to control herself. Finally she said in a low voice, "Ever since she left Ytarn of Arilikan, I've been expecting her to reappear and help us. Now—"

"Now it's up to us," said Archer.

She looked down at her long hands. The fingers were laced together. Slowly, deliberately, she separated them and spread them over her knees.

Watching, Archer was sick with fear for her, and love of her. "There must be a way out," he said with difficulty.

She tried to laugh. "In other circumstances—if he were not what he is—I would ask you to challenge him."

"Challenge?"

"It is the right of any who objects to a marriage." She shrugged. "But he is a magician, Aach'—it cannot be done."

"No. It can't," he said slowly. But the idea rooted in his head. Challenge the Sr of Nym? How did you fight a magician if you weren't a magician?

Impatient suddenly, he didn't want to talk about the Sr of Nym, or the Melaklos's madness. He only wanted to gather Nayan into his arms, to comfort her and himself.

He saw that her eyes were bright with tears held back. Without willing, they both were on their feet and standing together, embracing in the protective circle of their arms, murmuring meaningless words of comfort.

"Lady Tsiel!" The girl attendant's voice cut across theirs. "The guard's back."

Tsiel drew back from Archer. "Back?" she said, in the voice of a sleeper reluctantly waking. "The guard."

Archer closed his eyes and cleared his head. "That must be my escort." He kissed Tsiel's forehead. "Don't worry," he said softly. "We'll get out of this."

Before going through the blue curtains, he looked back. She was standing before the stone bench, straight and proud, head high in defiance.

The guard took him to the main room of the Hall, the long raftered wooden chamber typical of the north. Trestles and table-boards lay along the walls. One table was set up, at the far end of the hall, and here the Sr of Nym sat eating and drinking pale wine. He called cheerfully for Archer to join him.

"How's the Melaklos?" he asked, as Archer sat opposite him.

Woodenly, Archer said, "Losing that duel unhinged her. She's crazy."

The Sr of Nym grinned. "Serves her right for making me give up that battle." He poured wine into a cup and pushed it toward Archer. "And the Lady? What about her?"

"She's all right," said Archer stiffly.

"Of course." The magician sighed happily. "But that's not important now. I want to talk about our—our partnership."

"What about it?"

"That portal you carry—ingenious. Self-shielded, selective, and small enough to hide: I've never heard of one that good."

There was no trace of sarcasm in his voice. Yet he must know the truth, Archer thought. He must know that Archer was not a magician and could not have made the egg.

Still, suppose that he didn't know? Suppose that for some reason he didn't know what had really happened in the caves? The Melaklos would know about that. He'd play along for now, Archer thought grimly. If this was a trick, better to let the magician think it was working.

Archer lifted his cup and drank. Setting it down, he said, "All right, it's a good piece of work. So?" That was the right tone: defensive, skeptical.

The magician's grin broadened. "I haven't actually seen it, of course," he said. "I've left you all your paraphernalia as—call it an act of faith. Could I see the portal?"

"No!" The word burst out before he could stop it. Archer bit his lip in vexation. He didn't want the Sr of Nym to handle the panorama egg.

The Sr of Nym eyed him for a moment. "All right," he said. "That can wait. I'll tell you what I want."

"You want men," said Archer harshly.

The Sr of Nym nodded. "Right. Men. See, Acha, tomorrow morning the Arilikan Fleet will be here. Tomorrow midday I'll marry Tsiel, and I won't be an interloper. If the Council insists, I'll sign peace agreements. What's a treaty to a strong man?"

Archer didn't answer. He felt disgusted.

The Sr of Nym went on, "After they've left, we'll get troops, re-man my ships. They're in the harbor, waiting. When we're ready, we start. Carefully. Send ships south to major ports—as trading ships, see? Gather them at strategic points. Then hit them all at once. There won't be much resistance: none of them has much of a fleet on its own."

Archer asked carefully, "Will it work?"

"Of course. All we need is legitimacy and the men. That's where you come in. We'll have to pierce the sector barrier within the shield of your portal, so the Brotherhood can't get at us."

"Hm." Archer was skeptical. "Are you sure it can be done?"

"Of course! It's good work, but not that good." The magician leaned over the table, holding Archer's gaze. "But it's a delicate job, you know—like cracking an egg with a stone club."

"Ye-es," said Archer thoughtfully, the skeptic being convinced against his will. "But can you trust me? Why not use the Melaklos? She's docile enough now."

The magician threw back his golden head and laughed. "The Melaklos? Come now, Acha. She's broken. Anyway, d'you think I can't guess what she is?"

Archer sat up straighter. "I don't know what you mean," he said evenly.

The Sr of Nym laughed again and shook his head. "I've fought her, I've seen what you can do. You sent her here with the Great Serpent, didn't you? To distract me from your own actions? It's obvious Acha. She's your acolyte."

Acolyte? Archer tried to figure out this new development. What was an acolyte? The word had vague religious connotations, but he couldn't recall just what it meant. He realized that the silence was getting too long, that the Sr of Nym might begin to suspect something. There was only one thing to say, and Archer said it. "How did you know?"

"It was obvious, once I knew what you were." The magician leaned forward, intense. "But what about it? Are you with me?"

Archer looked at him stonily. "What's in it for me?" he said.

"For you?" The Sr of Nym flung out his hands. "Power, man, power! An empire!"

Archer shrugged.

"And something else." The Sr of Nym grinned. "Something extra. Your black-haired sea-woman."

"Tsiel?" Archer said, keeping his voice casual. "What about her?"

The grin became a leer. "There seemed to be a certain—affection."

Archer wanted to smash the handsome grinning face. He put his hands under the table to conceal their shaking, and said roughly, "So?"

The Sr of Nym shrugged. "I'll be married to her, of course, but that's strictly business. I like my women a little—nearer my own age, shall I say?"

Archer clenched his hands until the nails bit into the palms. The son of Lerkan was selling her like a temple prostitute!

"Well?" said the Sr of Nym eagerly.

Archer couldn't stand him any more. He stood abruptly, rocking his bench. "I'll think about it," he said. He marched toward the far door and the red-haired guard.

"Acha."

He turned.

The Sr of Nym was smiling. "About that idea of Tsiel's—challenging me, you know. I wouldn't try it, if I were you."

Fuming, Archer turned on his heel and left the room.

Chapter Seventeen

Winter: first quarter, day twenty-one (cont'd.)

"I lied to both of them," said Archer hotly. "I don't mind lying to him, but to Nayan? I don't like it."

"It is necessary," said the Melaklos wearily. "He may suspect that I am not as mad as you say I am, but he must not *know*."

Archer paced across the cell and looked back at her. She huddled in her gray cloak against the wall under the window, staring into space with tired eyes. She had not moved or changed expression when Archer returned, or while he told her of his conversations with Tsiel and the Sr of Nym.

"Is he bluffing?" Archer demanded.

She raised her head and looked at him without speaking.

"Does he know I'm not a magician? Or doesn't his mental contact reach through portals?"

"Probably not," she said slowly. "They usually do not. Archer, you have not yet told me what happened after I left Ytarn."

Surprised, he stood looking at her for a moment. He was so used to her knowing things that at first he thought she was joking. Then he saw the infinite weariness in her eyes, and knew that she was too broken and tired to jest. He crossed the floor and sat beside her and told her, as quickly and completely as he could, everything that had happened, from the Council meeting to the wreck at Sorovel-Tsieln and the days in the caves of the Kial. She listened in silence.

When he finished, she sighed and said, "You have done well."

He shook his head and hastily asked, "Who was the Owlet?"

She looked at him for a moment, then said, "Had he not been deliberately crippled—mentally distorted—by his sorcerous master, he would be the greatest sorcerer who ever existed." She moved a hand as if to dismiss him. "What else requires explanation?"

Her speech was more formal than ever, he thought, as if to shield herself from despair. He said gently, "What threw me across the room when I hit you?"

"A defense mechanism, a shield that reflects power against the user of power."

"Didn't you use it against him?"

"There are ways to break it," she said wearily. "Why ask useless questions? I am capable of speaking to the point."

Worried, he stood up and began to pace the cell. He had lied when he told Tsiel and the Sr of Nym that the Melaklos was completely broken by defeat, but it wasn't a complete lie. There was something in her now that he didn't like. She was capable of betrayal now. Still, she seemed sane enough. And she could probably help him find a way to defeat the magician.

He said, "Will this plan of his work?"

"Not if you are his helper," she said dryly. A small sarcasm, but it promised hope. "It might work," she went on. "It is a careless plan, but he has been careless all along. His pursuit of Nayan was clumsy; his use of Algundor was absurd."

"It hasn't defeated him yet," Archer pointed out. He turned and started back down the cell. "He's awfully young. I was—"

She made a small impatient sound. "What did you expect? I can tell you: an old man in long dark robes and a pointed hat, with a gnarled staff, a long white beard, and eyes burning like coals under bushy eyebrows. The distorted image of Odinn, in fact."

Archer was startled. "Odinn? Wasn't he a god?"

"Yes, Odinn, Wotan the one-eyed, bearer of the ashen spear. A type of *der spielmann*." She sighed and dismissed Odinn with a quick gesture. "We have until tomorrow noon, Archer."

The cell door opened and Roal came in, pale and shaken. He smiled thinly at Archer.

"My mother spoke of you," he said, in a voice that he barely kept steady. "She said that you are a good man."

Uncertain, Archer questioned, "She told you about *his* plans?"

Roal nodded. "I'll have to be in the ceremony, if she agrees to it."

"She may refuse?" Archer crossed to the boy. "Will she refuse?"

"I don't know. She's my mother and your lover, and he

192

threatens to kill us both. But she's also the Tsiel Tsieln. If she denounces him before the assembled leaders, she'll destroy his chances for a legitimate position in Arilikan."

"Leaving him to continue as he began," said the Melaklos quietly, in English. "With your help, Archer—and with or without your consent."

Archer said sharply, "You always have a plan. What do you suggest we do?"

She shook her head wearily. "I cannot think, Archer." Panic edged her voice. "There is a pattern here, but I cannot see it. Archer and Tsiel and the Sr of Nym. Magic and trickery, marriage and challenge. Power and the absence of power, the missing stair. There is pattern here."

Suspicious, Archer tried to read her face. Her words sounded like ramblings, but he thought that there was a message in them—a pattern. She had given him a key to the Sr of Nym's defeat, but what was it?

She met his eyes. He thought he saw, burning behind the weariness, the light of judgment—the look she had worn when she offered him the panorama egg.

Nonsense. She was too broken to test him still. He turned away from her and saw Roal's worried young face.

"There's got to be a way," he said, more to himself than to the boy. "After all, this is his last chance."

"Ours, too," said Roal.

Pattern. Pattern without pattern. The sunlight on the floor was a pattern, a rectangle broken by the shadows of the bars. Archer stared at it without seeing it.

There had to be a way out within the pattern.

The Melaklos was asleep under the window, hidden in her gray cloak. Her puzzling phrases went through Archer's head.

"Archer and Tsiel and the Sr of Nym." A triangle, a classic triangle in an odd way. The main actors in the drama.

"Magic and trickery, marriage and challenge." Magic? That was the Sr of Nym. Marriage was obvious. Challenge—Tsiel had mentioned that. It was Archer's right to challenge the Sr of Nym. But a magician fights with magic, and how does a non-magician meet him? With trickery? Was that what the Melaklos meant?

"Power and the absence of power, the missing stair." Archer hit the floor in frustration. That didn't make sense at all. Power? Absence of power? The Sr of Nym had power and he didn't, but what was the missing stair? All he could think of was a line from somewhere, about the shock of stepping on a stair that wasn't there.

Exasperated, Archer got up and paced the cell again. Roal watched him silently.

Challenge. That was what Archer wanted to do. Fight it out with the Sr of Nym, face to face. Romantic idea—ridiculous.

But he didn't think it was ridiculous. He had to admit to himself that he liked it. That was what it always came down to in the stories you grew up with: two people fighting it out face to face.

He was a romantic. The Melaklos had said so, and she was right as usual. He wanted to kill the black knight, who looked like Siegfried, and carry off the princess, who was thirty and not really beautiful. Fanciful perhaps, vainglorious—and what was wrong with that? It wasn't a dream to be afraid of, or ashamed of. It was the dream. Not even the Melaklos laughed at that. "I believe in dream," she had said to him.

Challenge. He was going to challenge the Sr of Nym.

Now all that he needed was a way to beat him.

He returned to the pattern of light on the floor. Pattern—pieces of a puzzle that fitted to make a pattern.

Absently, Archer emptied the small pouch that hung at his belt. He arranged the contents of it in the barred light, as though they were the pieces of his puzzle.

King Lear, water-stained and faded. A piece of scented wood he'd been carving into chain. Firestones wrapped in cloth. The bottle of sleeping pills. A spiralled copper ring. His pocket knife. The panorama egg.

What could he use as a weapon?

He rearranged the things. The firestones and the ring went together, for Tsiel and Roal. The wooden chain was the Sr of Nym—he put it near the firestones. The magician would be near Tsiel tomorrow. The book was the Melaklos—he set it aside. The knife and the sleeping pills were left. He frowned at them.

How do you fight a magician when you aren't a magician?

By trickery. You cheat. If it's cheating when he has powers that you can't fight on even ground.

Archer touched the book, the bottle. An idea was struggling in the back of his mind. An absurd idea, a plan so ridiculously impractical that—that it might work.

He'd have to have allies. Tsiel would have to help—or Roal. And the Melaklos.

He picked up the bottle of pills and set it down between

the firestones and the wooden chain. Then he swept everything back into his pouch.

Elated, he went to wake the Melaklos. She could advise him, tell him what chance he had. And she had a role to play, whether she wanted it or not.

He knelt beside her before waking her. She looked vulnerable. He remembered suddenly evenings in the mainland forests, talking with Lash and Nayan about the Melaklos—discovering that no one ever saw her asleep. He was glad that he never had. In sleep the lines of her face smoothed out, the close-lying skin was no longer tight over her alien bones, and this made her look impossibly old. She looked like one who has grown up too fast, and aged when contemporaries were still in their first youth.

Archer touched her shoulder, calling her softly.

She sat up suddenly, throwing her arms out in defense.

Startled, Archer just managed to duck. "I've got a plan," he said urgently.

She stared at him, her eyes huge and dark with sleep. Finally she said in a slow voice, "Archer? A Plan?"

Rapidly, in English, he said, "First I need two answers."

"Ask," she said.

"First: you told me that if the Sr of Nym went to sleep or was knocked unconscious unexpectedly, his barrier would collapse. Is that still true?"

"Yes."

Satisfaction tinged Archer's voice. "Second: can he be bluffed?"

She considered it. "Not in an area of his knowledge."

"But outside his knowledge?" he persisted.

She shrugged. "Anyone can be bluffed in ignorance."

Archer could have laughed. He leaned forward and said, "Now listen. Here's my idea."

By the time he was halfway through his explanation, she was sitting up straight and listening intently. When he finished, she threw back her head and laughed—laughed aloud for the first time since he had met her.

"Beautiful," she said, and her voice was full and rich again. "I had faith in you, Archer, but not enough."

"Then you think it'll work?" he asked anxiously.

She smiled. "It's audacious enough to succeed," she said.

There were arrangements to be made with Roal, instructions to give him. The Melaklos talked to him, so that the Sr of Nym could not overhear the plan through Archer's ears.

Archer kept his back turned while the Melaklos worked with the contents of his pouch. He knew what she was doing, but all the Sr of Nym would have to go on was one small sound: the sound of a tearing page.

Now that he had outlined his idea to the Melaklos, he didn't like it. It was too uncertain. He wanted to give it up—but the alternative was bondage to the Sr of Nym for Tsiel and probably for himself as well. That was infinitely worse than being killed in a duel.

The Melaklos hobbled back across the cell, lame from her long sleep. Roal supported her, face flushed and eyes alight.

"Well?" said Archer, shortly to cover his uncertainty.

"I'm sure she'll do it," said Roal enthusiastically. "If she announces your challenge before the assembled leaders, he won't be able to avoid it."

"Good enough," said Archer. He looked at the Melaklos, who again sat against the wall. "You'll be my acolyte, then—my assistant?"

"I shall be honored," she said with a twist of her mouth.

Archer took his pouch from her and dug out the *King Lear*. "We'd better rehearse a bit, I guess," he said. "How much of this do you know?"

"All of it."

Chapter Eighteen

*Winter: first quarter,
day twenty-two*

Early the next afternoon, the red-haired jailer and two islander ships'men from the Fleet took Archer and the Melaklos to the terrace room. The terrace was heavily curtained and canopied to hold in the heat of the twenty great braziers that burned around it. The island leaders were assembled at long tables around three sides of the terrace; the outer side was empty. Here the canopy curtains were half raised to show the icy sea far below.

Archer and the Melaklos passed through an open corner of the table formation and into the center of the open space. Here Archer turned around, seeking Tsiel and the Sr of Nym.

They sat together at the center of the long side, with the two-handled marriage cup shining golden on the table between them. Roal sat on the other side of his mother, flushed and angry. He and Tsiel wore white, the color of mourning.

Tsiel rose and said in a clear cold voice, "Here is your challenger, maker of magic. It is his right."

The Sr of Nym stood also, looked at Archer doubtfully.

Happily Archer thought, *he's afraid. He's convinced himself that I'm as powerful as he is, if not more.*

The Sr of Nym looked around the company. The bewildered leaders looked back at him belligerently. They might not be sure what was happening, but they understood challenge.

The Sr of Nym flushed to the roots of his golden hair. "Accepted, then," he snapped. He glared at Archer. "Who stands with you?"

Remembering the formula the Melaklos had taught him, Archer said, "My acolyte." The Melaklos, draped and hooded in her gray cloak, inclined her head. Insolently Archer smiled at the Sr of Nym and said, "Who stands with you?"

The magician's flush deepened. "No one," he said. "I don't need help against such as you."

"Very well then," said Archer. He bowed to Tsiel, who

tried to smile back. Then Archer turned and paced gravely toward the open wall, the Melaklos beside him.

"Are you sure the shield will work?" he muttered to her.

"It should." She sounded tired. "You'll be sustaining it, not I. It will protect only you. I don't know how long it will last."

Archer turned at the wall, whispering, "If Tsiel does her part, it shouldn't take more than fifteen minutes."

"We're on stage," said the Melaklos quietly. She bowed to Archer and moved to a stone bench at the wall. She stood on the bench like a gray statue.

Archer shuddered. If she overbalanced, she would go over the low wall, and the drop ended in rocks. He bowed to the Sr of Nym and took *King Lear* from his pouch. He and the Melaklos would be impressive and hypnotic, so that no one would react fast if anything went wrong.

The Sr of Nym began to speak quickly, gesturing with one hand. As acceptor, he opened the duel.

He heard the Melaklos's dry murmur, "Let the comedy begin."

The Sr of Nym flung his hands out toward Archer.

The air around Archer bellied inward, then sprang back. The Sr of Nym swayed as his bolt of power returned to him. The Melaklos's shield was working.

Archer's turn. Had Tsiel done her task? Watching her, he opened the *King Lear* and began with Lear's first long speech:

"Meantime we shall express our darker purpose.
Give me the map there. Know we have divided
In three our kingdom. . . ."

He read the lines like a chant, without attention to the sense of them. When he paused, the Melaklos responded in a voice like a deep-toned bell:

"We have this hour a constant will to publish."

Archer read the next seven lines, watching Tsiel. She looked straight at him, but one hand stole toward the marriage cup. In it was something white. A page from the book, Archer knew, twisted into a spill. Her hand hovered over the cup.

Lear's speech was finished; Archer turned to Edgar's first soliloquy and chanted,

"Thou, nature, art my goddess; to thy law
My services are bound. Wherefore should I. . . ."

The Sr of Nym's hand moved like a striking snake. He caught Tsiel's wrist, twisted it until she dropped the paper on the table.

Archer's heart raced. This might be the end for them.

"Who, in the lusty stealth of nature, take," intoned the Melaklos.

Mechanically Archer continued.

"More composition and fierce quality...."

The Sr of Nym looked up from the paper, smiling triumphantly. He vaulted over the narrow table and strode toward Archer, holding the paper like a talisman.

"Got 'tween asleep and—"

"Stop this nonsense," said the Sr of Nym. "You're a fraud."

Archer looked around as if in panic. The councillors were on their feet, muttering. They didn't know what was happening, and they were angry.

"All right," Archer said desperately. He lifted the cup and drained it slowly, lowered it and glared at the Sr of Nym.

The young magician smiled. He moved his hand and the knife vanished. Then he raised the marriage cup and drank it empty. He took both cups to the nearest table, returned and smiled evilly at Archer. "Now we continue," he said.

"Wait a minute," said Archer. "I don't think I want to—"

"We continue," repeated the Sr of Nym. He raised his voice. "You challenged me before the council. You have no choice."

Archer glanced at Tsiel. Her face was unreadable. If she had been successful—if the Sr of Nym had not caught her too soon—then everything was going well despite his catching her. They would know soon.

He turned back to the Sr of Nym. "All right," he said. "We continue."

The Sr of Nym bowed and retreated to the center of the open space.

"Now, gods, stand up for bastards," intoned the Melaklos, solemnly and out of place.

How long was it going to take? Surely they had been going for more than fifteen minutes. If Tsiel had been successful, then the Sr of Nym had drunk twenty sleeping pills with that cup of wine. He should be out cold—unless Tsiel had failed. Unless the Melaklos had not powdered the pills into that screw of paper. Unless the Sr of Nym was immune to them, despite the Melaklos's assurances. Unless, unless, unless—there were too many chance.

Something hit Archer. He staggered back a step. The Sr of Nym chanted and flung his hands out. It was as if he threw a bolt of power. Archer recoiled from the blow.

The shield was failing. Weary, he looked for the Melaklos. She stood before a table of councillors, hooded so that her face was hidden. The councillors looked hypnotized, with glazed eyes and half-open mouths. Only Tsiel and Roal were wide awake, looking from Archer to the magician with anxious uncomprehending eyes.

The voice of the Melaklos came clear, in cadence: "I think you'd better speak."

With an effort, Archer pulled himself back to the duel. He looked down at the book. It was open to the bookplate, with its stylized fool's cap and Patterson's flowing signature. Archer opened to one of the marked places and read automatically. It was the Fool's prophecy; they had already used it at least twice.

"When priests are more in word than matter."

The Melaklos chanted the next line in monotone, every syllable the same length: "Wen brey wares mar their malt with water."

The sound lifted Archer. He echoed it: "Wen no bleys are their tay lor's tu tors."

Sung like that, it lost all relation to the play. Archer straightened his back and lifted his head, feeling like a priest at some strange ritual.

The Sr of Nym chanted louder, trying to drown him out.

Archer's weariness dropped from him. He sang his next line in his deepest, strongest voice, "Ven slan dares do not leave in ton gays."

The Sr of Nym faltered. He had moved during the duel—he stood beside the open wall now. He leaned on it, breathing hard.

Feeling the beginning of triumph, Archer walked deliberately toward him, chanting. The Melaklos, at the far end of the terrace, mirrored him. They stood at opposite ends of the wall. The Sr of Nym glanced at the Melaklos, turned to face Archer.

He was having trouble keeping his eyes open, Archer saw. He blinked and shook his head, trying to shake off sleep. His mouth moved. "Fraud," he whispered. He drew himself up, gestured at Archer.

Archer scarcely felt the blow. He closed the book and took the panorama egg from his pocket—anything for a good prop. He held it before him like a talisman, pacing toward the Sr of Nym and chanting.

"Ten combs day tee may who lee vaze to see it."

"Vain go ing sall be you zed weet feet," responded the Melaklos.

"Get back." The magician stumbled away from Archer and sank onto a bench.

Anxious, Archer looked past him at the Melaklos, but her face was still hidden. He chanted, "Dees pro pace see mare lean sall mak kay."

"For I lee vay bee foe ray hiss tee may," the Melaklos finished.

Archer stepped forward, thrust the egg at the Sr of Nym.

The magician struggled to sit up. His head lifted. He glared at Archer. His lips writhed, one hand moved. Then he collapsed.

They had done it. Archer stared at the Sr of Nym, not yet believing it.

"Hola!" Tsiel cried. She leaped to her feet and over the table, Roal behind her. The councillors stirred and looked about, bewildered.

Elation struggled through Archer's weariness. He turned to meet Tsiel.

"Archer." The Melaklos's voice was low, urgent.

Her hood was back. Her dust-colored face was drawn, looking at the fallen Sr of Nym.

She said in English, "The barrier's still up. Archer, he's still conscious."

Frightened, suspicious, Archer turned to the fallen magician.

The Sr of Nym stirred. He pulled himself to his knees, to his feet, clinging to the wall. His beautiful young face was distorted with hate. He looked at Archer, at the Melaklos. His gaze shifted again. His mouth worked, his slurred voice was venomous. He lifted a hand, gestured weakly. His eyes burned through their growing glaze, staring at Tsiel. He drew back his hand to fling the spell at her.

Everything went into slow motion for Archer. He saw the Sr of Nym's hand start forward, knew that he could not reach him in time. Felt the panorama egg in his hand, cold, heavy with its crystal cover. Heard the Melaklos's voice in his

201

head: "It may kill you. I am not certain." Saw her, beyond the Sr of Nym, moving in a long slow step—she knew his thought, she was saying, "No." Then he saw Nayan's horror-frozen face, and he could move.

In slow motion, he threw the egg with all his strength, straight at the Sr of Nym. It floated toward the magician. The Sr of Nym's hand was unfolding, the long fingers uncurling to hurl his curse.

The egg hit the side of his head. He went back like a sleepwalker; his eyes blazed, started to close. He floated toward the floor.

The egg rebounded lazily over the terrace wall. Archer, leaning to look after it, saw it fall and fall and fall, shining in the pale sun, until it struck the icy rocks below and sent up glittering splinters of crystal, and then he was falling and falling and falling too.

PART THREE

Chapter One

Wednesday, December 8th— Tuesday, December 14th

There was light through his eyelids, and faint noise, and an odd familiar smell. Archer sniffed. It was a white smell, and it stung faintly. Antiseptic. He couldn't place it.

A door opened and closed, he heard footsteps. Someone picked up his left wrist. He opened his eyes.

They focused slowly. A face swam into sight above him: a youth—no, a young woman with short hair. She wore white, and an odd useless little cap that he should recognize. She smiled at him.

He cleared his throat and said, "*K'mai svel?*"

"Beg pardon?"

Surprised, he said, "You speak English?"

She smiled indulgently. "Of course. This is New York, you know." She made marks on the clipboard chart she held, and smiled at him again. "I'll tell doctor you're awake," she said.

"Wait a minute," said Archer desperately. "Where am I? What day is it?"

"This is the Sandemann Clinic," she said. "It's December eighth. You've had a long nap!" She smiled archly.

"Two weeks?" said Archer.

"That's right." She left, still smiling, turning at the door to say, "Doctor'll be in soon."

Archer scarcely heard her. Two weeks. That was what the Melaklos had set the panorama egg for, that night in kos-Alar. She had set it for two weeks after the day he had left, and now it *was* two weeks after that day and he was back in New York. Back to stay. The panorama egg was shattered.

He could not assimilate the thought. It numbed him, the way great grief does. He stared at the ceiling, trying to grasp it.

When the doctor came, brisk and important, Archer listened to him without hearing what he said. Dr. Boyd would come in the evening, the doctor said after a while, and left at last.

When they brought his dinner, he forced himself to sit up

and eat. At first he was dizzy, but the nurse propped him with pillows and his head cleared fast. The food on his tray looked strange, but it smelled all right. He reached for the fork. Then he saw his hands.

They were a stranger's hands, pale, pudgy, with a narrow gold band on the third finger of the left. A wedding ring, he thought, but the words were meaningless. He moved the hands; they responded to him. But he remembered his hands as being leaner, harder, weather-burned, scarred from travel and swordplay.

Swordplay, he thought dully. Sure. These hands hadn't held a sword of any kind since he stopped fencing six years before.

Slowly, because there was nothing else to do, he picked up the fork with his stranger's hands and started to eat.

Dr. Boyd came in the evening, filling the pale room with his explosive personality. He didn't tell Archer much.

"Frankly, I'm not sure what's wrong," he said. "Your secretary called me two weeks ago—said you'd collapsed in your office and been taken to emergency room. I had you moved here. Been running tests—nothing conclusive. I want to do some more before I let you go."

"What's wrong with me?" Archer said tonelessly.

Boyd shook his head. "You've been more or less cataleptic all this time. I'm not sure just what you've got, but it's probably some form of epilepsy."

Astonished, Archer said, "Epilepsy?"

"Sure." Boyd gestured again, nearly knocking the plastic water pitcher over. "Epilepsy isn't always convulsive. In some forms of petit mal, the victim just blacks out for a few seconds or minutes. Such a short seizure may not even be noticed by anyone around him. Cataleptic trance has been known to last for hours or even days—but your case isn't quite typical. As I said, I want to run some more tests now that you're conscious."

Archer looked toward the curtained window. He didn't care what Boyd thought was wrong with him. He just wanted to go home and be alone to straighten his mind out. He said, "When can I leave?"

"Four, five days—we won't take too long." Boyd snagged his hand in a venetian-blind cord. As he untangled it, he said, "By the way, where's Diane? We've been trying to get in touch with her."

"Diane?" He tried to remember. Where was she? Oh, yes.

"She's gone to the Caribbean with—with a friend," he said aloud. "She should be back any day."

Boyd nodded. "Good. Your office says to take all the time you need for recovery. Oh, and someone's called a few times from Ragnell's Cove. English accent, good voice—name's Patterson, I think."

Archer sat up. "Sir Henry Patterson?"

"That's it." Boyd stood up and strode to the door. Looking back, he grinned and said, "We'll be in early with the black boxes. Pleasant dreams." He went out and closed the door.

Pleasant dreams, Archer thought sourly. What would Boyd think if he knew what Archer's dreams had been? If it had been a dream. Whatever it had been, Boyd must never know. No one must ever know, Archer thought bleakly. They'd think I was crazy. I can't tell anyone.

Except Sir Henry. Archer settled into the bed. Yes, he could tell Patterson. He had to talk to someone. He reached up and turned off the light, closed his eyes and waited for sleep. He could sleep now: he had a goal.

They didn't let him have any visitors during the five days of testing. He bore it all patiently, just wishing that they would finish and send him home. Finally came the day when they wheeled him out and put him into a hired car and he was driven home.

The house was strange. He went through it on tiptoe, as if he feared to wake it. It was familiar, but not with the familiarity of something known. It was familiar as if he had seen it once in a dream and never quite forgotten it. He had to think to remember what the rooms were. He looked into all of them, but found nothing to tell him that he was home. Finally he retreated to his den.

Here he locked in a drawer the reminders of his adventure: the full bottle of sleeping pills, and the faded *King Lear*, with no water stains on its covers, no dog-eared pages, no sonnets in the Melaklos's neat microscopic script, no missing leaves—just the play and notes, and the bookplate with the stylized fool's cap and Patterson's signature. After the bottle and book were locked away, he did not look at them, nor did he look at the panorama eggs that filled the shelves, his collection.

Dreams fade. Even the most memorable of them sink into recesses in the mind, to rise only when some chance association reminds one of them. Archer told himself this constantly, trying to convince himself.

207

But the dream did not fade. He remembered Nayan/Tsiel's face more clearly than the face of his wife, and the Melaklos's dry voice was easier to recall than Diane's high-cultured tones.

Give it time, he thought. Ignore it and it will fade. Find something to do.

He tried to read, but he couldn't keep his mind on the words. He found himself re-reading pages without absorbing what was in them. Television was more of a failure. He stared at it without seeing or hearing it, his head full of the world called Dolesar, This Place, and the people he had met there.

He walked. Every morning he let Mrs. Oliphant, the daily woman, in at nine and went out to walk. He ate lunch at the nearest eating house, if at all. He walked until the early dark drove him home to stare unseeing at the walls or the babbling television.

Other things disturbed him. He was clumsier in movement than he was used to being, slower. He ran out of breath too fast. On his third morning home, he saw himself in the mirror as he shaved and realized what had happened. It was like seeing his hands all over again.

When the egg fell from the terrace, he was Aacha, strong and fit after most of a year spent traveling in Dolesar. When the egg broke, he was again Archer, fat, out of condition, dying. He stared at the image in the mirror, at the pasty face and puffy features. His eyes ached; he hadn't cried since he was eight years old.

Self-consciously he went to his den and rummaged for his address book. He had regained his health by a definite routine—the Melaklos fitness program. Silly thing to call it. What was in it? Two and three workouts a day with swords. Archery. Coarse plain food. And walking, lots of walking. He could duplicate all of it. He found the telephone numbers of the archery club he had quit two years ago, the fencing club he hadn't been to for six years. He picked up the telephone receiver and started to dial.

Then he realized what he was doing, and put it back. He sat staring at it. He couldn't duplicate the Melaklos's program. It might drive him mad. It would be catering to the dream.

He dropped his head into his hands and groaned.

He stayed home that morning. He had two telephone calls. The first was from Whistlin at the office, asking how he was and talking gleefully about the partnership. Archer had to concentrate to remember who Whistlin was and what he was talking about.

Diane called at eleven. He picked up the receiver, and her high clear voice said, "Hal, darling!"

Who was Hal? He thought about it, realized with a start that this was what she called him. She was his wife, he told himself. Her name was Diane. He said, "Hello, Diane."

"Hal, darling, where have you been? I've been trying to catch you for four days!"

"I've been away," he said, not quite truthfully. He looked at the photograph of Diane on his desk, trying to recall what she looked like.

She said, "I'm in Los Angeles, darling. I'm coming home."

He said carefully, "What about Paul?"

She laughed, a silver sound over the wires. "I got tired of him. You were right, Hal, he's a bore. I'm coming back to you—if you want me."

Automatically he said, "Of course I do." But he was appalled to realize that he didn't care. She was coming back? How kind of her. She's coming back and I'm glad, he told himself fiercely. He cast about in his mind for something to offer her in return. He said, "Diane, I've got the partnership."

"Hal, darling, how wonderful!"

Her voice was around him like a warm flood. But through her voice he kept hearing echoes of a fuller, clearer voice: Tsiel's, Nayan's. The voice of an imaginary woman. He shook it off and concentrated on the portrait of Diane on his desk. It was a duplicate of the one on his office desk: Diane, blonde and beautiful, arrogant in peacock-blue satin.

He remembered the first night she had worn that dress. She had sat at her dressing table in an apricot-colored slip, smoothing makeup on her forehead, looking anxiously at the skin around her eyes, touching the corners of her mouth.

In that moment of remembering, Archer understood his wife for the first time. Understood what kept her so frantically active, kept her going to plays and parties that left her exhausted and haggard, made her find lovers who were young and dashing. She was afraid. Afraid of Time, of the marks that it left at the corners of her eyes and mouth. Afraid that if she stood still, he would catch up with her and wither her golden beauty. Archer felt like crying out to her in pity. She was so vulnerable, so ridiculously afraid.

He had never felt sorry for her before.

It was so new a feeling that when she said, "Hal? Are you

there?" he almost couldn't answer, for fear of saying something that would hurt her.

He cleared his throat, said, "I'm here."

"Listen, Hal darling, I can't get away today or tomorrow, but I'll come on the first plane Thursday. I should get in between eight and ten—I'll call from the airport, all right?"

"All right," said Archer with an effort.

"Thursday morning, then." Her voice caressed him. "Good-bye, Hal darling. I love you."

"Good-bye, Diane," he said. He cradled the receiver, still dazed from his moment of realization. Diane afraid—it was a strange thought. Silly girl, silver girl—

Then, unwillingly, he rememberd Tsiel—Nayan who was Diane's age and looked younger because she was not afraid. He had thought of that on the night when he first saw her clearly, sitting in a wine shop in kos-Alar with torches highlighting the lovely bones of her face.

He shouldn't think about Nayan. But he couldn't help it. What had happened after he was snapped back? Had the barrier collapsed, was the Sr of Nym defeated? If he had escaped his vengeance would be terrible—

Fiercely Archer told himself, Diane's coming home. That's all that matters!

He got up and collected his hat and coat. Maybe if he walked he could get the dream out of his mind. If it was a dream.

What was Tsiel doing now? Was she thinking of him?

He slammed the door as he went out.

Chapter Two

Tuesday, December 14th— Thursday, December 16th

Archer met Sir Henry Patterson in the streets of the old town, and stood under the bare elms talking to him. He had not sought the old actor out, as he had planned—he hadn't really wanted to share the dream with anyone. Now it was good to talk to Patterson. It made the dream ghosts retreat into the shadows of his mind, to wait until he was alone again.

Not wanting to be alone with them, Archer talked to Patterson for hours, under the elms and then in a drugstore where they went for coffee. Patterson watched him with obvious concern. Archer wanted to tell him about the dream, but he couldn't speak of it in public. He was delighted when Patterson invited him to dine the next night.

Going home, he decided that he would tell Patterson all about the dream. Some dreams could be exorcised that way. Maybe it would work with this one.

"I believe in dream."

Frightened, startled, Archer looked around the icy street. No one else was out, but he had heard the Melaklos's voice as clearly as though she stood beside him. He stood still and listened, but he heard nothing further, and nothing moved against the thin snow.

Hallucination, he told himself angrily. *I've got to get rid of that dream.*

But did he want to get rid of it?

He faced that question finally, sitting behind the desk in his den that night. Did he want to get rid of the dream?

No. It was a beautiful thing, like a secret jewel in a secret box in his head. If only it would fade a little, and not be so painful when he thought of it! It hurt to recall Nayan's face, her voice, the touch of her long strong hands. It hurt to remember crisp autumn mornings in the forest, the dark silent rivers, the glittering winter sea. It was too clear, too real. It mattered too much to him. He loved Nayan more than he had loved anyone in his life. He loved her so much that the smallest memory of her was like a knife in his heart.

Even the memory of the Melaklos was painful, her odd alien face, her dark dry voice, the half-hatred that he felt for her. It was she who had given him this torment, this memory that was so beautiful that it hurt. He wondered where she was now. Making a dream for some other fool, perhaps, with her mirror-mask face and her distant eyes.

If only it would fade.

If only it would slip into that misty half-world of dreams, then he could look at it as if it were one of his panorama eggs, the most precious of all. He would treasure it, savor it in the long quiet evenings. Parts would fade almost completely, parts remain clear but far away, comfortably far away, distant enough for him to be sure that they were dream.

If only it would fade!

Terror came in the next day's mail. It was Wednesday, a pale gray day with slow snow falling. Archer walked all day, keeping his mind firmly fixed on the evening's engagement with Patterson. Once or twice he recalled, with vague surprise, that Diane would be home the next morning. He returned to the house in the early dark, with just time to read the mail, change clothes, and walk to Patterson's house.

The mail was on his desk: a few late bills, a dozen Christmas cards, three packages. Christmas packages, of course. He set them aside with the cards for Diane to open. The address on the smallest caught his eye.

His heart beat painfully while he studied the package. It was a four-inch cube, addressed simply to "Archer" in a quick neat block printing. There was no return address, and the postmark was so blurred that he could not read it. The package was so light that it might have been empty.

He tried to ignore it while he opened the other mail. He opened the bills and the Christmas cards, read through every one carefully, read the advertising fillers with the bills. He put them all carefully back into their envelopes and stacked them for Diane. Finally only the packages were left.

He set two of them aside impatiently, eyes fixed on the little one addressed to himself. It was a Christmas present, that was all. Nothing to be afraid of.

But he was afraid of it all the same. It might contain something that would prove he was insane, or make him insane. There was only one way to find out.

He couldn't make himself touch it. He stared at it.

The ticking of the wall clock was loud in his ears. He looked at it. Just time to change and walk to Patterson's house. He got up, walked slowly to the door.

He had to know! He turned, strode back to the desk. Standing beside it, he unwrapped the package with shaking hands. A cardboard box, filled with wood shavings. Gingerly he lifted the top layer of them away.

The panorama egg lay nested in the box.

Archer stepped back, stumbled against his chair. He kicked it crashing into the wall. His heart pounded, choking him. He had expected this when he noticed the package, but it terrified him all the same.

The egg lay in its nest of shavings, dusty brown speckled with dark. He could see the larger dark spot in the large end, the peephole. Some scent drifted into the air. He sniffed, trying to capture it.

Sharp, astringent. The smell of *tsol* wood.

Archer fled the room.

He was incoherent when Patterson let him in. He knew it, but couldn't help himself. Patterson said nothing, just took his coat, then led him to the library, gave him hot water and brandy, and waited. Archer shivered in one of the armchairs before the fire, trying to collect himself.

He was in Patterson's library, he told himself. They would have dinner in a little while. He had walked all the way without a hat or scarf, but he didn't recall being cold. He couldn't remember the walk at all. The panorama egg—but he didn't want to think about the panorama egg. It was better to think of Diane. She would be home in the morning. She would call from the airport between eight and ten, and he would go get her, and they would go somewhere far away for Christmas, somewhere where he wouldn't be reminded of panorama eggs.

Diane will be back tomorrow, he told himself firmly. He tried to smile at Patterson.

"Better?" asked the old actor.

Archer nodded. "Don't know what came over me," he said uncomfortably.

Patterson talked of nothing in particular before and during dinner, and Archer gradually calmed and regained his poise. By the time they went to the library for coffee and brandy, he was laughing and talking, his panic gone.

In the library, Archer settled into one of the big chairs and looked around. It seemed forever since he had been here, but the room was not changed. The old-ivory walls, the mellowed oriental rug, the dark wood, the chairs, all were the same. The ornaments on the mantelpiece were the same: the candelabra, the three china eggs, the ebony clock, the capering bronze jester. Over them hung the Berini portrait, Patterson fifty years ago as Lear's Fool.

I'll speak a prophecy ere I go.

Archer shuddered and looked away from the portrait. *King Lear* would never be the same for him, not since that night when he saw the ostrich egg and met the Melaklos.

Casually, he said, "There was a woman here the last time I came, Miss—what was her name?"

"Mera Melaklos?"

"That's it." He had forgotten that she had a first name. To him, she was the Melaklos. He said, "Have you seen her lately?"

Patterson chuckled. "Not since that night. She'll be back next week, though, to spend the holidays with me. She keeps her own high holidays. Next week's the hiemal solstice: midwinter, winter festival."

Archer spilled coffee on his knee, but hardly felt it. "Winter festival?" he said incredulously. Winter festival in Ytarn, himself and Tsiel ignoring it while they prepared for the fleet to sail. Autumn festival in kos-Alar: torch-lit streets, drunken nights, Nayan leading the chants in the temple in her rich clear voice. Festival.

Patterson looked at him curiously. "This seems to mean something to you," he said.

"It does," said Archer slowly. Now was the time to tell Patterson about the egg and the dream. But was it a dream? The egg was in the den in a cardboard box. Was it a dream?

"By your face, you could a tale unfold," said Patterson.

Unsteadily Archer laughed, catching the tag. "A tale whose lightest word would harrow up thy soul, freeze thy young blood."

"And make my two eyes, like stars, start from their spheres?" said Patterson. "Very well. Speak; I do attend thee."

"It started with the Melaklos," said Archer slowly. "It started here that night."

Slowly at first, but quickly growing more animated and more rapid, Archer told Patterson everything that had happened, from the Melaklos's appearance in his office to the arrival of the egg in the mail. The actor listened in silence, getting up a few times to refill the coffee cups.

As he talked, Archer was surprised at the way everything unrolled before him, every event in its own place, instead of the jumble that had filled his head for a week. He remembered and described everything: the egg itself, the first confused days in the other world, the long time of traveling, meeting Nayan and Lash in kos-Alar, the Festival, the roundabout journey to Ter-Lashan, Nayan's disappearance, the endless waiting, Lash's return, Archer's own rebellion, the journey to Ytarn, the long cold voyage north, the caves of the Kial, the events on Tsiel itself.

When at last he finished, he was exhausted, but his head was clear for the first time since his awakening in the hospital. He sat staring at the fire, sipping cold coffee, until Patterson spoke.

Chapter Three

Thursday, December 16th

"It came in the mail, eh?" said Patterson thoughtfully. "Have you looked into it?"

Archer shuddered uncontrollably. "No." He realized something more, and laughed unsteadily. "Do you know, no one in this world has seen it, except for me and the Melaklos?" He laughed again. "No one."

"Steady, now," said Patterson. He poured brandy into balloon glasses on the tea table. "That disturbs you: why?"

"Why?" Archer stared at him. "Can't you tell?"

"I believe that I can, but I'd rather hear you say it." Patterson handed him a brandy glass and settled back with the other.

"All right," said Archer. He swirled the brandy, watching it, collecting words. Finally he said, "Before that package came, I was sure the whole thing was a dream."

"Sure?" said Patterson.

Archer took a deep breath. "All right. I hoped it was a dream. Because if it wasn't, I was crazy or the Melaklos hypnotized me. Or it was real. But it couldn't be real." He took another deep breath. "Things like that don't happen," he said. "It scares me. I don't want to believe that it could be real."

"Why not?" said Patterson quietly, inexorably.

Irritated, Archer started to speak angrily, but met Patterson's steady gaze. Archer collected himself and said, "It violates the laws of the world I know. It's the impossible happening." He leaned forward. "Wouldn't it frighten you?"

"It does frighten me," said Patterson slowly. "Now and always."

Eagerly, Archer said, "You've had an egg, too?"

Patterson shook his head. "No. But I can't reassure you and tell you that yours is a dream or a trick. That's what you want me to do, but I can't tell you that."

Archer sat still. He felt that he had been somehow betrayed. He *had* wanted Patterson to reassure him.

Patterson said, "You see, I believe in dream. I believe in

the impossible. So do you. That's why this scares me, why it scares you. You can't be frightened by something you don't believe in."

Archer looked at him doubtfully, looked around the room. It was real, solid, tangible. But rooms in Dolesar had been equally solid, equally tangible. Were they equally real?

Patterson said, "What about the rest of the story? What happened after you were sent back? Does the egg tell you anything?"

This was an aspect that Archer hadn't considered. He thought about it. "He must have lost—the Sr of Nym," he said finally. "If the Melaklos could get out to send it, the barrier must be down. So the brotherhood—that's some kind of wizards' guild—must have him." He thought further. "Then Tsiel would be ruler again—except that she was going to abdicate and leave the rebuilding to her son. He's younger than she is—"

"So I should hope," murmured Patterson.

"—And stronger. She was going to be his advisor." He stopped abruptly. He could see Tsiel's face as it had been at the Council when she announced her intention to abdicate, the high scorn for Algundor, the concern for her own people, her high-souled pride. The memory turned his heart over.

Patterson said, "Why did she send the egg?"

Startled, Archer took a few seconds to understand him. Then he said, "I don't know. To give me a choice, I guess. I can stay here or go back." A new idea caught him, and he added, "It may not even be the same world in there now."

Patterson said, "Assume now that it is Nayan's world."

Obediently Archer considered. "Choice," he said helplessly. "You're right, I do believe this. But I know that belief is insane. How can I choose between sanity and insanity?"

Patterson raised his eyebrows and said nothing.

Compulsively Archer continued. "And it's a choice I've got to make soon. Diane's coming back in the morning. If I don't do anything by then, I probably never will."

"In which case, you will have made your choice," said Patterson.

He was right, Archer thought unhappily. He couldn't get out of choosing—between sanity and insanity, reality and dream, Diane and Tsiel.

He said aloud, "It's funny. I know which is the right choice. Diane. Tsiel's only a dream. Dreams fade, don't they?"

Patterson said nothing.

Insistent, almost pleading, Archer said, "Dreams fade, don't they?"

"You needn't convince me," said Patterson.

Archer sat back and sipped at his brandy. Patterson was right. The one he had to convince was Archer. Thinking aloud, he said, "I love Tsiel. I know that now. I haven't seen Diane for nearly a year, and I don't know whether I'll love her when I see her again." He looked at Patterson helplessly. "She's my wife. I've been married to her for ten years." He lapsed into silence again, turning his glass and staring at the fire.

Patterson set his glass on the table and leaned forward. "Archer," he said, "I want an honest answer. You're trying to choose between them on a basis of duty—which needs you more. So tell us, tell us, pray, which does need you more? Which is incapable of simple survival without you?"

Surprised, Archer thought about it. "Tsiel can survive without me," he said reluctantly. The truth hurt, but it was to be faced. "She's lived without me for thirty years. She's got her country, and her son. She can survive."

"And Diane?"

Archer shied away from the answer even as he gave it. "Yes. If I die, she'll be well off. And her family has money. But she needs—"

"What?"

Archer hesitated, then said, "She needs protection. She's afraid of growing old."

"Can you protect her from that?"

"No," said Archer honestly. "But I can help her live with it."

"Can you?" said Patterson. He smiled. "You are amazing."

"You sound like the Melaklos," said Archer before he could stop.

Patterson chuckled, then asked, "What is Tsiel afraid of?"

"Tsiel's not afraid of anything," said Archer immediately.

Patterson nodded. "So," he said, and put the tips of his fingers together.

He's going to sum up, Archer thought, and felt like laughing.

Patterson said, "Neither of them is incapable of survival without you. Diane needs protection, but Tsiel doesn't. You love Tsiel, but you aren't sure about your feelings for Diane. Is that correct?"

"It isn't that simple," Archer snapped. "I'm not sure of

anything any more." He tried to shake off his growing anger. There was no point in shouting at Patterson.

He looked at the objects on the mantelpiece, tabulating them to help him regain his temper. Three china panorama eggs. The bronze jester. The ebony clock. The—he went back to the ebony clock. He got up to look at it more closely.

"What's up?" said Patterson.

Archer found his voice. "It's seven-thirty in the morning. I've kept you up all night."

He walked home, although Patterson offered to drive him. He turned at the corner for a last look at the old actor, standing in his doorway looking out over the snow in the quiet elm-shaded street.

Once home, he went to his den without stopping to remove his coat. The panorama egg was still in its box. He sat behind the desk and took it out, laid it on the blotter. It rolled, stopping against the frame of Diane's portrait. That seemed oddly appropriate. He left it there, looking at it.

In the soft light of his desk lamp it seemed almost alive. It had the same quiet color as the face and hands of the Melaklos. He wondered why she had given him this second chance. This last chance. She had said, hadn't she, that a second passage from his world would kill him.

He tried to think that he was saying farewell to Nayan, but it was too hard to do. He remembered her too well. She was too vivid, and he loved her too much. She loved him, too—it was funny. He wanted to help her rebuild Tsiel.

Diane's portrait rebuked him. There was an appeal in her eyes, something he had not seen there before. A trick of the light? Or of his mind, which knew how vulnerable she was. He would stay and help her as much as he could, shelter her. Eventually Tsiel would fade into a memory, poignant but no longer painful. Eventually.

He rubbed his forehead fretfully. He was in that late stage of wakefulness when every sense is heightened, when colors burn the eyes and the skitter of a dry leaf across concrete makes the heart leap. The ticking of the wall clock was like a hammer in his ears.

He looked at it. Eight-thirty. Diane would call any time now, and his dilemma would be over.

He looked at the portrait, the egg. He was too tired to think clearly. His mind went in circles: Diane, Tsiel; sanity, insanity; reality, illusion; Diane, Tsiel.

I believe in dream, said the Melaklos in his memory.

But dreams fade.

Maybe if he put his head down, it would clear. He lowered it to the desk top. His eyes closed.

Sound ripped the air. Archer sat up, clutching at the desk. His heart raced painfully.

The sound again—the telephone, shrill, piercing. He stared at it, trying to remember what it was.

Diane. At the airport. He had to go get her. Yes.

It rang again.

He could not move.

Insistent, it shrilled again.

With one convulsive motion he swept it to the floor. It jangled and crashed into silence. He sat back, feeling his heart slow to its normal pace. His head was clear. He was happy for the first time since his return home.

He reached for the panorama egg, picked it up. He leaned back, caressing it as if it were the most precious thing in all the world. Slowly he raised it to his eye.

Chapter Four

Tuesday, December 21st

It was Midwinter Eve. Soon it would be midnight, and then Midwinter—the day of the winter solstice.

Sir Henry Patterson and the Melaklos sat before the library fire, drinking red wine and talking at intervals. He lounged in one of the armchairs, watching her curiously. She sat curled on the rug like a gray cat, blinking into the fire.

Patterson broke the silence. "Mera, m'dear, what did you do with Archer?"

"Mm?" She turned her head lazily. "Archer? He's dead, isn't he?"

"He is," said Patterson. "I went to his funeral this morning." He set his wine glass on the table and looked directly at the Melaklos. "There were some odd things about his death."

She said nothing, just sat with her head turned from the fire. The flames cast strange shadows over her face.

He said, "Archer dined with me last Wednesday, and told me an extraordinary tale. A tale about a panorama egg."

She checked a small quick movement.

Patterson went on. "When we went home, he was upset and undecided. His wife says that she called him from the airport at nine. The telephone rang several times and then went dead."

The Melaklos watched him without winking.

He leaned forward to emphasize his next words. "She hired a car and drove home. She found Archer sitting in his overcoat in his—den, I believe she said. He was dead. His hands were in his lap, clasped together as though they held something small and fragile. The medical men had to pry them apart."

The Melaklos was still silent.

"His hands were empty," said Patterson.

She spoke at last. "What is this to me"

He shook his head. "It won't do, Gideon Crawle, it won't do. He told me all about it."

"About what?" she said evenly.

He leaned forward and touched her right cheekbone. "There's a scar there, m'dear. It wasn't there two weeks ago. That's where he hit you in the cell."

Her head went back. "All right," she said. "He told you? I rather thought that he would."

"Where is he?" said Patterson.

She shook her head. "He's dead. As far as I know, he's quite happy."

"As far as you know—" he began, but she shook her head again.

"I am thy fool my old," she said. "I cannot lie to thee."

"You could lie to the father of lies," he said.

She smiled with one corner of her mouth. "But not to thee, my old. So I will say nothing."

"The pattern of all patience," he muttered. "Tell me one thing. You're a wearer of masks. What mask did you wear for him? The poor man didn't know whether to fear you, hate you, or be grateful to you."

"I wore many masks," she said vaguely. "I cannot remember them all. I have worn masks so long, my old, that I cannot remember what my face is like—if I have a face." She laughed. "Like Peer Gynt."

Patterson picked up the wine glass and sipped at it. "Peer Gynt and the onion," he said. "Every layer of the onion a life, or a mask, with the truth at the core."

"But there was no core," said the Melaklos.

For a time they were silent again. This time she spoke first. She turned around completely, leaning her back on the hearth and hugging her knees.

"I didn't transport Archer for my amusement, my old," she said. "I liked him. He was trapped. I gave him a chance to escape."

"But why make him almost hate you? Why couldn't he like you?"

"He had to rebel," she said earnestly. "In accepting the egg, he rebelled against the things that trapped him here. But in the egg, in Dolesar, he depended upon me. If he had liked me, he would not have minded that. He had to dislike me so much that he hated being bound to me by need. I made it so. And in Ter-Lashan he rebelled."

"He rebelled to go to Ytarn and find Nayan," said Patterson.

"Yes." She released her knees and sat up straight. "Do you see, my old, that was when I knew that he would win. He

222

was right when he said that I had planned everything—I knew what I had set into motion. I knew that he had the imagination and the strength to win. But as long as he obeyed me and let himself depend upon me, his power was useless."

Patterson regarded her thoughtfully. Finally he said, "Why did you send him the egg again? Why not let it be a dream?"

"I wanted to know," she said. "Most people, offered a possibility of dream, would reject it. I wanted to know if he was strong enough to accept it without prompting."

Doubtfully he said, "Are you sure most people would reject dream?"

"They'd be afraid," she said. "Afraid that it would be false, more afraid that it would be true. I had to know if he had the courage to believe the impossible."

Patterson shook his head, still doubtful.

She leaned forward. Her eyes were large and dark in her shadowed face. Softly she said, "If dreams were to sell, what would you buy?"

He stared back at her for a long time. Then he looked around the room. "I have what I need," he said slowly. "I have most of what I want. Dream? I don't know. I'm not desperate enough."

"Exactly," she said, nodding. "He was desperate enough, and strong enough, and courageous enough. When I gave him the choice again, he took it. I wondered if he would."

Patterson chuckled suddenly. Reproachfully he said, "But you've never offered me a panorama egg."

She laughed, a full rich sound that Archer had never heard. It filled the room, light, warm. "You, my old? You have never needed such a thing."

There was another silence in the fire-lit room. Once she looked up and said, "I told him that another passage would kill him here. Thus are all dreams made true, ever to last." Then she was silent again. They looked at each other, Patterson with his comical face lit by the fire, the Melaklos with her fool's face, a mirror of his, painted with motley shadows.

Finally he said, "What about you, m'dear? You are the maker of visions, you are the dreamer of dreams. What are your own dreams, Merakin? What dream world do you want?"

She looked at him somberly. Her voice was so low that he could scarcely hear it. "All worlds are dream to me, my old," she said. "It is my curse. I live in dreams and wear the masks of dreams. I should like to find a world that is real."

223

Patterson looked away from the wistful twisted smile on her alien face. He stood and stretched elaborately, looked at the ebony clock.

"Midnight, m'dear," he said lightly. "Your year is turning." He poured wine into their glasses; it shone like rich flame.

She took the glass he offered her and lifted it toward him. "To the circle's end," she said. She sipped at the wine. Then, with a quick movement of her wrist, she flipped the rest into the fire. She set her glass on the tea table and turned her head to Patterson. Her face was composed, her voice light and careless.

"I told you the last time I was here that Andersen wants to consult you. He has an idea about...."